A Chance in a Million

The Chances
Book 5

Emily E K Murdoch

DRAGONBLADE PUBLISHING, INC.

ARE YOU SIGNED UP FOR DRAGONBLADE'S BLOG?

You'll get the latest news and information on exclusive giveaways, exclusive excerpts, coming releases, sales, free books, cover reveals and more.

Check out our complete list of authors, too!

No spam, no junk. That's a promise!

Sign Up Here

www.dragonbladepublishing.com

⁓

Dearest Reader;

Thank you for your support of a small press. At Dragonblade Publishing, we strive to bring you the highest quality Historical Romance from some of the best authors in the business. Without your support, there is no 'us', so we sincerely hope you adore these stories and find some new favorite authors along the way.

Happy Reading!

CEO, Dragonblade Publishing

Five Gold Rings
Four Calling Birds
Three French Hens
Two Turtle Doves
A Partridge in a Pear Tree

The De Petras Saga
The Misplaced Husband (Book 1)
The Impoverished Dowry (Book 2)
The Contrary Debutante (Book 3)
The Determined Mistress (Book 4)
The Convenient Engagement (Book 5)

The Governess Bureau Series
A Governess of Great Talents (Book 1)
A Governess of Discretion (Book 2)
A Governess of Many Languages (Book 3)
A Governess of Prodigious Skill (Book 4)
A Governess of Unusual Experience (Book 5)
A Governess of Wise Years (Book 6)
A Governess of No Fear (Novella)

Never The Bride Series
Always the Bridesmaid (Book 1)
Always the Chaperone (Book 2)
Always the Courtesan (Book 3)
Always the Best Friend (Book 4)
Always the Wallflower (Book 5)
Always the Bluestocking (Book 6)
Always the Rival (Book 7)
Always the Matchmaker (Book 8)
Always the Widow (Book 9)
Always the Rebel (Book 10)
Always the Mistress (Book 11)
Always the Second Choice (Book 12)
Always the Mistletoe (Novella)

Always the Reverend (Novella)

The Lyon's Den Series
Always the Lyon Tamer

Pirates of Britannia Series
Always the High Seas

De Wolfe Pack: The Series
Whirlwind with a Wolfe

Noble titles throughout English history have, at times, been more fluid than one might think. Women have inherited, men have been gifted titles by family or gained them through marriage, and royals frequently lavished titles or withdrew them as reward and punishment.

The elder Chance brothers in this series agreed to split the four titles in their family line during the Regency era, rather than the eldest holding all four. It is a decision that defines their brotherhood, and their very different personalities.

Now with the next generation, one Chance father has allowed his son to inherit his title before his own demise, echoing kings and queens who have abdicated their titles throughout history. Perhaps his brothers, the uncles of this next generation, will follow suit...

Get ready to meet a family that is more than happy to scandalize Society...

Chapter One

December 30, 1839

T HEY ENTERED LIKE a flock of swans.

Silly thing to think, really. Victoria's cheeks blushed at the thought, but she had not been foolish enough to utter it aloud, so—

"'Swans'?" her mother murmured, fluttering her fan before her lips to prevent anyone deciphering her words. "What are you talking about, Victoria?"

Victoria swallowed hard, her attention still fixed on the family that had just entered the Bath Assembly Rooms. "N-Nothing."

She was not the only one who had turned to watch one of the *ton*'s most prestigious families enter. Everyone knew the Chance family.

"Honestly, you must pay more attention to yourself if you wish to…"

The words continued, but Victoria's attention did not. Her gaze was flickering over the elegant shawls across the shoulders of the Chance ladies, the way the Chance gentlemen stood so tall, so relaxed, so absolutely certain they belonged there, in the center of things.

It was intoxicating. Alluring, even. The way they moved about the world, as though each and every Chance family member knew that they would be welcomed with open arms. As though the world were holding its breath waiting for them. To be a Chance… Well, it would be the closest thing, outside of the nation's young Queen Victoria herself, that she could imagine to royalty.

"Victoria Ainsworth, are you listening to me?"

Victoria started away from the Chance family—one particular member, really—and instead alighted on... Ah. The unimpressed look of her mother.

"You are staring," her mother hissed, color high and dark eyes glaring. A ringlet of brown-and-silver hair bounced against her cheek as her lips moved. "Staring, in the Assembly Rooms! How many times have I told you—"

"I know, I know," Victoria said wearily, trying to keep her expression neutral. It would never do for the world to see just what she thought.

"—and yet despite knowing, you intend on vexing me by—"

"I did not do it to irritate you," Victoria could not help but say.

It was, of course, the wrong thing. Her mother's high color was now turning an interesting pale white. "And who were you looking at with such interest, such—oh. The Chance family."

Victoria forced down a smile as her mother's feathers, significantly ruffled, started to calm. It was hardly her daughter's fault, after all, if she was caught staring at the Chance family. Everyone stared at them any opportunity they got.

"Well. I suppose I can understand your curiosity," her mother said stiffly. "Though they're not the sort of people who would talk to the likes of us."

It was Victoria's turn for her color to heighten. Shifting her fan from one hand to the other, as though that would calm her nerves, she swallowed hard to ensure her voice was level when she spoke.

When she did, it was in a low voice. That barely mattered. The buzz of interest when the Chance family had entered the Assembly Rooms was more than enough to cover her words.

"I know that, Mother. But I thought—"

"Ladies of good family do not think," her mother snapped. "Really, Victoria, sometimes I think—"

"Ah, Mrs. Ainsworth, how pleasant to see you."

Victoria stiffened as a woman she vaguely recognized approached the pair of them. An impressive jaw, sparkling intelligent eyes, and a gown that spoke more of last decade's fashion than this, she was more than a little imposing. Judging by her mother's reaction to the woman, it was someone important. Only the very rich or the very noble made her mother beam so awkwardly.

"Lady Romeril, what a pleasure," murmured Mrs. Ainsworth as she curtseyed low. "I had not realized you were in Bath. How does the Season treat you?"

"Oh, very ill, very ill. I find Christmas to be most tiring and I am glad to be almost rid of it," said the older woman without curtseying. Her gaze raked over Victoria, then immediately pulled away. "Tell me, Mrs. Ainsworth, have you tried the waters?"

"Oh, yes, indeed," replied Victoria's mother, fluttering her fan in her nerves. "In fact, when I first arrived here in Bath…"

Victoria took a slight step back, her heart starting to race against the boning of her corset. Neither of the women took the slightest bit of notice.

Another step. Still nothing.

Five steps later, Victoria was carefully positioned behind one of the resplendent columns by which she had been astonished in the Assembly Rooms, free from her mother's careful eye and able to look at the room.

A gaggle of young ladies, around her age, giggling over the punch bowl. A pair of gentlemen, perhaps her mother's age, debating something—politics, probably. A set of dancers, ten pairs, striding up and down the set to the pace of the elegant music created by the musicians positioned at the opposite end of the room. Smoke pouring from the card room just to her left and laughter pouring out with it. So many people milling about, feathers and jewels and canes and the flutter of gloves…

It took a great amount of self-control not to immediately look at the one family that drew her attention.

Victoria's breath caught in her throat as she finally permitted herself to look again at the Chance family. A few of the younger generation, her generation, had disappeared. The daughter of the house appeared to be dancing, and one of the brothers was arguing with his mother—seemingly over the way he had tied his cravat.

The temptation to walk over there to overhear them was strong. Victoria managed to force it down.

Only then did she look at the eldest brother. Thomas Chance. Lord Thomas Chance, eldest son of the Duke of Cothrom.

"—leave him alone," Victoria managed to catch before someone's laughter drowned out his words until, "—take it up with his valet, not Leo."

Victoria leaned against the pillar, the cooling marble necessary as the heat of the room—and the effect of Lord Thomas Chance—worked on her, skin prickling.

She was not going to obsess over the man anymore, she told herself firmly. *A year was more than enough. He probably does not even remember you.*

"—and I heard most of the Chance money is gone!"

Victoria froze.

The voice was a young man's, not a person she knew, and he was talking loudly just on the other side of the pillar—the pillar hiding her from view.

"No! Surely not. The Chance family is one of the wealthiest—"

"They *were* one of the wealthiest," chimed in the voice again, a certain smugness in every syllable that Victoria did not like. "You know there were four brothers, and they've all grown and married and had children—"

"They don't look like children to me," returned his companion, his voice deeper and with a dark tinge to it. "Why, Lady Maude looks ripe and ready for picking if you ask—"

"She'd never have you, so don't even think about it," snapped the first voice. "Didn't I just tell you there's no money? Dowry's all gone—"

"Oh." The second voice sounded disappointed.

"—and all because that Lord Thomas doesn't know when to stop playing cards, I heard!"

Victoria gripped the pillar, using it mostly to keep herself upright. Thomas—*her* Lord Thomas, the reason the Chance family was ruined?

Not that he was *her* Lord Thomas, obviously, she attempted to correct herself as her frantically beating heart fluttered, her lungs tight, her fingers white as they gripped the pillar. Obviously.

"—the old spendthrift is nothing like the old block," the gentleman's voice continued, almost gleeful as he recounted the disaster that had obviously hit the Chance family. "Old Cothrom had never done anything but keep the family under control and solvent, and in just the last year—"

"So you're saying he'll be up for a flutter later, then?"

Victoria closed her eyes for a moment in horror.

"Haven't you been listening to a word I've said? Come on, you'll find much better victims in the card room—less willing, but more solvent. Anyway, don't you owe John Knight a hundred pounds?"

"The man cheated, I tell you, and what's more…"

What was more, Victoria never knew. The voices moved away; two gentlemen older than herself appeared in view as they strode past her pillar, Victoria pressing herself foolishly against the marble to hide.

Their absence did not end the ringing in her ears.

"Didn't I just tell you there's no money? Dowry's all gone and all because that Lord Thomas doesn't know when to stop playing cards!"

It was foolish of her, Victoria knew, but to hear such words spoken about the man she…

But she was being ridiculous. Young ladies did not fall in love with gentlemen they met a few times over the Christmas season just over a year ago.

Yes, they had danced together. He had looked at her, Victoria thought dreamily as she leaned back against the pillar, and held her hand, so lightly yet so warmly. He had smiled, laughed at something she'd said—what, she could not remember. It probably had not been that amusing. But Lord Thomas Chance had laughed, and red-hot wax had poured through her center, and she had known she would never be the same again.

He had complimented her shawl. Or was it her headband—a ribbon?

It did not matter. Victoria could still feel the connection, one borne of knowledge that there was something between them, something greater than anything she had ever shared with anyone.

"You dance most elegantly, Miss Ainsworth."

That had been it. Victoria smiled, oblivious to the dancers before her as they meandered up and down the Assembly Rooms. She was no longer in Bath. She was in Almack's, in London, and it was Christmas Eve, and she was being led back to her mother by Lord Thomas Chance.

"Why, thank you. I must say that you are hardly shoddy in your footwork yourself."

She had been bold to say such words, and her cheeks burned even now recalling them. And Lord Thomas had laughed, his eyes crinkling in the corners as his pupils sparkled, and he had said...he had said...

"You give me vitality, Miss Ainsworth. It is thanks to you that I dance so well, if I do at all."

Her spirits had lifted then and they lifted now. Victoria could feel heat pooling inside her again, falling through her stomach and resting between her hips. That sensation only Lord Thomas had ever sparked, a discomfort that had blossomed when his gaze had darted to her mouth then back to her eyes.

"And I hope, if I may be so bold," Lord Thomas Chance had said in a low voice, his tone muzzy with need, or at least she had thought so at the time, *"that you and I may dance again, Miss Ainsworth."*

"Oh, yes..."

And they never had. Not in all the days of the following year. Never again had Victoria found herself standing opposite the man who—

"It's Miss Ainsworth, isn't it?" came a voice.

Victoria smiled. At some point in her remembrances, her eyelashes had lowered, losing herself in the memories of the delectable Lord Thomas—

"Miss Ainsworth?"

Victoria froze. Her eyelashes fluttered open. Her lips parted.

It was Lord Thomas Chance.

"I never forget a face," he said cheerfully, inclining his head lightly and glancing about the room. "Never thought I'd see you here. Been in Bath long?"

Victoria opened her mouth. Not a single syllable left it.

"It's getting awfully hot in here, I must say," said Lord Thomas, pushing back his sandy hair with a careless hand, a gold signet ring on his smallest finger, making himself even more handsome than Victoria had thought possible. "Don't you think?"

Say something. For the love of God, say something!

"H-H-Hot," Victoria managed to stammer.

Yes, he was making her ridiculously hot—but he didn't need to know that.

Her fan. She was holding a fan!

Relieved to find something to do with her hands, Victoria snapped open the fan and fluttered it before her eyes. She ceased immediately, as it had replaced Lord Thomas in her view, and she knew which one she'd rather look at.

Oh, this was foolhardy. The man probably had no memory of her at all—though he *had* recalled her name.

"I told my mother it would be too warm in here, but she would not listen," Lord Thomas was saying with a wry look that spoke of charming eldest sons and their devoted mothers. "She was the one who reminded me of your name. Said I should come over here and see if you required any assistance."

Victoria wilted, her shoulders slumping and the hand clutching her fan falling to her side.

He...He was only here because his mother—his *mother*—had asked him to approach her? Hadn't even remembered her enough to recall her name? Had to be reminded of it...by his mother?

Oh, this was mortifying. From such heights of delight to such depths of shame, how was she ever to survive it?

Victoria tried to swallow, tried to recollect herself, but her mouth was dry and the thought of her mouth had made her look at Lord Thomas's lips, and now she was thinking what it would be like to kiss him and—

"I say, you do look warm, Miss Ainsworth," said Lord Thomas quietly, stepping toward her. "Do you feel quite well?"

I could throw myself into your arms, Victoria could not help but think, her mind racing. He would have to catch her, and she could pretend she had sunk into a faint—a swoon, because of the heat. His hands would press into her arms, and he would draw her into him and—

Pull yourself together, Victoria!

"I am quite well," she said aloud, though how, she was not sure. "It...It *is* a tad warm."

"My sister, Maude, always says public balls are far too crowded," Lord Thomas said with a casual flick of his head over his shoulder.

Victoria looked past him and saw the elegant and refined Lady Maude Chance chatting animatedly to a young lady she did not recognize. "I...I quite agree."

"Yes, most people agree with Maude—it's safer," said Lord Thomas with a chuckle.

Victoria's pulse skipped a beat as she joined him in merriment.

To an outsider, perhaps, a casual observer, it would have appeared that she was flirting—*flirting!*—with Lord Thomas Chance.

Not that I am doing such a thing, more's the pity, Victoria thought, trying desperately to put together a coherent enough thought that she could say out loud. She would love to flirt with the man, but she was hardly the flirtatious sort, and when one had spent the last year thinking about the man before oneself, and then he stood there, proud and tall in his brushed wool coat, carefully fitted across a broad chest—

"And you are enjoying yourself in Bath?"

Victoria had just been about to ask what happened to people who did not agree with his sister—a clever ruse, she considered, to get to know the Chance family a little better as well as to insinuate herself into said family—and she had to make such a quick change of topic that her tongue tumbled over the words.

"And what happens to people who—enjoying myself. Yes, yes. Bath. Nice place."

"Nice place"? What on earth had happened to her brain?

The part of Victoria watching this in horror was sobbing in a corner, but try as she might, the part of Victoria standing before Lord Thomas Chance and looking like a complete fool did not seem to be able to move.

Oh, he was handsome. And charming. Delightful company, and an excellent dancer—

That was it. What if she asked him to dance?

It was not the sort of thing of which her mother would have approved, but from what Victoria could see, her mother was out of earshot and would likely as not never hear about such a thing.

"—come here each year for Christmas, along with a few other families," Lord Thomas was saying, "and I must agree that—"

"Dance?" Victoria blurted out.

There was a tightness paired with rising heat from being in the presence of a man over whom she had obsessed for the last year, and it sadly meant that the carefully constructed sentence had descended to a single word.

"Dance?" Lord Thomas blinked. His long, golden eyelashes were awfully delicate. Then he glanced over his shoulder and nodded as he turned back to her. "Yes, they're dancing."

Victoria almost rolled her eyes. *I'm not an idiot!* she wanted to shout. *I'm a clever, witty, usually charming woman!*

Except when I'm with you. Apparently.

"Y-Yes," she said, hating that her voice failed her at such an opportune moment. Well, this was it. She had to say it. "Do... Do you... Would you like to dance, Lord Thomas? With me, I mean?"

It had taken every iota of bravery she possessed to say such a thing. Out loud! To a gentleman! In public!

Ladies simply did not ask gentlemen to dance. It did not happen. Until it did. Until she had said those words.

Victoria looked up into those dark eyes, deep and passionate as they always were...and found they were not looking at her. They did not appear to be looking at anything. Lord Thomas had that vague, faraway sort of look in his eyes that Victoria recognized as utter distraction. It was the expression her mother fell into whenever Victoria attempted to tell her about an interesting new play that had debuted on the London stage.

Looking surreptitiously over her shoulder just in case there was something Lord Thomas was looking at—*not a woman*, Victoria thought to herself, and that was her main concern—she took a deep breath as she turned back to him.

"I said, Lord Thomas," she repeated, hardly knowing from where her bravery came, "would you like to dance?"

"Mmm?" said the tall gentleman, clearly not listening to a word.

Victoria bit her lip. She was hardly going to ask a third time—not when it had been so mortifying the first two times, and there did not appear to be a way to make the man pay attention.

What on earth could have distracted him? He did not appear to be looking at anyone in particular. Perhaps it was these debts she had heard talked of—the money troubles he had apparently managed to get the family into.

It was most unlike him, though. At least, unlike the little Victoria knew of him. But then a few conversations, a dance that had utterly changed her life but Lord Thomas barely remembered... It was hardly a deep connection, was it?

"Well, I hope you have a pleasant time in Bath, Miss Ainsworth." Lord Thomas Chance gave her that smile—that smile Victoria had seen him give countless other young ladies, the one where he wasn't even properly looking at the person to whom he was speaking. "Good evening."

It was about to become too late—she needed to do something, say something, anything to catch his attention—anything to make him stay here, talking to her.

Fear pounding through her veins, Victoria swallowed hard then managed to splutter, "M-My lord—"

"Leo, you foul fiend, don't tell me you've gone into the card room without me!" Lord Thomas Chance laughed as he slapped one of his brothers on the back. He was somehow several feet away and as he continued talking, he strode forward and the crowd swallowed him up. "What did I tell you, never risk a hand of cards without..."

Victoria remained, fixed to the spot by the pillar. She watched as Lord Thomas and his brother laughed together, pushing through the growing crowd easily, until they turned into the card room and slipped out of sight.

Only then did she realize her lungs had not moved for what felt like an age.

The air burned in her lungs as she drew in a long, gasping breath and it mingled with her disappointment.

A year. Over a year, just, a year spent wondering exactly what she would say to Lord Thomas Chance when she next saw him.

And now it had happened, and...

Well, she had not quite made a complete fool of herself. *That,*

Victoria thought fiercely, *would have required me to have actually made any sort of impact upon the man at all.*

But she hadn't. He would go home tonight, she knew, barely having registered that they'd conversed.

Oh, it was all so foolish. Why had she managed to let the opportunity slip through her fingers? Half the *ton* was interested in making the acquaintance of Lord Thomas Chance, and the other half wished to marry him. There she had been, unsurrounded by other young ladies, with his full attention...

And she had said nothing more interesting than... Victoria could not recall having said anything interesting, now that she came to think of it.

Leaning heavily against the pillar, the cool marble doing nothing to calm the frantic thoughts in her mind, Victoria took another deep breath.

Well, it was a new year in a few days—and wasn't there that tradition of making a resolution as one entered a new year? Something to improve in oneself, or the determination to do something different?

Victoria drew herself up and swallowed, hard.

That was what she would do. The upcoming year, the year of 1840...she would seduce Lord Thomas Chance.

Chapter Two

January 3, 1840

T HOMAS CHANCE WAS attempting to think of a solution to the laundry of St. Thomas's. And he would have done, too, if his head hadn't been attempting to unscrew itself from his neck.

He groaned in agony. Then he groaned again, in the desperate hope that the agony would be frightened away.

"You bring it upon yourself," said Alexander, his dark eyes sparkling with mischief as he spoke with a tone of delight.

Thomas groaned again, then opened his eyes to glare at his younger brother. "You'll bring it upon yourself if you're not careful."

"I told you whisky after port was a bad idea," said his brother, wagging a finger and a grin on his face. "And what did you say?"

Thomas groaned.

"Yes, something like that," said Alexander, snorting as he entered the library and dropped onto the sofa with a book in hand. "And I said—"

"'You'll regret it in the morning,'" muttered Thomas, sinking deeper into the armchair, which was as far as he'd managed to get that morning. "And you were right, damn you."

They were always right. There was something infuriating about having two younger brothers, both absolute dolts, who managed to be right about this sort of thing. Most infuriating.

And he would tell them how infuriating they were, he was certain, once this pounding headache had disappeared and the light stopped making his eyeballs ache.

There was a snapping sound and Thomas winced. "Can you not be quiet?"

"I don't think so, no," mused Alexander. When Thomas opened his eyes, his brother was holding a large atlas he had apparently snapped shut. "There's not much point, either."

Thomas frowned. "There isn't?"

"Certainly not," said his other brother, striding in with a smug look on his face. "Father is on the hunt for you, and I can tell you now it won't be a quiet conversation."

Bringing a hand over his eyes and wishing to God he had not drunk a single thing last night, Thomas groaned.

Of course Father was on the warpath. Of all days to have a hangover worse than death, it had to be the one Father decided to… What was it Mother had said just the other day? *"Have it out."*

"I don't have anything to say to him," he muttered to the floor.

The snort could have been either of his brothers, but the snicker was most definitely Alexander. "You know what he's like—holier than thou—"

"Not that it's very difficult, when Thomas is the *thou*." Leopold grinned. His rangy, athletic frame was mostly hidden by his jacket, but there was a strength in his shoulders in particular that made him dangerous in a boxing ring and impossible to shove. Not that his brothers didn't regularly try.

Thomas glared, but it did not appear to make much difference.

"He's the head of the Chance family, and it's a great deal of responsibility," reprimanded Alexander, though there was a glint in his eye that told Thomas quite plainly that he thought the whole thing amusing. "We've heard all the stories, about how hard he had to work to keep his brothers in line—"

"I always thought Uncles Frederick, George, and John got the worse end of the staff in those stories," Thomas said, interrupting. That was it, push the conversation onto someone else. "After all, they could not be *all* bad—"

"You're worse," Alexander said bluntly. "Spending everything—forging Father's signature!"

The last few words were spoken in a hiss, as though at any moment their father would walk in on them. Which, as it was his library, was very possible.

"And spending Maudy's dowry... You're a fool, Thomas, and you can't keep hiding what you've done forever," said Leopold in a similarly low voice.

Thomas rolled his eyes—anything to distract himself from the acute discomfort he felt at their accusations.

Well, not *accusations*. What was the word for it, when someone accused you of something terrible, and they, to your own detriment, were actually right?

"I never intended for it to get so out of hand," he muttered, carefully examining his thumb.

Anything rather than look up at his two younger brothers. Barely men, and here they were, castigating him for something that was entirely not his fault! How could he have known he would grow so invested? How could he have predicted how difficult it would be to walk away?

"The family fortune is gone and it won't be long before Father finds out," Leopold was saying quietly. "He might throw you out."

Thomas snorted with a shrug. "I'll go to my club."

"And pay for your room and board with what money?" The bluntness of Alexander's words scraped across Thomas's already painful conscience.

They were right. *Damn them.*

And the guilt Thomas had pushed aside for months, the knowledge he had been a complete fool, the certainty that it was all going to come out, the one thing his father feared and loathed in equal measure—scandal—about to roost in the Chance household yet again...

It was all his fault.

Thomas shifted uncomfortably in the armchair. "I'll fix it."

"I think the time for that ended last year," Alexander said seriously. He had moved now from the bookcase he had been perusing and was now standing a few feet from the eldest Chance brother with a somber look. "Look, Thomas—"

"I don't need your help," Thomas said automatically.

The very idea! He was the eldest Chance brother—the eldest son of the eldest Chance brother. Father and his three brothers had produced countless children, but he was the most responsible.

The most irresponsible, a quiet voice in the back of his mind muttered.

Thomas ignored it. He also ignored the glances his two brothers exchanged. "Look, I said I'll fix it—and I don't need you to berate me. You can't berate me more than I berate myself!"

"Clearly not enough," said a deep voice.

Thomas rose to his feet, his legs forcing him upward before his mind could engage. It was one of the things one did when the Duke of Cothrom entered a room.

"Good morning, Father," said Leopold quietly.

"How are you today, Father?" asked Alexander, his voice taut. "I was just thinking, a ride would be—"

"Out," said William Chance, Duke of Cothrom, in a low voice.

He did not need to repeat himself or explain he meant for one of them to stay. Desperate as Thomas was to catch his brothers' eyes, they did not meet his gaze as they left the library, closing the door behind them and leaving him to face their father.

Thomas swallowed.

It was ridiculous, really. William Chance had been a prim and proper young man, by all accounts, and had aged into a prim and proper gentleman with graying whiskers and a sharpness about the eyes. Though he had gifted all of his sons his height, he alone was starting to soften in the middle as the years crept up on him. He was not a harsh man, nor a cruel one. In many ways, he had been a loving and present father.

But there was something about his fury that burned through the silence that made Thomas feel he was five years old again and had been caught stealing butter from the kitchen.

The fact that it had been for the stable cat had been irrelevant. Sons and heirs of dukes, he had been reminded at the time, did not steal. The very thought!

William Chance, Duke of Cothrom, expected his sons to be above reproach. And now...

Thomas cleared his throat. "Look, I can explain—"

"I very much doubt it." said his father stiffly. "Sit."

Legs folding under him without conscious thought, Thomas hated how he returned to a state of childhood whenever his father gave him that look. It was the look that said: I know what you did, and I know you've tried to hide it, and I cannot decide which is more disappointing.

"You," said the Duke of Cothrom slowly as he lowered himself onto the opposite sofa, "have spent all my money. Correct?"

Wishing the floor would swallow him up, never to return him to consciousness, Thomas forced himself to meet the man's eyes then immediately wished he had not. He nodded.

"When I gave you equal access to the estate as my son and heir," his father said, "it was because I trusted you. I expected great things from you. My solicitors advised against it..."

Thomas swallowed.

"I didn't even think to keep an eye what you were doing. I didn't think it necessary. You have let the family down," his father said quietly. Thomas almost wished there was malice in his tone, anger, fury—but there was naught but disappointment. "Especially your sister. No dowry, I have discovered."

The knot in his throat would not disappear, no matter how many times he swallowed. "I can—"

"Explain, you said. I don't think so. There is nothing you can do to—"

"I intend to marry a fortune."

Thomas was not sure what had possessed him to say it. The thought hadn't occurred to him, it had *spilled* from him, pouring from a place inside he had not known was there.

The Duke of Cothrom raised an eyebrow. "Marry. You."

"To a fortune, yes," Thomas said hastily, spotting the prospect to at least attempt to show willingness. "I am of age, I am your heir— heirs need heirs, so I should marry. Why not marry money? Fill the coffers of Cothrom with—"

"With someone else's money," interjected his father, rolling his eyes. "Like your Uncle John."

Thomas hesitated, unsure if his father was censuring him. "Uncle...Uncle John?"

His Uncle John, Marquess of Aylesbury, was an absolute rogue—in the best sense. He was probably Thomas's favorite uncle. The man knew his way around a deck of cards like a rascal and always had the most hilarious stories to share of when the four Chance brothers had been younger. He was, ever since Thomas could remember, devoted to his wife.

And he married her for money?

"Aunt Florence—he married her for her dowry?"

For a moment, his father hesitated. Then he gave a curt nod. "It was agreed beforehand. Between them, I mean. A marriage of convenience."

Thomas nodded, though he wondered why on earth his uncle had bothered. Would it not have been easier, surely, to just pick a suitable one, one noble enough to interest and rich enough to suit, and marry her?

"Well, you are to be married, then," said his father with a sigh. "To whom?"

Thomas blinked. "To whomever."

The Duke of Cothrom rolled his eyes again. "I see. Well, I am going to give you something that should aid you in your quest to find a pliable and wealthy bride—and it may just give you a sense of responsibility too, something of which you are in dire need. I discussed it with your mother, and she has given me her full support in the matter."

Trying not to let his irritation show, Thomas attempted to appear intrigued. "Oh?"

"*Oh*, indeed," his father said testily. "It is irregular, but I have spoken with my solicitors and with the House of Lords—"

"House of Lords?" Thomas repeated, eyes widening. "But why would—"

"—and they agree that though it is unusual, there is no technical reason it cannot be done," continued his father tautly. "I signed the paperwork this morning."

Thomas waited for his father to explain, but all the man did was look at him. It was a careful, considered look, and it made him most uncomfortable. "Well? What is it, this gift?"

The Duke of Cothrom smiled. "I'm giving you the duchy."

Four hours later, Thomas could still not understand it.

"You are quite sure you did not misunderstand," Alexander said slowly, handing him the deck of cards to shuffle in the refined air of the card room at the Bath Assembly Rooms hours later. "You could have misheard him. Perhaps he said—"

"He was most definite," said Thomas, still in shock. "He's rescinded the title, passed it on to me before he dies. I...I am the new Duke of

Cothrom."

It was impossible. It was ridiculous. It was madness!

It had been done that morning. His father had shown him the paperwork, explained it all, then left him, hardly able to think...as the Duke of Cothrom.

Thomas dropped the deck of cards onto the table between them, then dropped his head into his hands. "What on earth am I going to do?"

"Do? Be the Duke of Cothrom, I suppose," said Alexander with a wry laugh. "Oh, come on! You were always going to inherit someday. Frankly, if our father and his brothers had not had such an unconventional arrangement to begin with, the three of us would have been born with titles from the start."

"Yes, but we weren't and I didn't expect to become the duke. Not now!" Thomas lifted his head and looked at his brother. "I thought Father—I hope Father will live another twenty, perhaps thirty, years! But now I'm the duke? What does that make him?"

His brother shrugged. "Wait until this news gets out in the *ton*. You're going to be absolutely bombarded."

"'Bombarded'?" Thomas repeated.

Words hardly made sense anymore. How could they, when the unthinkable had happened?

"Well, I am going to give you something that should aid you in your quest to find a pliable and wealthy bride—and it may just give you a sense of responsibility too, something of which you are in dire need."

Responsibility? He was the new Duke of Cothrom. His father had said something about meeting tenants, talking to the steward, organizing his sister's next ball, ensuring the invoices on the desk were paid—a litany of problems that were now, apparently, his.

How did one go about being a duke?

It wasn't something Thomas had ever particularly worried about. It was an eventuality, yes, but it would happen so far ahead in the future, he had not given it a second thought.

"Your Grace," said a voice.

And the worst of it is, the very worst, is that—

"Cothrom."

—that I can't ask my father for help, Thomas thought darkly as he leaned back in his chair and pulled a hand through his hair. The man wouldn't help him. The whole point was to make him feel ridiculous and start shouldering responsibility. But how could he—

"You're going to have to get used to that," said Alexander with a snort of laughter.

Thomas blinked, frowning at his brother. "To what?"

"To answering to your title."

"No one said my—"

"'Your Grace,' 'Cothrom'—two new ways people will talk to you." Alexander wiggled his eyebrows. "Would you like to start practicing?"

For a moment, Thomas could do nothing but stare. Then his lips parted in a laugh, the whole nonsense of the situation pouring through him.

Him, a duke!

"Now that's the response I expected," Alexander said meaningfully, pulling the deck of cards out of Thomas's unresisting hands. "You really are a dolt, you know that? Do you know how many men in Society would kill to have a duchy fall into their lap?"

Thomas chuckled, shaking his head ruefully. "I suppose quite a few."

"Maybe more men of Papa's generation should step aside, let the younger bucks take charge," mused Alexander, as though he'd been put in charge of re-organizing Society. "After all, we can't all wait around forever for the heads of families to—"

"*Alexander!*"

"Well, I can't believe I'm the only one who has thought it." The youngest sibling grinned. "I'm sure Leopold will now consider it, with him becoming the heir and all that."

Thomas would have punched his brother lightly in the arm, but that would been moving, and he couldn't be having with that. Besides, he probably shouldn't. Dukes did not go around hitting brothers.

He was a duke. The Duke of Cothrom! He was powerful now, respected—he could have any heiress he wanted, likely as not just for the asking.

Everything was going to be fine. He would marry well, restore the family coffers, and then he could go back to St. Thomas's and—

"Father said something ridiculous about your wedding."

Thomas's laughter faded. Alexander was looking at him with a sharp, almost too-knowing look, and he had spoken quietly in case they were overheard. Not that it was likely. The card room at the Assembly Rooms had filled up fast, every table packed with gentlemen playing whist and poker and a whole host of other games. Smoke filled the place along with the scent of deep, rich red wine.

"Your wedding," his brother repeated with an arched eyebrow.

Ah, yes. He still had to find an heiress to marry.

"If you were going to marry an heiress, say…oh, next week," began Thomas, leaning forward over the card table. He lowered his voice, though the noise of the room sufficiently muffled their conversation. "Any heiress you could have. Which one would you choose?"

For a moment, Alexander just stared. Then he said slowly, "You're pulling my leg."

"I'm the Duke of Cothrom now," Thomas said with a grin, power rushing through him, heady like the finest port. "I could marry *anyone*."

"Give over—"

"I'm serious. I need to wed, and I can't imagine any Society mama saying *no* to me, can you?" Thomas felt a lightness in the limbs, the sense of giddiness reaching his head.

Well, why not? Pick someone, anyone, and let the whole disaster pass him by. He'd want a pretty woman, naturally. *Can't marry someone you don't want to look at.*

"You are honestly asking my opinion of what woman to marry—like you've entered a haberdasher's and are considering a row of silks for a cravat?"

Thomas ignored the incredulous tone of his brother. He wouldn't understand. How could he? *He* hadn't spent the family funds. He didn't have to marry a fortune. He wasn't a new, shiny duke.

"Heiresses in the *ton*—heiresses in Bath, if possible," Thomas insisted. "Pretty enough to look at, well connected enough to suit—"

"You're talking absolute—"

"I'm serious, Xander. If it's the only way I can restore the family fortunes, restore Father's trust in me…" Thomas had not intended to let his true feelings show, but he couldn't help it. His pain, the self-loathing at the fact that he had managed to get himself into this situation, slipped out.

He met Alexander's eye and did not look away. His brother examined him for a moment, then sighed and turned to look through the door into the main Assembly Rooms.

"Heiresses," he said with an air of finality. "Right. Well, I suppose there is Marjorie Dalton."

Thomas moved the name about in his mouth, as though he were tasting a fine wine. "Miss Dalton…?"

"Lady Marjorie, the Earl of Burnell's daughter," his brother corrected him sternly. "The junior branch of the family—you know the Daltons well enough. Her dowry is forty or fifty thousand, so I hear. Nice enough family, beautiful, charming, if you ask me…"

Alexander kept talking, but Thomas found it hard to concentrate. A few steps behind an older lady his mother's age or older, a young woman had just stepped across the doorway wearing a soft-blue gown. The swish of the material accentuated the lightness of her movements, the delicacy of her waist.

And a memory stirred. A memory from not too long ago, and

another one too, that was harder to place.

"Miss Ainsworth," Thomas said without thinking.

"—and she—who? Oh, Miss Ainsworth. Yes, I suppose she is an heiress," said his brother lightly. "But Lady Marjorie, she—"

"Miss Ainsworth—an heiress?" Thomas stared at his brother. Surely not. He'd never heard such a thing. "Truly? She doesn't have a fortune, does she?"

Alexander shrugged. "Would you call five and forty thousand pounds a fortune?"

Thomas swallowed. *Yes, he would.* From memory, she had not been that bright—a little vacuous and eager to please. *Interesting.*

"But Lady Marjorie—"

"Well, I can make the decision easy enough," said Thomas firmly. He wasn't going to permit any feelings—not that he had any, he hardly knew the women on the *ton* outside of his family—to get involved. This was a marriage of convenience, even if he didn't see the point in explaining that to the lady in question. Whichever one she would be. "Ready?"

He pulled a shilling from his waistcoat pocket.

His brother's mouth fell open. "You—You're not going to make the decision about the woman you marry based on a coin toss?"

Thomas shrugged. "Why not? There is surely an equal likelihood of me getting along with either woman. They're both young, pretty, rich—"

"Thomas!"

"It doesn't matter to me which woman it is," he said, trying to forget the way his father had looked at him that morning. "I will restore the family fortune, and make sure Maudy has her dowry. You have a better idea?"

Alexander frowned but said nothing.

"Heads it's Lady Whatsherface—"

"Lady Marjorie," said his brother, a strange look passing over his face. "But—"

"Heads it's Lady Marjorie, tails it's Miss Ainsworth," said Thomas, straightening his back as he turned the shilling over and over in his hand. It was warming to his touch and he could feel his pulse thrumming against it, quickening in pace as he beheld the coin.

This was it. His whole future was about to be decided, and by the toss of a coin. But was it truly any different, really, than Society's usual methods?

Thomas tossed the coin.

His eyes followed it, unblinking, as it soared up in the air between them and then started its descent downward. Pulse thundering, ears unable to hear anything as the roar of his pulse echoed—

The coin landed.

On its side.

"Blow me," said Alexander slowly.

Thomas stared, unable to believe his eyes.

"What are the chances of that?"

"I...I would guess a chance in a million," said Thomas quietly, hardly daring to pick up the coin. It was still warm as he removed it from the table, his mind spinning.

He tossed it again. The impossible did not happen a second time, and it took a moment to realize that it had therefore selected for him a bride.

He leaned over. "Tails."

"Well, there you have it!"

Thomas looked up and saw his brother grinning.

"Well, it's a very good jest," Alexander said, "but you're not actually going to—where are you going?"

"To speak with my future bride," said Thomas airily, with far more confidence than he felt. "I'll see you at home."

"But, Tommy—"

Ignoring his brother's frantic words, the new Duke of Cothrom strode out of the card room and into the hustle and bustle of the Assembly Rooms. The place was packed; as usual, too many people had been let in, and Thomas's gaze raked over lords and ladies and footmen and gentlemen and—

There. There she was.

The woman he supposed to be her mama no longer in sight, Miss Ainsworth was standing by one of those pillars—and it was the pillar that jogged his memory. Yes, it had only been a few days ago, hadn't it? He'd spoken to her briefly by a pillar. What she had said, he could not recall, nor any of the answers he had given. He'd spotted Packham on the other side of the room, reminding him of the fifty pounds he owed him.

She was alone, which suggested no one wished to speak to her. Perhaps her conversational skills were as dull as he recalled. Perhaps he would be bored stiff in her company. Perhaps her companionship would be intolerable.

But that was what gentlemen's clubs and his siblings and cousins were for. She could have her life under his roof, and he would have his, wherever he might go.

Well, no time like the present. Miss Ainsworth, and her five and forty thousand pounds, would soon be his.

Thomas made sure to hold his head up high—like he'd seen his father do—as he strode across the room. Pushing past people who attempted to gain his attention, he firmly ignored them, keeping his focus fixed on the woman who was about to solve all his problems.

When he reached her, however, he noticed three things.

Firstly, he had not prepared anything witty or charming to say, which was most remiss.

Secondly, Miss Ainsworth was alone and therefore gave him all her attention.

And thirdly, Miss Ainsworth was far prettier than he had remembered. In fact, she was beautiful. A lavender scent wafted around her, intoxicatingly sweet. Golden hair cascaded into a plait woven with gold thread then piled upon her head in a way that drew the eye—his eye—to the curve of her neck, then lower to the curve of her—

Thomas jerked his head up from where it had been, staring agog at her breasts, to see her cheeks flushed and her eyes bright.

Speak, man!

Allowing a broad grin to spread across his face, Thomas said, "I... Uh..."

How did she do it? Completely dazzle him, and just by staring! Staring, leaning against a pillar, a pillar he very much wanted to pin her against and taste—

"Hello," said Miss Ainsworth quietly. "Your Grace."

Chapter Three

I T WAS LIKE being in a dream. Victoria had almost had to force her mother to admit that there was no harm in her attending the Assembly Rooms twice in a week, and she had spent most of her time fetching and carrying glasses of punch for Mrs. Ainsworth. She'd been so hurried the last time, Victoria had spilled a slosh over her gloves, now in her mother's reticule. The moment she had managed to get away, she had seen him.

Just out of the corner of her eye. It had been the briefest glimpse, yet more than enough to get her pulse racing.

Tempting as it was to walk back across the open doorway to the card room, where she had spotted Lord Thomas Chance gazing out at the dancing in the Assembly Rooms, Victoria had managed to stop herself.

And now, here he was. Standing before her. Taller than her, dark eyes flashing with something she did not understand, saying…nothing.

Well, not entirely nothing.

"I… Uh…"

Victoria could not help but smile. This was something so far out of the ordinary that she hardly knew what to say herself. What was Lord Thomas Chance doing, staring like that? Like…

Well. Like he liked what he saw.

This rarely happened to her—and it certainly had never happened with someone as handsome and charming as Lord Thomas Chance. Oh, all the Chance cousins were charming in their way. It appeared to be bred into them.

But Thomas—Lord Thomas.

No, that was no longer his title. Her mother had informed her only moments before. Everyone was talking about it—the Chance family foregoing tradition yet again.

Steeling herself to be more forward than she had ever been in her life, Victoria swallowed. "Hello, Your Grace."

The new Duke of Cothrom blanched. "I—I haven't gotten used to that."

Victoria nodded, uncertainty prickling at the edges of her mind. Was that too direct? She had not actually heard the full story, just that somehow, for a reason no one knew, the Duke of Cothrom had given the title to his son Thomas.

The man she had longed for, pathetically pined over for so long…was now a duke.

And she needed to say something, Victoria realized, as the silence eked out longer and longer. Lord Thomas Chance had already been a delectable enough prospect for any young lady in the *ton*, and now that he was the new duke, there would be plenty of ladies who would see the opportunity to become a duchess and would wish to grasp it with both hands.

What would it be like to grasp Thomas Chance with both hands? Her fingertips grazing his shirt, the heat of his—

Victoria cleared her throat and hoped to goodness the desire in which she had allowed herself to indulge had not been visible on her face. *The very idea!*

"I only just heard," she said softly as Lord Thomas—His Grace— stepped to the left to avoid a footman carrying a silver platter of empty punch glasses. "I suppose you knew your father would—"

"No. No, it was all rather a horrendous surprise, to tell the truth."

He spoke with such honesty that Victoria's gasp got tangled in her throat.

Oh, this was what she had longed for—a conversation with Lord Thomas that was intimate, and open, one that suggested she was more to him than just any woman with whom he might converse.

But she must not get ahead of herself. It would not do to forget she was supposed to be seducing him.

As Victoria threw back her shoulders and took a deep breath, just like her mother had always told her not to, a flicker of delight soared down her spine as she watched the new Lord Cothrom's eyes widen, drop to her not-inconsiderable bosom, then swiftly lift back to her eyes.

Pink seared across his cheeks, just for a moment.

There, Victoria thought, a strange new thrill roaring through her. She could flirt, even if her mother said that young ladies did not do such a thing.

Young ladies wishing to catch a duke had to flirt.

"Well, la! I suppose I should indeed call you 'Your Grace' from now on," Victoria said as brightly as she could manage with her lungs so tight. "You'll be ready for the finer things in life now, I dare say."

The moment the words had escaped her lips, she regretted them.

What on earth was she saying? Did she not know that Lord Thomas—that His Grace had barely two pennies to rub together thanks to his own foolishness?

Victoria was still certain there was more to the story. The new Duke of Cothrom could surely not be so foolish. There was undoubtedly someone else involved, someone Lord Thomas was protecting.

Lord Cothrom, that was. Oh, Lord, this was getting complicated.

"I would rather you called me 'Lord Thomas,'" he said quietly, taking a step closer.

So she could hear him, Victoria tried to convince herself, her pulse quickening with every inch he moved closer. Oh, she had never been this close to him, not outside of a dance. And that had only been once.

How did he do it? There was something about the man, something electric, something that grasped deep within her and demanded to be recognized. She became naught but a moth nearing a flame, unable to look away, unable to think when he looked at her like that. When his mouth curved. When his eyes flickered to her breasts again and—

Victoria swallowed. She was letting this opportunity get away, one she could never have dreamed of.

Lord Thomas Chance was always dining with the very best, attending balls with the finest of Society, invited to gatherings by the most elegant of the *ton*.

Tracking him down, she had thought, would be difficult. And now he was talking to her!

"Though as the duke, there are responsibilities and grandeur I had not expected," the new Duke of Cothrom said airily, puffing out his chest in a way Victoria had never seen before. "I suppose I shall have to catalog the vast estates I now manage, speak to those who labor on the land…"

He continued in the same vein for a great deal of time, Victoria's shoulders slumping with each passing minute.

This was not the Lord Thomas she knew. The man she had met just over a year ago…he had been charming, yes, but he made himself the butt of his jokes, was affectionate when speaking of his family, and had genuine interests. He'd had passion, a passion for justice. He had spoken powerfully on the poorhouses, spoke against criminalizing vagrancy.

Victoria remembered the moment she had made him laugh, and it had felt like…like the rest of the world had fallen away, and there had been only the two of them.

Just her, and him, laughing because she had been witty.

And now…

"—gems, and statues, that sort of thing," the new Lord Cothrom said, waving an airy hand. "One can easily forget, you see, just how fabulous are the riches of one's home if one does not catalog them.

EMILY E K MURDOCH

The Reubens, and the Gainsboroughs…"

Victoria tilted her head slightly as though that would aid in her understanding. What on earth had gotten into the man? If he had been anyone else, she would have said he was…

Well. *Boasting.*

It wasn't natural, and the strangeness of his manner began to grate.

This wasn't the man she had planned to seduce.

"—and… I'm boring you, aren't I?"

Victoria did her best to lie with a winsome expression. "No! No, not at all. I—"

"I never expected to be a duke. Not really," he muttered, all the bluff and bluster gone. Suddenly, the man with whom she had fallen so helplessly in love had returned, his cheeks red. "You don't expect your father to die, do you?"

"No," Victoria said softly, pushing aside the pain. "No, you don't."

Somehow, Lord Cothrom appeared to realize he had said something indiscreet. "I do apologize, Miss Ainsworth, I… Your father?"

Drawing herself up as best she could, Victoria nodded. "Five years ago. It was quick, and the doctors tell us it was painless, and that is all one can hope for."

He looked stricken, his shoulders sinking—his evident pain that he had hurt her, undoing all the distance he had wrought with his speeches about gems and land. "I am so sorry. Please, forgive me, I did not intend—"

"I know," Victoria said softly, reaching out and placing her hand on his. "I know."

Then she looked down, her lips parting in astonishment.

She had not intended to do it. The movement had been one of instinct, of reassuring someone who had not intended to hurt her that she was not, in fact, much injured.

But she had not remembered that she had removed her gloves. And the new Lord Cothrom, he wasn't wearing any gloves, either.

The whole world spun on the briefest of connections. Victoria could almost feel the earth changing its course as the attention of her mind focused on nothing but the caress of his fingers, the way they moved, almost imperceptibly, underneath hers.

And then she removed them.

Well, she could hardly keep them there, could she? There would be a scandal. Someone would see. Touching Thomas Chance like that for more than five seconds, she could not be held accountable for her actions.

Victoria swallowed. "You always were easy to talk to."

She felt a fool admitting it but softened as she saw the wide smile she elicited.

"You think so?" The Duke of Cothrom leaned forward. "I am glad. I enjoyed our conversations last year—no, I suppose technically, now the year before last—very much. It is pleasant indeed to see you in Bath, Miss Ainsworth."

Warmth rushed through her. How was it possible for such inane words to have such an effect on her?

But then, she had not intended to fall in love so quickly. She had not expected to one day meet a man who would touch her heart so instantly, so painfully.

And now here she was, talking to him!

"Yes, my mother and I are here for the winter," she said, hardly sure how she was able to get one word out after the other. *Now flutter your lashes, just like you see the coquettes of Society do...* "It's so important to be warm, don't you think? Bath is so wonderful for warming oneself. And... And yourself?"

"The whole senior Chance branch is here," he said with a snort that could have been laughter and could have been derision. "And my Uncle John and his family. My sister is determined to avoid finding a husband despite our mother's best attempts, God help us, and my brothers... Well, the less said about my brothers, I fear, the better."

He had always had a way of putting her at ease—putting anyone at ease, she supposed, but Victoria felt whenever she was with him that she was the only person in the room. In the world. Even that time the other day when he'd seemed so distracted. Nothing else had mattered.

"I would have loved siblings, but alas, it was not to be," she said, looking up through fluttering eyelashes. Was this working? How did one tell?

Thomas Chance most definitely laughed this time. "And in my view, you have made a lucky escape! Siblings are not all what they are cracked up to be, and I have three—and goodness knows how many cousins. To be honest, I lost count. My father, he always said…"

Something of the charm died away in the man's expression and Victoria felt the lack of it immediately. It was like stepping outside into the cold Bath streets without a pelisse just as the first flakes of snow started to fall.

Blast. Well, there was nothing for it now. She could hardly ignore the obvious, and it was best that they deal with it head on.

"I am sure your father is confident in you. I mean," Victoria added as Thomas raised a quizzical eyebrow and her body threatened to explode with heat, "he would not have given you the title, and in such an odd manner, if he did not believe… Well. That you could do it."

"'Do it'?"

"Be the Duke of Cothrom," said Victoria, flushing at the intimacy with which she spoke. It had been so long since they had spoken, spoken properly. This was the sort of conversation that he would surely be having with a trusted friend. Not a woman who had foolishly fallen in love with him then never done anything about it.

"The whole of Bath appears to know all about it, far more than even I do," he said wryly. "But it's astonishing how quickly news can get about the place and be twisted in the telling. I heard a ridiculous story once about…about your dowry, for example. That it was five and forty thousand pounds."

The Duke of Cothrom's dark eyes met hers, unwavering, yet with a tinge of uncertainty.

Victoria's lips parted. If it had been anyone else, she would have reprimanded them in no uncertain terms, before tapping him with her fan and sauntering away! The very idea of bringing up such a topic, and in public!

But it wasn't anyone else. It was Lord Thomas Chance. It did not matter that he was the new Duke of Cothrom—he was the man who had made her laugh, who had put her at her ease, who had danced with her and discussed Shakespeare and Marlowe and the poets.

And the casualness of his manner made Victoria realize just what the brigand was up to.

She almost laughed aloud.

"—and I heard most of the Chance money is gone!"

She should have guessed—it certainly should have struck her when Lord Thomas had made a beeline for her after he'd left the card room. This wasn't a seduction. At least, not from his side. This was not even a wooing.

This was all part of his plan to restore his family's fortunes.

Perhaps if it had been another man, Victoria would have been offended. That nasty Colonel Lloyd, for example, or the odious Lord Zouch.

Any other gentleman speaking to her like that in an attempt to woo her merely for her dowry? She would have been swift to return to her mother, and hope to goodness she would never have to see the offender again.

But Lord Thomas Chance?

Victoria forced aside her grin and considered, her mind racing, as she thought what to say in reply.

Well, it was hardly a secret. Her father's death had left her mother a wealthy woman, and a separate pot of money had been put aside for when Victoria was married.

And Lord Thomas Chance needed a pot of money, did he not?

The Chance family fortunes were spent and it was all his fault, if the rumors were true. He needed to marry, and marry well. Marry extremely well.

Marry someone like her.

"Miss Ainsworth?" Lord Cothrom said, concern puckering a line between his eyes. "I have not offended?"

Victoria tried to keep calm. "Offended? N-No. Not offended."

Because it was so obvious, wasn't it?

Lord Thomas Chance, now Lord Cothrom, was considering her, Victoria Ainsworth, for his wife *because of her money.*

She, Victoria Ainsworth, was already in love with Thomas Chance, Duke of Cothrom.

So...why not? Why not permit him to woo her? Why not encourage him, even, to pursue her, flirt with him, give him the show that every young eligible woman offered a courting gentleman—the very thought made her stomach lurch—all the way to the altar?

She could pretend to be a coquette, with nothing more impressive in her mind than the next visit to her modiste. She could chatter gowns, and parties, and all the sorts of things eligible ladies of the *ton* spoke of. And she could lull him into a type of affection, dangle her dowry before him, and...marry him.

Her mother would not approve.

Mother will never have to know.

"Miss Ainsworth?"

Victoria swallowed. Perhaps she should be concerned—it was hardly the best way for a marriage to begin. But then, how many arranged marriages began with less chance of success? She would be a duchess. She would be *his* duchess. It wasn't as if he had nothing to offer her, even if his aim was clearly her fortune. Why not be happy, if she could?

Why not, indeed, grasp happiness?

Not that she would be grasping Thomas anytime soon... Not in public, anyway.

"Miss Ainsworth?" The Duke of Cothrom was frowning, guilt searing across his face again. "I have offended you, after upsetting you about your father. Oh, hell, whom I've just mentioned again. And now I've cursed. Miss Ainsworth—"

"You were asking about my dowry," Victoria said, cutting across him as nerves danced up her. "Five and forty thousand pounds, I think you said."

His eyes met hers. "Yes."

"Well, I am afraid I will have to disappoint you," she said as lightly as she could manage. The musicians were starting up again, and though a part of her wished they could be dancing, it was perhaps safer to have such a conversation here, out of the way. Where they could talk privately.

The Duke of Cothrom's smile faltered. "Disappoint me?"

"My dowry is not five and forty thousand pounds," Victoria continued, a giddy sensation flickering inside her.

His posture drooped. "Ah, I see. Well, that's a shame—"

"It's actually closer to fifty thousand now," she interrupted, watching his face carefully.

Yes, there was the relief and the delight. Was there desire there? What could she do, in the next few days and weeks, to transform that mercenary interest into something so much greater?

His eyes blinked rapidly. "Fifty—fifty thousand?"

Victoria nodded airily, as though she discussed her dowry all the time. "Yes, my father made some good investments just before he died and they have already started to prove fruitful. Wonderful, isn't it?"

And she did not miss the calculating look that disappeared almost in an instant as Thomas Chance nodded. "Yes. Yes, very wonderful, in fact."

Victoria tried to tell herself this was no different than any other courtship. Fine, so Thomas only wanted to woo her for her money. She knew that—an advantage not every woman had in her situation.

He would woo, and she would simper. He would corrupt her, and she would seduce him. *We will fall in love*, Victoria thought with a surge of excitement, a grin unbidden on her lips. And they would be happy.

"Tell me, Miss Ainsworth," the duke said, taking another step closer to her, now almost pressed up against her.

Victoria closed her eyes, just for a moment, to imagine it. His breath warm on her neck, her fingers in his hair, all alone, the two of them indulging in the desire they both—

She almost jumped when he next spoke. Her eyes snapped open.

He was a great deal nearer than she had thought—a great deal. Just as she had imagined, Thomas Chance's breath blossomed on her neck, making her skin tingle.

"Tell me...have you ever explored the environs of Bath?"

Victoria looked up into those dark eyes and saw desire...but for her money, she told herself firmly, not for herself.

Not yet.

"Y-You know, I haven't," she said, trying not to think about what this must look like. Honestly, it was a miracle her mother hadn't stormed over there and demanded the man propose on the spot.

Now she came to think about it, that wasn't the worst idea in the—

"In that case, I would be honored if you would accompany me on a carriage ride tomorrow," said the man she adored.

"Why, thank you, Your—"

"My barouche is very comfortable," Thomas Chance continued, a wolfish grin on his lips. "I think you will find it more than adequate for our needs."

Victoria swallowed.

Dear God, the man moves quickly. When he had said a carriage ride—

well, any well-bred lady like herself would presume he meant a chaise and four, large enough to encompass herself and a companion, likely as not her mother. To keep it all aboveboard.

Clearly, Thomas Chance did not wish to keep things aboveboard.

How would she explain this to her mother? The prospect of her daughter becoming a duchess might not even be enough to sway her to allow the encounter without a chaperone.

That would be a problem for the next day.

Attempting as best she could to push aside all the images of what a barouche ride with a scoundrel like him would be like, Victoria forced herself to nod. "That... That sounds adequate, yes."

Adequately scandalous. Adequate to start a thousand and one rumors through Bath. Adequately small enough for his knee to brush up against hers, to feel his heat, to—

"In that case, I shall call upon you at eleven o'clock, Miss Ainsworth," said the new Lord Cothrom brightly. "I...I admit, I look forward to it."

And there's no need to look so surprised, Victoria thought wryly as Thomas Chance took one further look at her bosom, then bowed so low, his mouth almost came into contact with her breasts, then departed.

Oh, he thinks he's so clever...

Chapter Four

January 4, 1840

"YOU JUST WATCH, I'll easily—damn!"

"Not as easy as it looks, is it?" Leopold shook his head, beaming. "Remind me, what was it you were saying about how you were the best in the family at—"

"Thank you, I don't need reminding," growled Thomas.

The rain had poured all morning, making his early morning walk impossible. It was only now that he couldn't have it that he realized just how greatly he depended on it.

He'd never much been one for exercise, inheriting the naturally lean Chance frame, so he had never paid much attention to the daily walk on which he took himself as part of his routine. Sometimes he even went out if the day was damp. But this morning, the rain had turned to sleet, which had turned to snow, and though it had warmed sufficiently to be rain again, he was no fool. He was not going out in that.

Something tightened around his torso. And would he be able to go for his ride? The barouche was all ready. He didn't want to let down—

"That's another two points to me, then," said Leopold smartly, updating the score with a most irritating grin. "You know, I thought you used to be good at this."

"Billiards is not a game for the weak," Thomas shot back, allowing a grin to slide across his face. "You'll soon make a mistake and—"

"'The weak'? You jest, sir," returned his brother.

Thomas grinned as he strode around the table to line up his next stop. "I think you'll find that's 'Your Grace.'"

He regretted the words as soon as they were out of his mouth. His brother's face did not alter, but it was the carefully considered expression that purposefully did not alter that told Thomas everything he needed to know.

"Ignore me," Thomas said abruptly.

Leopold's jaw was tight. "I generally do."

"No, I am serious. I should not have said—"

"You are the duke now. There's nothing to be done about it," Leopold said lightly. Too lightly. "Come on, play your shot."

Thomas turned to the table, in the main to prepare for his shot, but partly because it was easier to look at the green baize than the carefully wooden expression of his brother.

Oh, everything was topsy-turvy. The whole family had been put out of kilter with this duke business—not that he had ever asked for it—and the letters from cousins would start arriving soon. There was even talk, apparently, that his uncles were considering handing over their titles to their eldest sons in turn. It was madness. It was foolishness. It was—

Well, it was their prerogative.

And it put the second-born sons into very strange positions.

It was all very well being under the authority of a father—that was expected. But to have to look up to a brother in the same way, to accept that all of a sudden, it was your sibling who was the head of the family while your father still lived…

Thomas almost bit his tongue as he lunged for a shot and completely missed.

"One would almost think there was something on your mind," Leopold said sarcastically.

Thomas swallowed hard before straightening up and shrugging. "I suppose there is."

"The heavy duties of duking?"

He turned, half-hoping his brother was intending to be unpleasant so the two of them could have it out, right here and now. But Leopold was smiling, a weary smile, admittedly, but one without malice or anger.

"Honestly, I don't mind," he said quietly. "You were always going to be the duke. It was never—"

"Yes, but it happening now," Thomas said wretchedly, twisting his billiard's cue around and around in his fingertips. "It's... It's..."

"*Odd*, I think is the word you are looking for," supplied Leopold with a brief grin before he studied the table between them and positioned himself for his shot. It was masterful. Thomas updated the points. "You'll be fighting off the ladies with that billiard's cue of yours."

Thomas snorted. Perhaps he was right. He'd never exactly had much trouble attracting the ladies to his cause at the best of times, but he hadn't been a duke then. Just a duke's son.

It was an interesting thought.

He knew how his father felt about matrimony, but really, a duke needn't be faithful...

Miss Ainsworth's pale bosom, the flush of red across her skin, made a rather jarring image in his mind at that moment. He had no need of other ladies, he reminded himself, until he'd made a conquest of this one. *The* one.

"He doesn't need help with the ladies," came a new voice, one that made Thomas flush at the insinuation. "Do you, Tommy?"

Maude, the eldest of his siblings, was leaning against the door-frame with a teasing laugh on her lips. Dark, naturally curling hair, a generally refined air and a sharpness in the eyes that brooked absolutely no critique, his sister had broken a fair few hearts in her day. *Not that this isn't her day, obviously*, he mentally adjusted hurriedly. But when one's sister reached thirty, it was natural to think her... Well. The word "spinster" had been banned by their mother, but...

"I haven't been *Tommy* for years," Thomas said, entirely ignoring the first part of her comment.

"And I quite disagree, the man desperately needs help with the ladies," Leopold said with a laugh, clearly delighted that it was now two against one.

Maude raised an eyebrow. "If that is true, why is the barouche prepared for the new Duke of Cothrom and his 'lady friend' so I can't use it to go to Milsom Street?"

Ah. Yes, he probably should have asked to use the barouche. It should have occurred to him that his sister might want to use it. *Damn.*

But then, Thomas reasoned as his chest swelled, did the Duke of Cothrom have to ask to use his own barouche? Surely, Father had never—

"Oh, Lord, he's thinking about being the Duke of Cothrom," Maude muttered in a not-so-subtle voice.

Thomas's chest immediately deflated. "I'm not—"

"You can tell so easily—it's all in the shoulders," said Maude, stepping into the room and taking the billiard cue out of his unresisting fingers. "Honestly Tommy, you are so easy to read. I don't know why you're thinking of taking that woman out in the barouche. Why not just tell her you want to marry her dowry and—"

"Maudy!"

Both brothers exclaimed her name in equal horror, though, Thomas thought, for different reasons.

As it was, heat was building in him that had nothing to do with the billiards table and everything to do with Miss Victoria Ainsworth.

"You can't just go about bandying suggestions like that," Thomas said forcefully. "And give me my cue back. You can't play—"

"Who says I can't?" said Maude, flaring up immediately.

"Look, the man wants to marry a fortune—" began Leopold.

"And what is wrong with that?" said Thomas, reaching to take the billiard cue from his sister.

She stepped away around the table. Oh, but she was infuriating. Were all sisters so purposefully irritating? And she always did it with a grin—that was the most annoying part!

Well. That and she'd taken his billiard cue. What on earth did she think she was going to do with it?

"Isn't marrying a fortune a tad uncouth?" said Maude, that eyebrow once again raised.

Uncouth? "I think it's the most ducal thing I could do," Thomas reasoned, reaching again for the billiard cue and once again having it moved out of his reach. "What better way to safeguard the family than to bring in a whole heap of—"

"And what does *she* think about this?" his sister shot back, a hand now on her hip.

It made her look so like their mother, Thomas had to fight the urge to instantly tell the truth and apologize. Sisters should not be able to so easily manipulate their brothers.

"Take your shot," she added to their brother.

Thomas looked at Leopold for assistance, but the man merely shrugged and began lining up his next shot.

"Miss Ainsworth," Thomas began, hardly knowing where the sentence was going.

"She'll see through you immediately," muttered his brother. He took his shot. He missed.

"Serves you right." Thomas smirked. "Maudy, give me back my—"

"And what makes you think I couldn't take the shot?"

Exchanging a look with his brother that was part mirth, part pity, Thomas grinned. *She is so much older than you*, he reminded himself. Thirty, a spinster by any definition—though he dared not say it—and just as determined to wed for love as their mother had been. She would need a large dowry to attract a man at her age, even if he fell in love with her. She should be permitted some fun, even if it was only a few attempts on the billiards table.

As long as she didn't rip the baize.

"Go on, then," Thomas said aloud, stretching out his hands in a gesture of invitation. "Have a try, but don't feel too bad if you...if you..."

His voice trailed away as Leopold gasped.

With a swiftness and adeptness he had never seen in a player, Maude stepped to the table without hesitation and potted the next ball. And the next. A swift sidestep around the table and two more balls were potted. Before Thomas could say another word, his sister had cleared the table and jumped up onto it to perch on the edge with a wry smile.

Thomas stared at her, then their brother. "But... But how... how did she—"

"I spend an inordinate amount of time at home, not permitted to leave on my own, and unwilling to go everywhere with Mother," Maude said matter-of-factly, though Thomas did not miss the sadness behind the words. "What do you *think* I spend my time doing?"

Leopold was laughing. Thomas had to admit he had been thoroughly schooled.

"Very good," he admitted. "Now, are you going to let Leo and me—"

"I am not," Maude said smartly.

Thomas frowned. "And why not?"

"Because, *Your Grace*—"

"Don't call me—"

"—because it has stopped raining. Don't you have a bride to charm?"

Whirling around to the large bay windows overlooking the street, Thomas saw that she was right. At some point during their conversation, the rain had ceased, and there was even the suggestion of sunshine peeking out behind the clouds.

"Your barouche awaits," Leopold said with a wink. "Now all you have to do is woo the woman."

All he had to do was woo the woman. When put like that, it sounded quite simple.

After all, he'd wooed women before. Now, he could even offer his bride the title of "duchess" far sooner than he'd once thought. How hard could it be?

As Thomas drew up outside the Ainsworths' home, his mouth went dry as he saw the door open and out of it appear…

How much had he drunk last night?

In his memory, Miss Ainsworth had been pretty, yes, with a bosom to sink into and a smile he'd wanted to claim as his own. But that was all.

This woman?

"Good morning," said Miss Ainsworth lightly, alighting down the steps onto the pavement to stand beside the barouche. "I was worried the rain would prevent our ride." She kept glancing over her shoulder and back to her front door, as if afraid someone else might appear to join them.

Perhaps she had not exactly been truthful to her mother as to her plans for the day.

If he were a gentleman, he should have insisted she bring a chaperone.

But he didn't have the time to be a gentleman. Bills would soon need to be paid.

But more importantly, the way her neck kept turning, the smooth skin tickled by the soft ringlets of her hair…

Thomas opened his mouth, any one of the clever and charming phrases he had used to such great effect in the past just ready to spill from his lips.

None of them did.

Miss Ainsworth's worthy smile flickered, just for a moment. "And... And yet the sunshine is here. How pleasant. La!"

Thomas was certain the day was pleasant—and if he had in any way continued to notice the weather, he was sure he would have seen it was fine. But that was not the fineness on which he was concentrating.

Miss Ainsworth was wearing a pelisse of elegant blue that tucked underneath her bust in such a way that...

Mouth dry, mind nothing but knots, Thomas cleared his throat in the hope it would encourage some words to come out.

The expression of Miss Ainsworth was bright. "Am... Am I to be permitted entrance?"

Thomas whispered, "Entrance?"

What was she talking about?

Miss Ainsworth tapped the side of the barouche with a gloved finger and a giggle. "Your... Your barouche. May I enter?"

Thomas blinked. Then suddenly, the realization he had just been staring like a complete imbecile dawning on him, reminding him all of the social niceties he had, up until this point, completely forgotten. Niceties like saying good afternoon, and how nice the weather was, and opening the door for her, and telling her how pleasant it was to see her...

Very, very pleasant.

Jumping up as though he'd been struck by lightning, which didn't feel far from the truth, Thomas almost tripped over his own feet to descend from the barouche.

"Good afternoon, Miss Ainsworth and how nice you are. You look. Nice weather!" he stammered in a medley of words mingled with confusion and—

Well, yes. Desire.

It was strange—most ladies looked *more* impressive under the kind candlelight of the Assembly Rooms, and it was only when one arranged to meet them in the clear light of day that a gentleman realized that... Well. They did not quite live up to the remembrance.

"Your Grace?"

But somehow, Miss Ainsworth was quite the opposite. Oh, she had looked pretty enough standing against that pillar—Thomas told himself as a particular part of him started to become like stone—but here, in the brightness of day under a growing sun...

She looked magnificent.

"Your Grace, may I?"

And the way she looked at him with such a knowing—

Thomas blinked. "'Your Grace'?"

"That is how I must address you now, is it not? I know you said you prefer 'Lord Thomas,' but I thought that would not do." Miss Ainsworth spoke lightly, though there was a slight quaver in her tone. "La, Your Grace!"

La? Nerves, perhaps?

She wasn't the only one. *Pull yourself together, man,* Thomas told himself firmly. *You're here to woo the woman, not be charmed by her in return. She's the one who is fortunate to attract you. You're a duke! You're here for her fortune and not much else.*

Right. Charm offensive. The old Chance charm. It had never *not* worked, after all.

"Miss Ainsworth, you may address me in any way you wish," Thomas said smoothly, reaching past her and allowing just a hint of his sleeve to brush up against her arm as he opened the barouche door. "Please."

He offered out his hand.

It was a simple gesture. It was also one he had performed countless times and for ladies of all ages and stations. Why, just last week, he had helped Lady Romeril into a carriage, and the day after, assisted his mother's lady's maid after they'd returned from the modiste.

Which was why Thomas had not expected much when Miss Ainsworth took his hand.

It was all he could do to stay upright. The heat that poured through the elegant glove as she took his hand—it was incomprehensible. Sparks seemed to soar down his fingers, his whole arm stiffening and his body rocking at the sudden impact.

Miss Ainsworth appeared unaffected. She released his hand without a second glance and settled herself in the barouche, pleated skirts spread out around her.

Then she looked at Thomas. "Are you quite well, Your Grace?"

Thomas blinked. He was still standing with his hand outstretched, hardly able to believe what had just happened.

This was ridiculous. He was here to woo her, not be wooed!

Clearing his throat loudly, he muttered, "Yes, yes, fine," as he snapped the barouche door shut and stepped around the carriage to take his seat.

His seat beside the woman he had decided to marry merely for her money.

He was not looking at her for only a few moments, not even a minute, but it was enough. When Thomas stepped up into the barouche and settled himself, he was perfectly able to do so without thinking of fingers, hands, or the hip he could feel beside him.

Almost without thinking.

"Now, Miss Ainsworth, I believe I promised you a ride around Bath's environs," he said briskly, picking up the reins and encouraging the pair of horses into a gentle trot.

"You did, indeed," came the giggling reply.

Thomas calmed his rapidly pacing pulse. That was it. All he had to do was lean into it. Despite what he told himself, there was no need to conflate urgency with boorishness. He may have taken this lady out without her chaperone, but he would not force her to accept him. He had a little time. At least, until the debts were called in.

"I wished particularly to show you the most delightful little hill," Thomas said, his voice strengthening as he slipped into the flirtatious rhythm he had used time and time again. "There is the most splendid view from there that I think you will appreciate, what I believe to be the second-most beautiful view in all Bath."

"Oh?" Miss Ainsworth's voice sounded intrigued, and as they continued along Milsom Street and started making for the edge of the city, she asked the question Thomas had known she would. "And what is the *most* beautiful view in all of Bath?"

"Ah, well, there's a difficulty there," Thomas said, settling into his seat and its well-worn cushions as he trotted out the lines that were equally as worn. "For I am afraid you cannot see the first most beautiful view in all of Bath."

She tilted her head. "I cannot?"

Thomas rewarded himself with a glance at his companion as the horses picked up pace and ignored the jolt of longing. "Only I can enjoy that view this morning."

As expected, pink seared across Miss Ainsworth's cheeks and she looked at her hands clasped in her lap before her. "Oh, la! Your Grace, you must not—"

"I do not think I like the formality of that phrase," said Thomas completely honestly. "Not with you."

"You... You do not?"

There was a breathiness in her voice now, one he knew well. He was usually able to get a lady to this stage within a few minutes of conversation, but there was something strange about his rapid success with Miss Ainsworth. It was... Well. Not as pleasant as he had expected.

Thomas glanced away for a moment, his gaze flickering over the hedgerows and tall oak trees lining the road leading away from Bath. The city was very much behind them now, yet the beauty of nature in winter was insufficient to distract him from his thoughts.

And the primary one was: *it shouldn't be this easy.*

It was strange. He had never worried about his ability to charm the ladies—why would he? But using these lines on Miss Ainsworth, ones he had perfected with others...

It felt wrong, somehow.

Damn.

What had gotten into him?

"I suppose you would like me to...to call you 'Lord Cothrom'?" Miss Ainsworth asked, her voice light yet weighty with meaning.

Thomas slowed the horses until they were at a gentle walk, then took the opportunity to look at his companion.

Miss Ainsworth was blushing very prettily and appeared delighted with him. Why shouldn't she have been? He was a handsome, titled, charming gentleman of good family and, until recently, good fortune.

A twist of guilt charged through him. And here he was, wooing her merely for her money.

"I said—"

"I am sorry, I did hear you," said Thomas, and before he could polish up the words with some Chance charm, the honest truth slipped out. "I was momentarily distracted."

"Distracted?"

"By you," he said simply.

Miss Ainsworth's cheeks pinked again, but in her pupils he could see precisely what Thomas had hoped for.

Desire. Want, longing, even perhaps a need. She needed him.

Which was precisely what he had aimed for. If he played his cards right, they could be engaged within the month. Sooner, perhaps.

And that was what he needed.

Thomas steeled himself, reminded himself just how much was at stake. The whole family, their place in Society—Maude's dowry. St. Thomas's.

He had to do this. Even if there was a modicum of guilt.

"I still don't know how you would like to be addressed," said Miss Ainsworth with a smile.

Thomas, he wanted to say. *Call me 'Thomas.' Call it out as you—*

"Lord Cothrom will do just fine," he said aloud, forcing down the instinct to open himself to her, to become vulnerable.

That must never happen. Of all people in the world, Miss Ainsworth must never know the true him, the Thomas Chance who made mistakes and let down his family so utterly.

No, best she only encounter the charming Duke of Cothrom, Thomas reminded himself sternly as he plastered a smile upon his face. That was the way it had to be.

"Tell me, Miss Ainsworth, how is your mother? I greatly wish to take tea with her…"

Chapter Five

January 6, 1840

A LL IN ALL, Victoria thought as she sipped her tea, *it is going well.* True, the conversation had not entirely flowed as she had hoped. Yes, there had been some quiet at the beginning. It could not be denied that there were lulls in the awkwardness in the room. But all in all—

"And what, precisely, are your intentions toward my daughter, sir?"

And it was all going so well.

Victoria managed not to snort into her tea and attract her mother's ire for being unladylike, having placed her cup back in its saucer before anyone spoke. The trouble was, the silence elongated out and out, until it was obvious Thomas Chance, Duke of Cothrom, had not replied.

He caught her eye. Victoria flushed.

Well, it was a very direct question—and one accompanied by the incorrect term of address, to boot.

She suspected her mother knew about the carriage ride the other day. Surely, someone about the *ton* had spotted them and made Mrs. Ainsworth aware of the fact that when her daughter had claimed to want to rest in her room, she'd actually brazenly left out the front door. Nothing untoward had occurred during the ride, but the mere fact of the matter was, Victoria had been in the gentleman's company unchaperoned.

Her mother likely thought, though, that it was best not to speak of the topic aloud. She knew her mother. If they didn't acknowledge it, it was if it hadn't happened.

But *something* had surely irritated her mother to this degree of restrained disrespect.

Besides, Victoria knew precisely what the Duke of Cothrom's intentions were toward her. He wished to marry her dowry, and if she happened to come along with it, so be it.

He would marry her, spend her money on his family, probably gamble a great deal of it away, and then...

Probably get bored of me, Victoria could not help but wonder as her attention flickered once more over the elegantly dressed gentleman on the sofa opposite her. He had on a high collar, a cravat with more knots than the Navy, and a charming smile that made her go so weak at the knees, it was a good thing she was already sitting.

Not that her mother appeared transfixed.

"I said," repeated Mrs. Ainsworth in a louder tone, "what precisely are your intentions—"

"I do apologize, Mrs. Ainsworth. I did hear you before, but I was considering my reply," interjected the genteel words of the Duke of Cothrom. "You see, your daughter means...means a great deal to me."

Victoria did her best not to snort.

Well, really! He barely knew her. How on earth could he say such a thing?

She, on the other hand, knew him. She had never believed in love at first sight, not until she had been introduced to the tall and painfully enthralling gentleman known then as Lord Thomas Chance.

Since that moment, she had... Well, not exactly *obsessed.* Obsessed was a strong word.

She had certainly been open to hearing information about the eldest Chance brother in the senior branch. Perhaps that was the best way to put it.

So she knew him. She knew how Thomas liked his tea—she had seen the widening of his eyes in surprise as she'd quietly instructed her mother to leave the slice of lemon in his cup. She knew where he bought his cigars, and who smuggled his brandy, and what sort of horses he liked to gamble on at the races.

She knew him.

Him, on the other hand? Victoria very much doubted he could have picked her out in a crowd...until someone, obviously, had mentioned her dowry.

He'd flattered her quite often these past few days, and she could hardly stop herself from reacting like a smitten fool, but she knew what he was doing when he spoke so prettily.

Intentions? Oh, his intentions were very clear, indeed. For now, Thomas Chance was only interested in her money.

For now. Victoria was determined to change that.

"Because there are gentlemen in the *ton*—I barely call them gentlemen, you understand—who would wish to court my daughter on account of her pair of immense—"

"*Mother!*"

"—investments, which consist of her dowry," finished her mother, her mouth agape. "Honestly, Victoria, I cannot think what else you were thinking I might say."

Heat scalded Victoria's cheeks as she looked at precisely what she had been thinking of. Both of them.

She wasn't blind; she saw the way men grew distracted by a subtle heave of her chest. It was one of her greatest assets. Greatest pair of assets.

When she looked up, Thomas Chance was most determinedly not looking at her assets.

Victoria permitted herself a small smile. "I am sure His Grace could not be thinking of mere money, Mother. Goodness!"

That was it—pretend she was foolish. Didn't gentlemen like foolish women?

"Of course not, of course not," said Mrs. Ainsworth quickly, waving a hand holding a teacup and threatening to spill tea over her own drawing room. "I speak naturally of other, lesser gentlemen. Not yourself, sir. My lord. Your Grace."

Grimacing was not an option. Victoria had been raised with the highest etiquette of the noblest houses—not that her father had had a title, but still. There was no harm in learning about the manners of the class one intended to marry into, as he had so often said.

So she was able to prevent any discomfort appearing on her face at her mother's words. By the looks of it, the Duke of Cothrom was doing the same.

"That is very kind of you, Mrs. Ainsworth," he said quietly. "I am sure there are mercenary men in the world."

Victoria watched carefully and saw a flicker of discomfort in his eyes. It was very slight. Unless one had been looking for it, she doubted whether it would have been noticed at all.

But it was there. So, he was having some qualms, was he, about pursuing her for the dowry alone? Well, that was progress.

It was certainly more honest than those ridiculous lines he had fed her during their barouche ride. Honestly—the 'most beautiful view of all Bath'? What rot!

"I suppose your new title has given you a great deal of new responsibilities," her mother continued.

"Oh, yes, a great many."

"And you are enjoying the new role, I suppose?"

Victoria saw it; the hesitation, the carefully arranged smile. What was he hiding?

"Yes, very much. It is strange, as you can imagine, inheriting while one's father is still alive, but I am hopeful he will be a great aid to me in this time of…of transition."

The duke spoke calmly, levelly, as though he was interrogated in this manner every day of the week. Victoria could see the discomfort, almost feel it in his frame. The tautness of his jaw, the way his shoulders did not move.

"Transition, indeed, a period of great change," said her mother slowly. "And I suppose during this period of change, you are thinking of the future. The responsibilities, I mean, to your line. In fact, you may be considering taking a w—"

"Madam, come quick!"

Just as Victoria was about to intervene to prevent her mother from being painfully blatant about her matrimonial hopes for her daughter, their housekeeper, Mrs. Stenton, burst into the room.

The new Duke of Cothrom spilled his tea on the carpet.

Mrs. Ainsworth cried out. "Mrs. Stenton, how many times have I—"

"I am sorry, madam, but a note just came from—from Lady Romeril!" their housekeeper said hastily. Her light, bulbous eyes were so wide, they almost popped out of her wan face.

Victoria almost laughed as she watched her mother freeze. Lady Romeril? Not a woman in their social circle. Though she had deigned to speak to them at events they had all attended, the woman was still far too high above them. A note from Lady Romeril? What on earth could that be about?

Her mother rose to her feet, spilled tea not worth thinking about when a note from Lady Romeril had arrived. "A note—from Lady Romeril? What does it say?"

"Oh, madam, I would not read a note addressed to you! Though... Well, it was not sealed, so a few words caught my eye..."

It was starting to become difficult to keep her giggles hidden, and it only became more difficult when Victoria happened to meet the duke's eye. His lips were pressed together, clearly keeping his laughter in, but it brought her attention very much to his lips...

His very kissable lips.

"Mrs. Stenton, what few words did you—"

"Something about a charity concert, and needing your input, and would you please go along to her townhouse at your earliest convenience to assist with the decisions, if it would not be too much trouble," said the housekeeper in a rush.

A small giggle managed to get past Victoria's lips, but she transformed it into a cough as her mother ran out of the drawing room.

"Mrs. Stenton, fetch me my pelisse! Order the carriage! Make arrangements for dinner without me—where, oh, where is my shawl?"

The housekeeper had followed her mistress's wake out of the room, and as the door swung shut, it muffled the chaos now erupting in the hallway.

Victoria's smile faded. Well, it was not exactly pleasant to have it made so obvious that her mother was desperate to make the acquaintance of fine ladies like Lady Romeril. Not in front of a duke, anyway.

When that duke was Thomas Chance…

He cleared his throat. "I am so sorry."

Victoria stared. *What on earth for?*

The strong scent of tea reminded her. "Oh, the tea—Mrs. Stenton will get that out in no time, I am sure. She is a wonder with a—"

"No, I actually meant…Well. About Lady Romeril."

Heat threatened to rise up her décolletage and neck, but Victoria attempted to keep her voice level and her demeanor calm as she said, "I don't know what you mean."

Her words sounded colder than she had intended, and for a moment, she worried that she had offended the man who had suffered through three-quarters of an hour with her mother.

But Thomas Chance grinned. "No, I actually… Well. Lady Romeril is a friend of the family. I thought it might be pleasant for us to have time to ourselves, so I thought… She did me a small favor."

It took a moment for the meaning of his words to settle in her mind. When they did, Victoria's lips parted in astonishment. "You— You orchestrated this!"

"And I cannot believe how well it worked," he said, rising from his sofa and stepping toward her own. When he sat beside her, heat seared Victoria's whole frame. "Very well, though I say so myself."

Fine. That was impressive, Victoria had to admit, though she did so silently rather than give him the satisfaction.

After all, he had doubtlessly performed the same clever trick on countless other ladies and their mamas. *Many of the young ladies*, she thought as she drew back, trying to prevent herself from leaning toward him, *probably gave in immediately to the man's advances.*

Unlike her. Obviously.

"What were we speaking of?" she asked as blandly as she could manage.

"I believe we were discussing my genius in creating a chance for us to be alone together," the duke said, his voice low and thrumming with possibilities.

Victoria swallowed. Hard.

It was not difficult to see exactly how the man once known as Lord Thomas Chance had gained his reputation as a charming gentleman. The man was attraction himself, paired with the devilishly clever conversation and the way he sat...

She looked away hurriedly. Dear God, did the man know he was doing that? Sitting like that, legs apart, making her look at—

"I actually think we were discussing the myriad and plentiful re- sponsibilities you will now be undertaking as Duke of Cothrom," Victoria said hurriedly, wishing for the first time in her life that she had a fan.

It is hot in here, isn't it?

"Oh, I'm not worried about it," he said lazily, leaning back and resting an arm on the back of the sofa. An arm that ended in a hand, with fingers gently brushing the velvet of the furniture. Brushing it mere inches from her face.

Victoria considered rising from the sofa and seating herself else-where. Then she looked at him, the affection she felt rising so potently, she could not move.

Perhaps it was time to stop playing the flirt. Her, that was. All this "la" business, it did not appear to be getting her anywhere.

"Not worried about it," she repeated, her voice quiet. "I suppose that bluff works on others, Thomas Chance, but it won't work on me."

His smile faltered, his eyes creasing as he beheld her. Victoria forced herself to maintain eye contact, knowing this might be the first time that she saw the real him. The Thomas Chance that he was, for some reason, so eager to hide.

"I don't know what you—"

"You know exactly what I mean," Victoria said softly, refusing to break their gaze. "You can try to hide it if you want, but...but you should know that it doesn't work on me."

He stared. "It doesn't?"

The front door slammed. That was it; her mother was gone. Aside from the servants, they were alone.

"No. It doesn't."

For a moment, she thought she'd gone too far, pushed him toward vulnerability too soon.

Then something changed. She could not have described it... A medley of a shift in his tension, a loosening of his jaw, an honesty breaking out in his eyes.

"You surprise me."

"Yet I am not surprised," Victoria said, hardly knowing where the bravery came from to say such things but unable to stop herself. "Gentlemen often underestimate a lady."

"I certainly underestimated you," he said seriously.

Somehow, he had gotten closer. Victoria had not seen him move, but there was a definite difference. From sitting right at the other end of the sofa, he was now but a foot away.

Well, that is sufficient, she attempted to tell herself. She was strong. She was not about to throw herself at him, after all.

Probably.

"I suppose you did," said Victoria, trying to speak lightly. "But you won't again."

She had expected a quip of a reply, something along the lines of *"Absolutely not"* or *"I won't be so foolish."*

But instead, Thomas quietly said, "I need a woman beside me with that sort of quality. The ability to surprise me. To be underestimated, to be sure, but then to…to use it as an advantage."

Stay calm, Victoria told herself sternly. *He wants your dowry, remember, and you want to seduce him and make him fall in love with you. You both have your plans. He's just progressing down his own.*

Now, what was her next move?

Dipping her shoulder ever so slightly to ensure that the duke gained an excellent view, Victoria said, "That is a rare quality indeed."

"Yes, and my future wife, for that is of whom we speak, must have other…qualities."

Yes, qualities like pots and pots of money.

"And you have a great number of those qualities," Thomas continued, his expression meaningful. "Almost all of them, I would say."

Resisting the urge to ask what on earth she did *not* have to offer him, for Victoria knew she would immediately attempt to demonstrate to him that she had it, she said instead, "I would rather you found a wife you liked. Respected, admired. Qualities or no qualities."

"You think a duke's wife should be merely charming?"

"I think a duke should be charmed by his wife," Victoria said, tilting her head. "I think he should be so charmed by her that any other qualities become secondary—"

"And do you intend to charm your husband, Miss Ainsworth?"

The way his lips curled around her name made Victoria want to rip off all her clothes. She managed to resist. "As a beginning."

Thomas shifted, his fingers brushing the velvet just in her eyeline. Oh, to be under those fingers, those gently stroking fingers...

"I think your future husband will be very fortunate indeed."

"Yes, he will," said Victoria softly, her cheeks pinking ever so slightly. "I can promise you that."

Was this still flirting? It didn't sound or look like the flirting she had seen. She had certainly never spoken to a man like this before. The way he smiled made a coiling ache settle between her thighs. *Dear Lord, who was swindling whom here?*

"Well, thank you," he said, his tone low and grave. "I do not think I have had such a...a refreshing conversation in a long time, Miss Ainsworth."

Victoria tried to ignore the frantic beating of her pulse. "It was my pleasure, Your Grace."

It was the word *"pleasure"* that did it, she was certain. She should not have been so bold, so direct. The word itself was incendiary, likely to spark something outrageous at the best of times.

Thomas Chance reached out and took her hand.

It could have been an innocent movement, one not likely to cause alarm in even the most austere of societal occasions, and so Victoria attempted not to allow her breath to shorten, her lungs to tighten. Tried not to focus on the softness of his fingers, skin on skin, reminding her of that moment at the Assembly Rooms that had become such a part of her dreams.

When Thomas raised her hand to his lips, however, Victoria found herself gasping, unable to stop herself.

"Miss Ainsworth," he said softly, pressing a kiss onto the back of her hand. And then a second. And then a third.

"I...I..."

Hating how inane she sounded, Victoria willed herself to do something, say something—but the trouble was, her instinct was to do something so extreme that the man would certainly not be returning for anything like afternoon tea again.

She was not in possession of herself, and before she could think about it, she had twisted her hand around so that when Thomas lowered his lips for another kiss, it was this time in the middle of her palm.

This time, her gasp was audible, laced with longing, and Thomas's gaze snapped up to meet hers.

"Miss Ainsworth?"

Victoria's breasts heaved, and though she attempted to say something, she found she could not for two very good reasons.

Firstly, she could not conceive of a single thing to say.

Secondly, because Thomas Chance's lips were on her own.

Whether he had been overcome by her boldness at turning over her hand, or the movement of her bosom, or something else, Victoria did not know. She did not know anything. Not with the heady pressure of his lips on hers, pleasure roaring through her body as heated prickles reminded her of every inch of her skin.

He had leaned forward, capturing her mouth with his own in a possessiveness that melted her core. Victoria could do nothing but accept the kiss, accept the indiscretion, accept his tongue as it laced along her lips, begging for entrance.

Who was she to deny him?

Victoria could not prevent a whimper as her tongue met his, a cascade of desire burgeoning inside her as her hands, suddenly freed, twisted up to his neck to pull him closer.

Closer—she needed him closer. She needed everything, all of him, all he would give her—

The kiss ended.

Panting, Thomas leaned his forehead against hers, just for a moment, then released her, leaning back onto the other end of the sofa as though he had been scalded.

Perhaps he had. *She* certainly felt a little warm.

She was also panting. Victoria placed a hand on her décolletage in an attempt to slow her breathing, but it had the unintended effect of drawing Thomas's attention to her breasts.

Not that she minded, particularly. The look of longing in his face was most agreeable.

"I...I did not intend that," he said quietly, meeting her eyes with an apologetic look.

There was no longer any time to steady herself. Victoria tried to keep her voice level and calm as she said, "I did."

The boldness with which she met his look of astonishment was mostly bluster, but she had no choice—he had to know, did he not, just how much she welcomed these attentions.

How much further she was willing to go.

After all, a woman did not seduce with heaving bosoms alone.

"You—You did?"

Victoria answered with a flicker of her eyelashes, hoping it came across as coquettish and charming, rather than as a woman still struggling to get her breath back after a kiss that had threatened to end her life.

"Dear God, I want to kiss you again," Thomas murmured, reaching out for her again.

And she wanted him to. But she could not just be one of those women who gave away kisses, could she? She wanted a proposal. A wedding.

A marriage.

Rising suddenly on legs that threatened to give way, Victoria said brightly, "Yes, I am sure you do, Your Grace—"

"Cothrom, woman, the least you can call me is 'Cothrom.'" He groaned, falling back against the sofa with lust in his eyes.

Victoria swallowed, reminding herself that though her mother had left the house, any servant could walk into the drawing room at any moment to clear the tea things away. It would not do to be found pressed against the sofa with the Duke of Cothrom ravishing her.

Probably.

Actually, now she came to think about it, that would certainly speed things along. A wedding to hush up a scandal. Yes, that would—

"You are far stronger than I," said Thomas in a low voice, rising and advancing with only one thing on his mind so clear, it was almost written on his face. "Victoria—"

"Miss Ainsworth," she said, taking a step back, only half knowing why she was retreating from this temptation.

"Victoria," Thomas repeated in a low, seductive voice. "You liked that kiss—"

"I didn't say I d—"

"And you would quite like another, wouldn't you?"

"Your Grace, I am a lady, and as you so cleverly pointed out, you have arranged to see me again without my chaperone present—"

He was advancing again and Victoria retreated step for step—until the back of her heel met a most inconvenient wall. "Wouldn't you?"

Victoria tried to catch her breath, but it was impossible—the man was impossible. The man was only feet away and if he kissed her like that again she would—

"Tomorrow."

Thomas halted, crossing his arms as though it was that or clutch her to him. "Tomorrow?" His gaze dropped a few inches, just for a moment.

Victoria watched him. "Tomorrow. I…I will kiss you again tomorrow."

His focus sharpened. "Is that a promise, Victoria Ainsworth?"

Oh, I would promise you a great deal more than that, she wanted to say, the words so desperate to be said, she had to press her lips together to keep them inside.

"I don't make promises to dukes," she said lightly.

Thomas frowned, a possessive look shadowing his face. "What other dukes are you talking to?"

"So lovely to have you here for afternoon tea, Your Grace," Victoria said breezily as she sidestepped him and advanced hastily toward the cracked-open door leading to the entryway. "We must do this again some—"

"Tomorrow, you said." Thomas's long stride meant he swiftly reached her, and it was only thanks to foresight that Victoria stepped away from the front door.

The front door that, it appeared, he had wished to pin her against.

Don't think about it, Victoria told herself sternly as her stomach started to churn and her knees quivered. *Don't think about it—*

"Tomorrow," she said quietly, hoping her eyes communicated far more than her tongue would permit. "Let's see what tomorrow brings."

Chapter Six

January 11, 1840

WELL, THOMAS MAY have been a total financial failure, but he knew how to found an orphanage—and keep it warm and the inhabitants fed. Mostly. It was small comfort, but there it was.

He had spent most of that morning at St. Thomas's, listening to the boys read and watching the girls learn their French. Despite the very little he could offer, in a strange way, it settled him. Made him feel…warmer. And within a few days, there would be a better laundry, piped water into the kitchens.

It was all going to plan.

"Your plan is idiotic."

Thomas sighed. *There was always one.* "Maudy, you don't know what you're—"

"Xander told me all about it," his sister said with a sniff as she rustled her skirts, the carriage bumping them slightly to the left. "And I think your plan is idiotic."

Trying not to roll his eyes, he eventually gave in. After all, it was dark. The evening had drawn in quickly and the night was clouded, the moon and stars hidden. There was no possibility she could—

"I saw that."

"Look, it's none of your business, Maudy," Thomas said testily, wishing to goodness he had not agreed to escort her to the Quintrell ball. "You just let me—"

"Lie to a woman and marry her for her money?"

It didn't sound brilliant, put like that. Squirming in his seat and telling himself he was only moving to get comfortable, Thomas said stiffly, "I wouldn't expect you to understand. You're only a lady, you couldn't appreciate just how much pressure—"

His sister's nostrils flared. "I'm sorry, is this the pressure you put yourself under because you spent all your own money, or the pressure you put yourself under because you spent all of Father's money, or—"

Thomas growled. "I don't want to hear it, Maude."

She sniffed. "Of course you don't."

Thomas glared. It was most irritating that his sister be so…so right. A most unpleasant habit of hers.

Because she was right. He was the one who'd gotten himself into this mess, but he was going to get himself out of it. Well. Miss Victoria Ainsworth's money was, at least.

And if they all knew…if they had any idea what he had spent the money on—

Thomas raised himself up and pushed aside the temptation to confess. What good would that do now? No good at all. Far better to sort this out through a little matrimony than a full-blown confession.

"We're almost there," he said aloud, "and I would be grateful if you—"

"Did not tell Miss Ainsworth she's been chosen at random to solve your money troubles?" his sister asked innocently.

Thomas decided not to tell her just how random the choice had been. Thank God Xander had kept that to himself, at least.

"Yes," he said shortly.

"But you're swindling her!" Maude said, real concern in her voice as the carriage rattled down another Bath street. "The poor woman, she has no idea you're merely using her for—"

"It's none of your concern, Maudy—"

"If she joins this family under false pretenses—"

"Enough," Thomas said sharply.

There was a particular sharpness to his tone that he could employ, when necessary, and he hated doing it. There was something of his father in it, which worried him. The man was kind, yes, and gentle, yes, but there was a sharpness, a directness, and miserliness Thomas could not help but dislike.

Was it possible... Was it there within him, if he looked deep enough?

"You *are* swindling her," his sister said quietly. "You are a lot of things, Thomas, but you are not a swindler. You are not a liar. I don't understand what's gotten into you."

"She has a large dowry and large—she has a large dowry," said Thomas, biting down the comment that most certainly would not have been appropriate to say to an older sister. Or any sister, for that matter. "What does she expect?"

"Oh, I am sure she realizes that sort of money has its own attraction," said Maude, waving a hand about the carriage. "It's almost physics, isn't it? That much mass, things are certain to gravitate toward it. I am just saying, I would not like to be pursued for my money—"

"Maudy—"

"—for only my money, I mean," she said, speaking over him as the carriage slowed. "I would hope any man seeking my hand would have an idea of who I was, who I am, besides my fortune."

Thomas swallowed hard. "And I do. With Miss Ainsworth, I mean."

"Do you?"

The carriage was almost at a stop, giving Thomas the opportunity to shuffle in his seat and avoid the question.

It had hit too close. To be sure, he knew a great deal about Miss Ainsworth. Her father was dead and she had a great deal of money. Her breasts were begging to be caressed, and she kissed like an angel. Or a devil. He wasn't sure which.

What else was there to know?

"Not that I will know again what it is to be pursued solely for my dowry," Maude said in a low voice as the carriage rocked, the footman descending to fetch their companion. "Now you've spent it all."

The guilt he had pushed aside for so long, managed to avoid as long as he didn't look at it in the face, reared its ugly head.

And it was ugly. Painful, scalding his heart, gripping it with a fiery intensity of agony that made Thomas want to close his eyes and grimace through the pain.

He had done this. He had ruined his family, brought shame upon his father, his name, and worst of all, had made it almost impossible for Maude to marry now. Not unless *he* married well. Extremely well. And quickly.

"I am sorry," he said quietly.

Maude sniffed. "Good. So you should be."

"But I will still pursue and marry—"

"Miss Ainsworth!" his sister said sincerely as the door opened and their guest was helped into the carriage by their footman. "How pleasant to make your acquaintance."

His sister's presence had been incentive for Mrs. Ainsworth to allow her daughter to join them without her. He'd never heard if she'd realized how she'd left the two of them alone the other day in her rush to join Lady Romeril.

He hadn't been alone with his prospective bride since. Hadn't seized his promised kiss.

"Miss Ainsworth," Thomas said hastily, heat splashed across his face. Had she heard anything? Was it possible to hear one's conversation through the carriage door? "Here, sit beside—"

"Me," Maude said firmly, casting him a warning glance visible even in the evening gloom. "We can't have you facing backward, can we? Here, place this blanket over your knees—what a cold night!"

"It is indeed, most cold," said Miss Ainsworth, settling herself and glancing briefly at Thomas. "Though I admit, I do feel significantly warmer now."

Thomas crossed his legs hastily as the carriage jolted forward and they began the final part of their journey.

Dear God, did the woman have any idea how that sounded? As though... Well, as though...

"—not much of a resemblance between you," Miss Ainsworth was saying with a nervous smile.

Thomas's stomach lurched. Ah. So she hadn't heard.

As he knew she would, his sister merely laughed. "Oh, you're not the first to look and fail to find it. We have different fathers, Miss Ainsworth—technically, Tommy, Leo, and Xander are my half-brothers."

He watched color rise on Miss Ainsworth's cheeks. Should he have warned her? Perhaps. It certainly would have avoided her awkwardly attempting to—

"I think a family such as that is a wonderful thing," Miss Ainsworth said amiably. "How delightful for you, to have three younger brothers."

"Not always," said Maude, rolling her eyes. "There's always one of them getting into a tremendous scrape. Some gentlemen just can't keep their hands off the ladies..."

Thomas wondered if he imagined the way Miss Ainsworth swallowed, her gaze darting his way.

Thankfully, it took but seven minutes to arrive at their destination, and Thomas was careful to rearrange his trousers after the two ladies had been helped out of the carriage by the footman. Only then did he descend onto the pavement, lit by glittering reflections of the light inside the Quintrell household.

"I do hope we are not too late," Miss Ainsworth was saying to his sister. "I know being fashionably late is starting to become the style—"

"Oh, a Chance does not follow the style, a Chance *defines* the style," Maude said with a grin, looping her arm around Miss Ainsworth's and marching her forward, away from her brother. "Come on, let's go inside."

Thomas had no choice but to follow the pair, trying not to think about how much he wished he had not agreed to chaperone his sister. It would have been far more enjoyable to have Miss Ainsworth to himself. Though in that case, her mother would have accompanied them, and he'd have had to devise another scheme for getting them alone, perhaps Lady Romeril pulling her carriage up beside them and inviting only the mother to join her. Leaving just Miss Ainsworth and him alone. Just him and her. Just him, pressing her against the fabric of the seats, her gasping under his fingertips as he wrought such sensations in her that—

"I said, give the man your hat, Thomas," said a sharp voice. "Honestly, away with the fairies again. Why are gentlemen so flighty, do you think, Miss Ainsworth?"

Thomas blinked. Somehow, they had managed to get into the hallway of the Quintrell ball, the sound of music and dancing pouring from under a nearby door.

There was a footman before him with his hands out for his gloves and greatcoat. Maude was openly laughing at him just behind the footman, and Victoria—Miss Ainsworth was beside her.

Thomas's stomach swooped.

"Hat, Thomas," his sister commanded as she rolled her eyes. "Men, eh, Miss Ainsworth? Absolutely useless."

"This one certainly appears to be malfunctioning," Miss Ainsworth said, a gleam of mischief in her eyes. "I suppose there is no way to revive him?"

Pushing aside all thoughts of just *how* the beautiful Miss Ainsworth could breathe life back into him—some parts of him more than others—Thomas hastily removed both hat and greatcoat, dropping them into the footman's arms before stepping smartly around him to claim—

"Ah, thank you, Thomas," said his sister archly as she slipped her hand into the crook of his free arm.

Blast. What a nuisance the woman was turning out to be. Ah, well, there was an easy way to solve this particular problem…

"Come, ladies," Thomas said as he stepped forward, one on each arm, his left arm jolting like lightning with Miss Ainsworth there. "In we go, what a fine ballroom—oh, Mr. Lister! Mr. Lister, you must come here and dance with my sister!"

Maude turned fierce eyes to him as she hissed, "What do you think you're—"

"It would be an honor, Lady Maude," simpered the young man. His moustache was barely grown and he was a head shorter than his sister, but that did not matter.

"I will see you after the dance, Maudy," said Thomas with a grin, disengaging himself from her arm. "Ah, a cotillion! A nice long one. Go with Mr. Lister."

There was absolutely nothing she could do, and she knew it. Thomas knew it. She knew he knew it. The look his sister shot him told him in very plain language that he was going to suffer for the indignity she was about to endure, and it would be a punishment of long duration.

But that was in the future. Right now, he was standing here at the edge of the ballroom with Miss Ainsworth on his arm and no sister to get in the way.

Perfect.

"I like your sister," said Miss Ainsworth quietly. "It is rare to meet a woman with such…such vitality."

Thomas snorted. "You are very circumspect, Miss Ainsworth."

"And you are once again underestimating a woman, Your Grace," she returned quietly. "Not a habit I recommend you form."

"Cothrom," Thomas said softly.

She flushed, as well she might. The ball was well attended, a great amount of chatter in corners and laughter in groups, but there was a chance someone could overhear them.

He was willing to take that risk.

"I... I do not think it appropriate to call you—"

"Probably not, but I'd prefer it."

It was the next stage of courting, Thomas was almost sure. Oh, he had bedded plenty of women—he had no concerns of technique there—but there had always been the understanding that whatever they shared, it would only last the night.

This was different. This would have to last a lifetime.

A shiver moved up Thomas's spine and by the doe-eyed look on Miss Ainsworth's face, she felt it.

"I...I don't think I should—"

"Oh, you *should*," Thomas said, squeezing his hand on hers as it looped through his arm. "There are plenty of things we should do. For example, I should dance with you."

Her eyes were bright. "You should?"

"I should court you publicly, while always looking for moments to be alone with you," he continued, allowing just a hint of the desire he felt to seep into his syllables.

"You should?"

"And I should make sure never to kiss you again until...until it is appropriate."

There it was—the flash of desire, one that Victoria...that Miss Ainsworth swiftly hid. But not swiftly enough. "You shouldn't?"

"Definitely not," Thomas said with a grin. "And yet you made me a promise."

"A promise?"

"And I did not see you the day following that delightful afternoon tea," Thomas said, lowering his voice and head so he could murmur into her ear. And get an eyeful of that delectable bosom. "And so you see, you owe me."

Her breathing had quickened now. He could sense it in the tightness of her grip on his arm. By God, he was good. Very good. He had wondered whether it would take long to have her eating out of the palm of his hand, but—

A flash of memory. The sensation of Victoria Ainsworth's palm against his mouth. Pressing a kiss into the warm flesh. Wanting more, *needing* more.

Thomas blinked. When the ballroom faded back into view, it was to see Miss Ainsworth with pinked cheeks.

"I think you'll rather find that *you* owe *me*," she said lightly, leaning into him so her hip pressed against his.

He swallowed a moan and tried to stay rational.

Fine. She was a woman who was far bolder than he had accounted for. Far more direct. Far more... Well, there was no other word for it: sensual.

He had not expected that. But it was a bonus, wasn't it, not a challenge? Did he not wish for a woman like that? Wasn't this going to make wooing and wedding her all the more interesting?

"You have never courted a woman before, have you?"

Miss Ainsworth's words cut through his muddled thoughts but unfortunately did not give his tongue much control.

"I... What?"

Her smile became wicked. "You *are* courting me, aren't you, Cothrom?"

Dear God, it was sweet nectar from the gods themselves, to hear that title on her lips. Just when Thomas was certain he would never grow accustomed to it, now he did not want Victoria—Miss Ainsworth to call him anything else.

Except *Thomas*, perhaps. Or *my dear*. Or *my*—

And that is where we stop, Thomas thought hurriedly, pulling on the reins of his untamed thoughts. He was not in the business of falling in love, most certainly not with the woman he planned to marry.

The very idea.

He had more important things with which to concern himself.

"I think we should dance," he said aloud.

Anything to shift his body inches away from hers to find some sort of equilibrium.

Her eyelashes fluttered. "D-Dance?"

That seemed to have unsettled her. Good. Thomas was tired of all the unsettling going in his direction—he was supposed to be the one making her fall in love with him. He wasn't supposed to...to *feel* anything.

"Dance," Thomas said firmly. "Come on."

The cotillion was already in progress, but that wasn't sufficient to halt him. He was a duke now, after all. What did he care about etiquette?

Thomas smirked at his sister's startled look as he joined the end of the set with Miss Ainsworth opposite him. He was the Duke of Cothrom now. Who was going to argue with him?

The dance was lively, requiring his concentration for the first few minutes as he gained his bearings. It would have been much easier to do if he had not been required, thanks to the steps of the dance, to come into frequent contact with a woman who made him want to do unspeakable things.

Like rip off that corset and plunge his head into her bosom, for example.

Thomas focused on not tripping over his own feet, touching Miss Ainsworth as lightly as possible, and not staring at the enticingly bouncing parts of her that called out to him.

It was a challenge.

"You are an excellent dancer," he said the next time their hands touched.

"You have excellent lines."

Oh, hell.

"It wasn't a line," Thomas protested as they joined hands to promenade down the set. "Well. Not really. I meant it."

Miss Ainsworth raised an eyebrow as they separated. When they came together again in the dance she murmured, "Gentlemen like you always have lines like that. You have a plethora of them, I suppose."

Yes. "No," said Thomas, rallying himself. "Not at all. You dance most elegantly."

"Another line?"

Yes. "What do you think of me, Miss Ainsworth?"

The look she gave him was so knowing, he would not have been surprised if the truth had been tattooed to his forehead.

"I think I am starting to get the measure of you, Cothrom," she said quietly as they stepped together again, Thomas standing perhaps a little closer than was strictly necessary. "And I would appreciate a conversation without any lines at all."

"Without...without any?"

Incomprehensible. How else did gentlemen speak to ladies? One prepared a series of lines that one knew ladies would enjoy. Platitudes, compliments, sweet words that said little but sounded impressive.

How else was a man to talk to a lady?

"Impress me," Miss Ainsworth murmured in his ear as she swept around him, her eyes surely far more suggestive than she had any idea of them being.

Desperately attempting to ignore the need filling his very bones, hoping against hope that Victoria could not see how eagerly his body responded to her, Thomas forced aside all thoughts of caring for this woman.

He could not care for this woman.

Hadn't he already proven that he was not to be trusted? Had he not already let his family down?

This was a business arrangement. Of a sort—she did not actually know it was a business arrangement, but other than in that respect, it was identical. He had no feelings in the matter. He offered a title—the most impressive title a lady could achieve. He had a good family name, and, if it was not too pompous of him to say, he would be pleasing for his wife to look at. And in exchange, he had an objective of his own: her dowry. He would get it. That was all that mattered.

Victoria laughed, throwing her head back charmingly as she relished the dance, her hands once again placed in his own as they turned in a circle.

And Thomas's heart twisted.

He had to uphold the family honor. Fortune was foremost on his mind.

"I suppose your new title has given you a great deal of new responsibilities..."

Mrs. Ainsworth was right: he had responsibilities now. Responsibilities to his sister, his brothers, his parents, to the Chance name.

And he—

"You're thinking, not dancing," said Victoria with a grin. "Dance with me, Cothrom."

Cothrom. The Duke of Cothrom. The burden of the responsibility weighed so heavily on Thomas's shoulders, he was astonished he was still standing.

"Come here."

A soft tug on his arm and somehow, she had pulled him away from the dancing to stand by the wall. Were people watching? Probably. Thomas discovered to his surprise he didn't really care, even if it was she, not he, who might suffer from the gossip.

If she did, he would just have to make it right. He planned to do so regardless.

"You're thinking too much," she said quietly, standing so close to him, Thomas could have kissed her if he had allowed himself to lean forward just an inch. "What are you thinking about?"

Thomas swallowed.

He could hardly tell her. This wasn't the time, nor the place—if there ever was one—to reveal there was absolutely no money in his family's coffers; that if he could marry her tomorrow, he would, because her money would be his family's salvation; and that if a mere coin toss had ended on a different side, it would have been Lady Whatshername here opposite him, flushed from the vigor of a dance, and not her.

It could have been so different. A chance in a million.

Thomas tried to smile. "Nothing. I'm not thinking of anything, I assure—"

"You can lie to yourself," Victoria interjected quietly. "You can lie to your brothers, your friends, even that clever sister of yours. But you can't lie to me."

Damn. He couldn't, worse luck.

Well, a hint of the truth, then.

"I was thinking about you," he said quietly. "I..."

He had intended to dress up the remark in platitudes, compliments, all the tried and tested techniques to make a woman melt before him.

And they faded away as he looked into her green eyes, alive with excitement and interest and...and something else.

"I was thinking of you, and how beautiful you are," Thomas said simply.

The flush was delicate, but it was most definitely there. "Another line. I see."

"It's not—Victoria!" Grabbing her arm to prevent her from stepping away, Thomas cursed his slip of the tongue. "Miss Ainsworth, I mean, it—it's not a line. Not for me, not in this moment. You are beautiful. Seeing you dance like that, free, and uninhibited... I've never seen anything so beautiful."

She hesitated, still turned partly away, but her expression softened as she looked deep into his eyes. Thomas forced himself to stare back, fought against the instinct to look away, to hide himself, to become just another laughing gentleman in a crowd.

Victoria's lips twitched. "Thank you. Shall... Shall we return to the dance?"

"You still owe me that kiss," Thomas pointed out, trying to pull her closer, other guests at the Quintrell ball be damned.

Her eyes flashed with triumph. "I know. Consider it in my keeping until I choose to bestow it on you."

Thomas's groan was so light, only she heard it, but he felt the response in her. "I hope that damned thing is earning interest."

"Oh, it is," Victoria said lightly. "It will be very interesting."

His jaw tightened as he tried not to grin. "Miss Victoria Ainsworth, you are infuriating."

"Why, thank you," she said, her eyes sparkling. "To the dance?"

Thomas nodded, pulling the arm of the most beautiful thing he had ever seen through his own. It was a good line.

"Seeing you dance like that, free, and uninhibited... I've never seen anything so beautiful."

What a shock to discover, as the words had left his mouth, that he'd meant them.

Chapter Seven

January 13, 1840

"WELL, ISN'T THIS nice," Victoria said as brightly as she could manage, her spirits sinking as her mother continued to refuse to leave. "So...so nice."

She glanced at Thomas Chance, Duke of Cothrom, and forced herself to immediately look away.

It had been on this very sofa that they had... That he had...

"Dear God, I want to kiss you again..."

Not that her mother knew anything about *that*.

"Very nice," agreed Mrs. Ainsworth. "I must say, I am delighted you accepted my invitation to tea again, Your Grace. You must have a great deal of calls on your time, and I cannot help but think that your acceptance is a suggestion of... Well. Of marked interest."

"Mother," Victoria said warningly over her tea.

"Marked interest, you understand me."

Victoria rolled her eyes and furiously did not look at her mother.

"In my daughter."

"Yes, thank you," Victoria said stiffly, picking up a plate of sliced sponge cake and proffering it toward the only gentleman in the room. Anything to do something with her hands, to keep herself from twisting them in knots in her lap. "Cake?"

Thomas Chance, most irritatingly, appeared to be enjoying this. "You know, I would like a taste of something sweet."

His voice had spoken low and her mother had been twittering on about the delicacy of his intentions—otherwise, Victoria would have been forced to throw the plate down and storm out of the room to prevent herself shouting at the pair of them.

Honestly, they were outrageous! Did they have to be so...so... Well. *So.*

"I am afraid cake is the only offering on the menu right now," she said as sweetly as she could manage.

Thomas leaned forward, carefully selected a slice of the sponge cake, and as he lifted it onto his small plate murmured, "'Right now,' eh?"

Victoria almost dropped the plate.

"—and I hear you and your sister had a wonderful time with my daughter at the Quintrell ball," her mother prattled on, evidently unaware her daughter was going to have to change her name and move to another part of the country if this continued. "She has always been an excellent dancer, my Victoria."

"Yes, I quite agree," said Thomas smoothly, not looking at Victoria as he bit into the cake.

She was watching him, though. How could she not? The way his lips curled around the cake, his mouth delicate yet possessive, tasting the sweetness eagerly, licking a crumb from his lower lip...

Something stirred within Victoria that absolutely should not.

"And an excellent conversationalist," her mother continued. "Not that she is doing much of that this afternoon. Honestly, Victoria, what has gotten into you?"

Victoria carefully placed the plate of cake on the console table beside her and had only a moment to gather her thoughts before turning to her mother. "Into *me*, Mother?"

"You're hardly offering our guest much in the way of conversation," Mrs. Ainsworth pointed out.

"It's quite all right, Mrs. Ainsworth," said Thomas in that low, gravelly voice of his that made Victoria want to drag him out of the drawing room and up to her bedchamber. "I am certain your daughter will offer me other things."

It was a good thing Victoria had not taken the sip of tea she so desperately wanted, for she would surely have sprayed it across the carpet—the carpet Mrs. Stenton had only just managed to clean since the time the duke had spilled his tea.

This was insupportable!

When Victoria, flushing heavily, managed to meet his eye, she saw he was grinning. Grinning! At her expense!

Well, two can play at that game…

"You really must ask His Grace about his other interests, Mother," she said as calmly as she could, noticing out of the corner of her eye a little stiffness in the man's frame. "He greatly enjoys the horses, I think. And card games. Don't you, Your Grace?"

This time, she faced him head on, a challenge in the lift of her eyebrow.

She had intended it as a jest. To make him feel uncomfortable as he had done to her. To show him that she, too, could provoke through the art of conversation.

She had not intended for the man's face to go pale, for his gaze to drop, the rest of his cake untouched on his plate as he swallowed hard.

"Oh, I do like a card game, Your Grace," her mother said happily without seeming to notice the change that had come over their guest. "My current favorite is whist, a most complex game at the best of times, but when played with Victoria—she has such a clever mind, you see, and…"

As the woman continued, an unsettling discomfort settled in Victoria's stomach. Thomas Chance had still not lifted his gaze, the uneasiness evident in the tension along his jaw, the way his fingers gripped the plate holding the now-ignored cake.

Oh, bother. What had she done?

"—and before I knew it, she had—Victoria? Where are you going?"

In truth, Victoria was not sure. She had stood up, knowing she had to do something, change something...and the easiest way was to leave.

With Thomas, of course.

"Lord Cothrom and I are going for a walk," she said firmly.

Her mother's mouth fell open. "Now?"

"Now," Victoria said resolutely.

"Now?" Thomas said, finally glancing up.

"Yes, now," said Victoria, feeling like she was stuck in a loop. "Come on. Let's get your greatcoat and gloves and hat from the footman and—"

"But it looks like rain," said her mother aghast, twisting in her seat as she watched Victoria stride over to the door. "And it's cold! It's January, Victoria. And why should the man appear now? You can't just—"

"Are you coming?" Victoria asked, opening the door and turning to the person in the room she had somehow offended.

Thomas hesitated. He was clutching the plate of sponge cake, mostly uneaten, and his color was still a mite pale. Then he nodded.

As Victoria could have predicted, her mother immediately became flustered.

"Oh, you mean—oh! *You*! You know, for a moment there I forget that you had—that you were... I thought my daughter meant your father!"

"Yes, I suppose that will be a hazard for him and me for a little while," said Thomas quietly.

Victoria's pulse pounded painfully to hear it. Where had the blustering, flirtatious, slightly outrageous duke she had known gone? Where was he? What had she done to destroy their connection?

"Yes, it is very strange," said Victoria, hardly sure what she was saying, "but then I think the Chance family does things differently. Will... Will you walk with me, Your Grace?"

And she stretched out a hand.

It was most uncouth. Unladylike. Her mother's widening eyes told Victoria exactly what she thought of that action, making it so obvious, so blatant that she wished to walk with him! Certainly not the sort of thing a delicate and refined young lady would do.

But most delicate and refined young ladies, Victoria thought, *are not faced with a man who looks like that and kisses like the devil.*

The duke rose to his feet and carefully placed his plate of cake on a console table. "I will."

His voice was low, earnest, and it shot tingles of heat up Victoria's spine as the two of them walked into the hall.

"But—but the weather!" her mother called, her voice carrying out from the drawing room. "Victoria, I cannot go for a walk in that cold with you, and you shall not go alone with a gentleman into the street."

"I shall ask Danvers to accompany us," Victoria said loudly, though she actually had no intention of asking her lady's maid. She raised a brow at the footman as he brought out their pelisses, hats, greatcoats, scarfs, and gloves, as if daring him to actually go and fetch the servant. "We shan't be long, Mother."

Victoria barely glanced at the duke as the footman opened the door for them and did not have to ask for his arm. Thomas merely took her hand without a word and placed it in the crook of his arm, as though it had always belonged there. As though she had always belonged by his side.

She swallowed, hard, as the front door closed behind them.

Well. This was not what she had expected.

"Where to?" Thomas asked quietly.

Victoria raked over his features, attempting to discern precisely what had happened. How had she managed to subdue this fine man?

"Anywhere," she replied softly, tugging the brim of her bonnet lower over her eyes so no one would identify her as un unmarried woman walking unchaperoned with a beau. "As long as it's with you."

A ghost of a smile and it was gone. Thomas stepped forward, steering her along the almost-empty Bath streets. The weather was indeed most unpleasant, and any sensible inhabitants had decided to stay indoors, where it was warm and dry. The whistling north wind was damp, bringing with it an icy sharpness that tore at the few remaining leaves in the trees and whistled around corners as they continued along the pavement.

Victoria did not need to ask where they were going. She could guess after about a minute. There was only one pleasant set of gardens in this direction of Bath, and that was Sydney Gardens.

The place was almost deserted. Frost still nipped at the blades of grass in the lawns, and the flowerbeds looked almost bare, most of their inhabitants bedded down for the winter.

Into this silent place they stepped.

Thomas had not said a word since they had left the steps outside her home, and Victoria could not bear it any longer.

"I am sorry," she said quietly.

He looked down, eyes heavy with meaning. "For what?"

"I...I am not exactly sure," Victoria said ruefully. "But I have hurt you. I said something that offended, that cut into you as surely as if I had wielded a knife. And for that, I am sorry."

Thomas had clearly not expected such a thing. His eyes widened, brow furrowing. "You apologize for something you do not know, or understand—something inadvertent, that was not intended to harm."

"Those are perhaps the most important apologies," she pointed out as their pace slowed and they rounded a bend in the path. "Anyone can apologize for the intended slights, the cruel words they crafted on purpose. But when a mistake, some ignorance, offends, an apology is necessary. How else can two people go...go on?"

The words almost faltered in her mouth, but she forced herself to say them.

Go on, she wanted to say, *to something more. To something just as real but more…more intimate.*

*Oh, I want to seduce you, Thomas Chance. I want to taste that mouth
again, know what it is to have your fingers in my hair, feel your breath on my
breasts, sense your invasive touch as you—*

"But you don't even know what I am taking offense at," Thomas
said, halting his steps and twisting so he could look directly into her
eyes. "I could be making a mountain out of a molehill."

Flecks of snow were starting to fall, but Victoria barely noticed.
How could she, when Thomas Chance was looking at her like…like
that?

"Are you?"

For a heartbeat, she thought he was going to lean forward and kiss
her. His head moved, inextricably inching closer and closer until his
lips were just inches from hers.

Then he straightened. "No."

Victoria attempted to swallow. It took her three attempts. "W-
Well, then. I apologize."

"And I accept your apology." Thomas gently bit his lip. "But don't
you think you deserve to know what you are apologizing for?"

"No," she said after a moment's thought. Tightening her grip on
Thomas's arm, Victoria started to walk slowly forward, sensing
somehow that he would speak more openly walking side by side. "No,
I think that is your right to tell me or not tell me. I could pry, yes—"

"And I would tell you." His voice was low, thrumming with promise. "If you asked."

Victoria glanced up and gave an awkward laugh. "But I don't
know if you want to tell—oh, Cothrom, I'm all of a muddle."

His expression sparked heat through her. "Good."

Her laughter was more natural this time and she elbowed him in
the ribs as she declared, "You know, I wouldn't be surprised if this
whole thing were a jest to make me uncomfortable!"

"And I suppose it could have been—except it's not," Thomas said
with a rueful grin. "Oh, hell. I can tell you. If there's anyone in the

world I should... But it's not..."

She watched him, reveling in the intimacy this moment brought. She could almost *see* the thoughts whirling around Thomas's mind.

He lost the family fortune. She knew that, even if he did not know she knew. The question was, could he bare his soul to her in this regard? Could he be deciding to be honest with her—something she had not expected?

As it turned out, she was half right.

"Let's sit here," Thomas said with a jerk of his head. "I know it's a little damp, but I think I'll feel more comfortable that way."

She did not question him, even as Victoria sat on the most definitely damp bench. Thomas positioned himself so close, her hip was pressed up against his. Even through the layers and layers of fabric keeping them apart, she could feel his warmth.

Victoria swallowed. *Well, this is it, then.*

Thomas leaned back with the elegance and confidence of a man who had been born to a title and had known, from a young age, that he would come into a better one. "It all started a year ago, I think."

She waited, unsure whether an interruption would break his concentration. Was she about to hear the full story—to discover precisely how and why the oldest son of the head of the Chance family had managed to lose tens of thousands?

As it turned out, she was not.

"There's not much to tell really, no great story, nothing to get excited about," Thomas said in a rush, his cheeks red—either from his words or the wind, Victoria could not tell. "I was foolish. I gambled. Horses, card tables—the sort of things that you jested with your mother about. That was why I felt awkward. I was a fool. I lost a great deal of money."

Victoria raised an eyebrow but said nothing.

Interesting. So he would happily tell her that he was a gambler, a bit of a spendthrift when it came to playing the tables and betting on the races. But he hadn't told her the whole truth, had he?

He hadn't admitted that the entire Chance fortune—at least, his father's—was gone.

"You judge me."

"I'm listening to you." she corrected in a quiet voice. They were still alone in Sydney Gardens, the threat of snow keeping people inside. Their breath turned to mist in the air. "I'm thinking."

"Thinking what a rotter I am—"

"Thinking you are hardly alone in the *ton* when it comes to losing a great deal of money at cards," Victoria said with a wry look. "I think even my father, at times, had a flutter. You are not so different from most gentlemen, you know.'

It was the wrong thing to say. Thomas stiffened. "I like to think that in your eyes, at least. I am different from most gentlemen."

Heat flushed up her décolletage, hidden by her pelisse and scarf but burning Victoria nonetheless. "I... Yes, of-of course you are."

"Am I?" Thomas spoke in a low voice, though there was no risk of anyone overhearing. He turned in his seat to face her, his eyes hungry, a pinched expression on his face she had never seen before. "I made some decisions, Victoria—apologies, Miss Ainsworth, and in some ways I think my family will never forg—"

"You may call me 'Victoria.' If you want." She had not intended to speak, but the need to hear him say her name, for the four syllables to be entwined by his lips, was overwhelming.

Thomas's eyes widened. "I... You... I can?"

Blushing furiously and wishing to goodness she wasn't, Victoria nodded. "I...I call you 'Cothrom,' after all."

"I would rather you called me 'Thomas.'"

His voice was low, and if she were not mistaken, his cheeks were reddening in color. It could not merely be the weather—surely, it was more than that. More than the cold. More than mere attraction.

Could it be—

"Not in company," Thomas added hastily, a grin loping across his face. "Now that would be scandalous. I would have to do something drastic if that sort of intimacy were overheard."

Victoria's mouth was dry and words simply would not come. "I...I..."

"I would introduce you to my family, but I would prefer to wait until...I mean..." Precisely what the man meant, he did not appear to know. "I am not in their good books at the moment, as I am sure you can imagine. If they only knew."

"Knew what?"

"What?" Thomas appeared distracted, only half-aware of what he was saying. "Oh, nothing."

Victoria frowned, but it did not appear that she was going to get much more out of him on that score. Something had changed in his demeanor; the openness, the willingness to talk had evaporated. Like frost in early morning sunshine.

She watched him sit, consumed by thoughts of his family and his obvious guilt. If only he had been truly honest with her—if only he had admitted that he had not just lost a great deal of money, but all the money his family possessed. Then she could tell him, in all honesty herself, that she...she was in love with him. That she would marry him, whether he loved her or not, if it would make him happy.

He might gamble away even her fortune. She knew many gamblers did—no lesson learned, they couldn't stop themselves. She might be forced to live a more impoverished life than she was used to, even if a duchess. But she found she didn't care. How could she not care?

Oh, the love she felt was an ache inside her lungs that never ceased. How she could care about someone so much, particularly when he was only interested in her wealth...

She was a fool. A fool in love.

"It's easy talking to you. I never thought—I mean, speaking of this sort of thing to anyone felt impossible," Thomas said with a dry laugh.

His breath blossomed out on the chilly wind. "But it's strange. I can talk to you about this. I can talk to you about...about anything, I think."

Victoria's heart skipped a beat. And that was why. Behind the rakish exterior, the bluff, the bluster, the fancy name and the fancy title, was the man she had fallen in love with over a year ago. The man who truly cared what others thought, who felt his guilt deeply.

She would have to seduce him as soon as possible. Make absolute sure they were discovered.

No time like the present.

"Do you want to kiss me, Thomas?"

His head jerked around. "I beg your pard—"

"You wanted to kiss me at the Quintrells' ball," Victoria said as confidently as she could. The gardens were still empty, so perhaps not the best place to be discovered, but still... "Well, you can kiss me now."

It was bold and direct, and indecent and outrageous, and she had said it.

And she was not blind. She'd seen the spark of desire in his eyes, the way Thomas shifted toward her. He wanted her. She wanted him. Why shouldn't they?

Getting caught would only lead her closer to her goal.

"You..." Thomas swallowed as he lifted a hand to cup her cheek. His glove was cold, but the gesture's heat melted through any hesitation Victoria may have had. "Victoria, you're so...so..."

Victoria's eyelashes fluttered shut as he leaned forward, anticipation flaring between her legs.

"So beautiful."

Her eyes snapped open and she leaned back. "I've heard that line before."

"No, Victoria, I—"

"I told you, I don't want lines," she said fiercely, all thoughts of kissing and its myriad delights forgotten. "I'm not just another woman you're buttering up to bed down, Thomas—"

"Victoria!"

"I'm different," she said, trying to keep the haughtiness out of her voice as she glared. "I'm not—This is meant to be—"

"Different," Thomas said quietly, brushing a thumb up her cheek. He had managed to move his hand with her, seemingly unwilling to release her.

Victoria swallowed. "Yes."

"Well, then, I should probably tell you that you are beautiful—"

Her heart fluttered, but her mind rebelled. "I swear, Thomas—"

"Because of your kindness. The way that freckle beneath your eye moves when you laugh. The gentleness of you, I..." Thomas swallowed. His eyes burned into hers. "I have never encountered anything like it. You apologize because you care about people, but most of all, you have this...this light. I can't explain it."

Victoria's mouth was dry again. She could attempt to blame the cold, wintery wind, she could argue it was because she had drunk insufficient tea that day...but it was Thomas, Thomas and his words, that were making her throat gasp for air and her fingers reach out.

They met the front of his greatcoat. Victoria splayed her palm against his lapels, just for a moment, then her fingers grasped the slightly damp fabric, pulling him an inch closer. And then another inch.

"Go on."

"I do want to kiss you, Victoria," Thomas said, a hunger in his voice she had never heard before. "And not just because you're beautiful, but because...because you're brilliant. You shine, Victoria, and everyone in your presence wants the light to fall on them. And I... I want..."

He leaned closer, and closer, and Victoria could not help but close her eyes as she welcomed the delicate brush of his lips against—

Footfalls.

The sudden absence of Thomas was painful. Victoria's eyes snapped open to see Thomas seated quite respectfully at the other end of the bench, looking in the opposite direction, as though he had never even been introduced to her.

A gentleman in a portly wig and a large cane inclined his head as he passed them. Victoria attempted to incline her own, but as it was spinning, she was not sure if she was successful.

"A walk."

She blinked. "Wh-What?"

"I promised you a walk," said Thomas with a wry grin. "And all I've done is prattle on."

The most delectable prattling. The most charming. The most—

"Come on," he said with a sigh as he rose to his feet. "I should take you back home. It's probably best I avoid scandal for another day…if I can."

Chapter Eight

January 18, 1840

G O AWAY. TURN *around, you blaggard, and don't look back.*
Thomas thought he should be commended for not actually saying the words out loud. They were on the tip of his tongue, desperate to be spat out at the rogue who had approached them.

Inserting himself into our conversations, making it impossible for me to talk to Victoria—to Miss Ainsworth, as she must be at the Assembly Rooms—on her own. It is despicable! It is deplorable! It is...

Downright disastrous.

Thomas straightened his back even more, as though that were possible, and tried as best he could to drown out the nonsense the man, whoever he was, was spouting.

"Such an elegant muslin, and the embroidering at the hems, most...most delicate," said the simpering man.

Thomas snorted as he watched the triangular-faced man's gaze drop to the edgings of Victoria's gown...around her bust. Yes, he was sure it was the embroidery that had the man's attention.

Victoria cleared her throat, the man's blotchy, pink face rose to meet hers, and Thomas crowed in the solitude of his own mind.

Yes! See, Mr. Whoeveryouare. She is not interested.

"Indeed," she said sweetly, "and is it the scalloped edge hem or the twisting fly knots of the embroidery you best admire?"

The man's eyes widened in panic. "I...er..."

"Was it the fineness of the weave of the muslin, or the delicate dying of each individual thread that had you transfixed?" Victoria asked, a little of the sweetness disappearing with every word. "Please, do tell, Mr. Halifax."

"It was…ah… In fact, now I think…think about it…"

She was a wonder. *Really, I should be congratulated,* Thomas thought proudly as he watched the woman he had decided to marry outwit the man before them. He was going to be the husband of a woman who actually had a brain, which was more than you could say for half the young things in Society these days.

To think, but for the toss of a coin, he would never have known that Miss Victoria Ainsworth was so…so interesting. So brilliant. So bright.

So beautiful.

The memory of the kiss he had not been able to take roared in his mind, but Thomas attempted to push it aside for now, even as the heady lavender of her scent threatened to send him straight back to that moment. He could indulge in that memory later.

"—oh, I do believe my party wish for my—that is, I must depart, Miss Ainsworth, so sorry…"

The man scampered away almost as fast as his legs, and the crush of people in the Assembly Rooms, would allow.

Thomas snorted. "What a fool."

"Yes," Victoria said thoughtfully, tilting her head as she always did when she was considering something. "He was rather silly. He should have complimented me on something easy to lie about. My jewels, perhaps. My hair."

Irritation sparked in Thomas's stomach, flaring like fire. "You—You mean you *wanted* him to compliment you?"

"Why not?" she returned, raising a sardonic brow. "Are you saying there is a reason why other gentleman should not compliment me?"

Thomas opened his mouth. He ran through the plethora of different options, discounted them all, and shut it again.

Hell. She had a point, not that he was about to admit it.

He had gone on a walk with Miss Ainsworth; had taken tea with her mother, twice, which was more than any man should ever have to bear; he had accompanied her to a private ball, and now the Assembly Rooms.

And still he had not spoken of his...intentions.

Not the real intentions. Not his hope that he could soon be putting her money to good use, spending it on a dowry for his sister and to pay off those last pesky debts.

No, the pretend intentions. The pretensions?

He had to marry her. He had to make Victoria Ainsworth his bride...and yet when it came to it, Thomas did not appear to have the right words to say.

"That is what I thought," Victoria said with a flicker of a smile. "Ah, and here comes Lord Zouch. Good evening, my lord."

The jealousy that had only just started to subside in Thomas flashed once more, this time a dangerous, red-hot bitterness that threatened to cause a scowl across his forehead.

Well, really! What did Victoria think she was doing, conversing with this other man, when Thomas was standing right here!

Standing there, a small voice in the back of his mind pointed out, *not proposing matrimony.*

Well, yes, Thomas argued silently with the voice who was most unwelcome. *Yet.*

Ah, so you have a plan then. Excellent.

"As a matter of fact I do," Thomas said heatedly.

Then he blinked. Lord Zouch and Victoria were staring, brows furrowed, puzzlement evident on both their faces.

"Ah."

"Indeed? How fascinating, Your Grace," said the lord vaguely. "I had no idea you had an interest in Ancient Greek."

Victoria was trying, and failing, not to laugh. Thomas could see it, the pinch of her lips, the widening of her eyes—he knew her features so well now, it was obvious. Blatant. There was therefore no need to drop his eyes to her breasts to see them shake in repressed mirth.

Dear God, why had he not proposed yet? To think, he could be sinking his face into—

"And whom do you prefer, Your Grace?" asked the lean and graceful Lord Zouch curiously. "Pliny the Younger, or Pliny the Elder? Assuming you are a full-breadth classicist, of course."

The square-jawed man laughed politely, as though what he had said were amusing. Victoria chuckled with him, tapping him with her—tapping him with her fan?

Thomas clenched his hands into fists by his sides but managed to keep his arms lowered, rather than cascading into the man's narrow nose.

This is just a marriage of convenience, he tried to remind himself, *just a convenience! She is a walking dowry, that's all.*

And that had been true, once.

"I don't care for either of them," Thomas said, striking out in the hope of making sense in a conversation that had entirely passed him by. "And you, Victoria—Miss Ainsworth, I mean."

Only the merest pink in the cheeks suggested that Victoria had been scandalized by the intimacy of using her name. Lord Zouch, on the other hand, blanched.

"Oh! Oh, I see. Well, I suppose I should offer you my congratulations, Your Grace—"

"No, no, you don't," Thomas said hastily, hardly knowing what he was saying. "You don't need to—"

"I don't need to, but I would like to," said Lord Zouch, offering out a hand. "Congratulations."

Victoria was laughing, not bothering to hide it, and Thomas was forced to maintain a stiff expression as he did not take the man's hand. "I regret you are mistaken. Victoria—damn, Miss Ainsworth and I—"

"Yes, I shall leave you to it," said Lord Zouch with a bow and just a hint of a regretful look. "Good evening, Your Grace, Miss Ainsworth."

He disappeared into what was fast becoming a crush, and Thomas groaned as he hung his head. He needed to tell her about St. Thomas's soon, and he had thought this the perfect moment. Now Lord Zouch had utterly ruined it. *What a beast.*

"I don't know what you're so worried about," said Victoria airily as she opened her fan and began to flutter it toward her admittedly pink cheeks. "I'm the one who will face a scandal if you don't propose soon."

She looked up through her eyelashes, a heady mixture of knowing woman and coquettish miss.

Thomas swallowed. "I...I suppose so."

"Though in that regard, I believe you will be like your brother—Lord Alexander Chance, isn't it?" Victoria said. "I have heard that he is quite the rakehell, breaking hearts all over London, Bath, Brighton—"

"Where did you hear that?"

Thomas had not intended to snap. He had not thought the insinuation would cause him as much harm as he felt, but there it was.

Victoria looked astonished. "Hear what?"

"That—What you just said," Thomas said, attempting to keep calm and failing miserably. Where was all this anger coming from—this defensiveness, this need to shield his wayward brother?

Because she wasn't wrong. Alexander had enjoyed more than his fair share of dalliances, and if he kept insisting on bedding widows, eventually, he supposed the news was going to get out.

But still. He hadn't expected Victoria, of all people, to start speaking of his brother's...exploits, for want of a better word, in the middle of the Bath Assembly Rooms!

"I couldn't say—"

"I need to know, Victoria," Thomas said urgently, dropping his voice as he stepped toward her.

He almost expected her to take a step back, but she held her ground, staring resolutely up at his face as though she had nothing to hide.

"And I said I couldn't say because I cannot remember," she said quietly, her eyes wide. "It's... Well, it's just something everyone knows."

Thomas swore

"Thomas!"

"Look," he said in a hiss, ignoring the way she'd exclaimed his name, though reminding himself he could mull on it later. "It's important to me, my brother's reputation."

Her face filled with curiosity. "Why?"

It was an excellent question, and one Thomas wasn't sure how to answer. Because he was his brother. Because Xander getting himself into scrapes was what he did, and what Thomas did was get him out of them.

Dear God, perhaps he had far more in common with his father than he thought.

As he ruminated on that unpleasant thought, he almost missed Victoria's next words.

"—personally think he should not be going about bedding widows and married ladies left, right, and center—"

Thomas growled. "No one has the right to judge my brother."

It was instinctive, this need to protect, and he did not like it. He had always left his brothers to their own devices, always trusted them to make their own mistakes. Lord knew, he had.

But being the eldest brother brought out something in him that he hardly knew what to do with. This was Victoria, the woman he intended to marry. Yet even her mere repetition of a rumor she'd had no hand in creating was making his blood boil.

Hell. Is this what my father feels like all the time? Is this some sort of...of duke thing?

"I do not judge him—I would spend half my life judging all the rakehells in the *ton* if I did," Victoria pointed out, aggravatingly calm in the face of his anger. "I just think... Well. He shouldn't."

"You have very strong opinions for a lady," Thomas said.

It was the wrong thing to say. Victoria glared, her frown pronounced over her expressive eyes. "You think ladies should not have strong opinions?"

Oh, no. This was a trap, and Thomas knew it.

He attempted to escape the net. "I didn't say that. I just—"

"Just what?" Victoria said fiercely.

"I just—well... Ladies, they don't..." floundered Thomas, wishing to goodness a lord would come and interrupt them. How had he managed to get into this argument? "They don't, that's all. Well, I suppose my sister, Maude, does. She would agree with you, actually. She's been saying to Xander for years—"

"So it's acceptable for a woman to have a strong opinion if she's a Chance?" shot back Victoria, almost laughing. "But no one else?"

It was a ridiculous thing to say, and Thomas was about to say so...but he hesitated.

Well, now she put it like that...

The music was growing louder, their voices raised over the din of the musicians and the stomping of the dancers, and yet somehow, the conversation felt...intimate. Personal. Private.

"Look, I'm not always right," Thomas said finally.

Victoria tilted her head. "You astonish me."

"I'm trying to admit that I'm wrong here," he said with a dry laugh. "Will you let me do that?"

"I don't know," she returned with a knowing look. "Are you actually going to say the words 'I was wrong'?"

Not if he could help it. But then, she knew that. He could see it in her eyes, see the intelligence gleaming.

Dear God, how had every other man overlooked this woman?

"Fine!" Thomas said, throwing up his hands and almost toppling a woman's befeathered headdress. "Oh, damn—fine, fine, I was wrong! There, are you happy?"

"Happier," said Victoria with a grin.

Somehow, she had stepped closer, her arm brushing up against his sleeve. It made Thomas wish his coat were elsewhere, his shirtsleeves rolled up, feeling the soft caress of her skin against his own.

"And besides, you know I'm right," Victoria said suddenly. "Your brother is doing far too much—I will not call it courting. I mean, there are probably broken hearts in a littered trail behind him, every time he—"

"What do you know of it?" Thomas snapped.

This time, Victoria jutted up her chin, as though prepared to debate with him. Him! About his own brother!

"You think merely because I have not—well, because I haven't...because I *haven't*, that I don't know what it is for a gentleman to take advantage of a lady?" she said in a low voice, cheeks pinking at the insinuation.

"You speak of that which you do not know." Thomas growled, fingers itching to take hold of the blasted woman and show her precisely what it was to be *taken advantage of.* "You can't possibly—"

"Oh, really?"

And before Thomas knew what was happening, before he could cry out or ask what on earth she was thinking, Victoria had grabbed him by the arm and pulled him, his feet almost tripping over each other, into a small alcove. Somewhere amidst the party, Mrs. Ainsworth might notice her daughter missing. However, the music was loud, the dancers cheering, the other patrons chattering—they could not be heard. They couldn't be seen, either. They were hidden now by a large fern in one of those ridiculously huge pots, but Thomas could not enjoy the moment.

Not with Victoria stabbing a finger into his waistcoat.

"You think that just because ladies do not speak of it, that they have no desire? That they do not want—want more than Society permits them? You think," said Victoria, her voice low and hot and angry, "that merely because a woman is not allowed to express—well, lust, that she does not *feel* it?"

Thomas could hardly believe what he was hearing. He had stepped into one of his delightful dreams and discovered a Victoria there outspoken about all the delectable things she wished to do.

Things he wanted her to wish him to do to her.

"You think that I don't see it?" Thomas growled back, unable to prevent the gravel slipping into his voice. "You think I don't see the way you look at me?"

Victoria's lips parted, but she was prevented from speaking because she was too preoccupied with gasping.

And that was because Thomas, rash anger and heat and need burning in his veins, had grabbed her shoulders, pushed her back against the wall, and pinned her against it with his body.

"Thomas!"

"I see the way you look at me," he said, glaring with barely contained need. "I see the way you watch me, how you hold yourself near me. You want—"

"And you want me," Victoria said with a gasp that most inconveniently pushed her breasts against him, making all rational thoughts flee from his mind. "I tasted it in your mouth when you kissed me. You want—"

Thomas swore again. "You're impossible."

"And you're incorrigible," she shot back, far faster than he could have imagined. *How on earth does the woman think with so much desire surely within her?* "You're the one courting me, Thomas—"

"Because you want me so badly," he growled.

"I'm not alone in that, I think." She chuckled as she glanced down.

Thomas glanced down in turn, bemused to understand what on

earth she was talking about.

Ah. Yes. That. Well.

"It's different for men," he said darkly, trying to ignore the very obvious sign of his attraction. The part of him pressing into her hip.

"Just because I can't show it," Victoria said softly, "doesn't mean I don't feel it."

Thomas was breathing rapidly now, trying to fight off the temptation to crush his mouth on hers to keep her quiet, hike up her skirts with one hand, and unbutton his trousers with the other.

This was not the time It was not the place.

It certainly wasn't part of the plan.

And then Victoria arched her back, ever so slightly, pressing her breasts into him as her hips ground against his—

"Damn it, woman, I'm trying to be honorable!" he exploded in a hiss.

Victoria grinned. "Not so honorable that you would propose to me."

And Thomas knew what he should say…and he did not say it.

How could he? The damned woman was tangling up his thoughts like threads woven into a tapestry, but the pattern was random, uncontrolled, undefined. He could no sooner ask this firebrand to marry him than he could ask the sun to shine all through the night.

He was not good enough for her.

He had known it the moment she had smiled, all those weeks ago. Had kept away from her, and others, knowing they did not deserve to have a husband who could not stop spending money on orphanages.

Victoria gave what could have been a sigh but sounded more like a whimper. His grip on her shoulders tightened, just for a moment.

"Let go," Victoria whispered, lifting her lips to his, straining under his grip in a way that made Thomas almost giddy with need. "Let go, Thomas. Take me…"

And that was when Thomas let go. He let go of Victoria completely and took two hurried steps back.

Dear God, that was close.

Breathing heavily and pulling a hand through his hair as though to settle his mind before looking up, Thomas saw Victoria was flushing pink and rearranging her hairpins.

Yes, that made more sense. Young ladies of impeccable breeding did not go around propositioning gentlemen.

At least, not in his experience. Perhaps Xander moved with a different crowd.

"I...I shouldn't have—"

"I never should have—"

Both of them broke off, Thomas allowing a grin to crease his lips. "Dear God, woman, you're a danger."

Victoria gave a laugh. "I suppose I am."

"And once again, I have underestimated you," he said ruefully, glancing momentarily at the tent in his trousers. "To my peril."

"I hope this will be the last time you underestimate me," she said, meaning laden in every word. "At least not to completion, anyway."

Thomas closed his eyes momentarily in an attempt to gain his bearings. He had not expected...

Well, this. *Her.* Victoria Ainsworth was charm itself, very pretty, and other than that, he'd had no fixed opinion of her. He'd thought her mind as empty as her corset was full. She had seemed like an easy woman to impress, to charm, and so she had been the tails of the coin.

And that had been it.

It? He'd never been more wrong in his life. Other than spending all that money on—

"And now I will leave you."

Thomas's head jerked up. "You will?"

"Well, you are hardly in a fit state to go anywhere," she said with a giggle, looking pointedly at his—

Thomas moved his hands to hide the... Well, the very obvious attraction he felt. "Ah."

"*Ah*, indeed," said Victoria with a twinkle in her eye. "Now, I am going to go back out there and find a gentleman with whom to dance—"

"*Victoria!*" he hissed, stepping toward her with a need he had not known he could feel.

She danced out of the way of his hands as she laughed. "That'll teach you not to follow through on your—"

"Victoria Ainsworth!"

"I'm not like all those other ladies you've bedded," she said, eyes bright and far too knowing. "I'm one in a million, Thomas Chance. And the sooner you understand that, the better."

And she was gone. The fern waved slightly in the breeze created by her sudden movement, and Thomas half-fell, half-leaned against the wall in a daze.

Dear God. What on earth was he going to do?

Chapter Nine

January 21, 1840

I T ARRIVED IN the second post of the day—and was almost missed.

"I'm certain it is intended to be addressed to Mrs. Ainsworth," Mrs. Stenton said sternly as Victoria picked up the heavy letter and looked curiously at the seal.

"I very much doubt it," breathed Victoria.

She didn't need to know who had sent it to recognize that seal. She'd seen it on carriages before, and on the small signet ring Thomas wore.

An elaborate, ornate C.

"Miss Victoria, what are you—"

"It's correctly addressed, and to me," said Victoria cheerfully as she ripped open the letter, casting aside the outer envelope and skimming the card it contained.

Her fingers tightened around the invitation. The invitation…to the Chance ball.

It would greatly please the Chance family if the bearer of this invitation—

Mrs. and Miss Ainsworth

—were to attend the annual Chance ball on the 21st of January, 1840.

Répondez, s'il vous plaît.

"What have you got there, my dear?" came her mother's voice from the drawing room. "More post? I hope it's something pleasant."

"More than pleasant."

Victoria had been certain, almost certain, that she had gone too far at the Assembly Rooms. Frightened him off. Made Thomas think she was a wanton woman who cast herself into the arms of any young gentleman who came along.

"And you want me. I tasted it in your mouth when you kissed me…"

Perhaps she had come on… Well. A little strong.

She had not seen him for the remainder of the night, heard neither hide nor hair from him since. Victoria had ensured she had not left the house ever since, desperately worried she would miss him—or worse, that she would not only miss him, but that he would speak to her mother.

Just that morning, she had started to give up hope. The *ton* was abuzz with news of this ball being moved up a week and she—the woman the duke was courting—had not been invited. She had not missed the slight. Evidently, Thomas Chance was not nearly so seducible as she had hoped.

And now…an invitation.

"A ball, and tonight," Victoria called out to her mother as she entered the drawing room. She would not think about what it meant to get the invitation only today. Thomas had hesitated to include her. But in the end, he had. "You poor thing."

Mrs. Ainsworth perked up her head from over her embroidery. "Why 'poor me'?"

"Because you have already accepted that invitation from Lady Romeril to play whist," Victoria said smoothly, lowering herself into an armchair and thanking her lucky stars her mother would not be accompanying her tonight. "Such a shame."

"I would say it is a shame for the pair of us," said her mother, returning to her embroidery with a look far too smug.

The excitement started to die away. "Why do you say that?"

"Well, it's not as though you could attend a ball on your own, could you?" her mother pointed out, far too reasonably for Victoria's liking. "It would be quite out of the question."

Victoria slumped against the back of the armchair.

She should have thought of that. Her mother was right; it would cause a stir if she were to attend alone, even if the Chances were one of the most refined and celebrated families in the *ton*. Perhaps because of that.

"What's that?"

Victoria looked up, but her mother seemed inexplicably to be pointing directly at her. "I beg your pardon?"

"That, written on the back of the invitation you're holding," her mother said with a frown. "Don't tell me you did not notice?"

Whirling the card invitation around in her hand, Victoria saw the hasty written words.

Lady Romeril happy to help. Tell your mother my sister will be your chaperone. T

A thrill flickered through Victoria as she read the words again. Lady Romeril—why on earth was she helping them? She had always thought the woman eager to be seen at the finest events of Society, not playing card games as a distraction. It was the strangest thing.

Still. If it meant she could attend the Chance ball without her mother...

"Lord Thomas—I mean, Lord Cothrom, has offered me his sister as a chaperone," Victoria said quietly. He'd thought of everything. He must really wish for her to attend.

"Did he now?" That had certainly gotten her mother's attention. The embroidery was placed on the cushion beside her and her mother's eyes became focused. "In that case, we will need to consider your ensemble. Gown—the blue, I think—"

"Surely, the green?" Victoria interrupted, leaning forward in anticipation.

"The way your cheeks pink in his presence? I think not," said her mother with a knowing look. "Trust me, my dear. You'll want to avoid green for a few months into your marriage when—"

"*Mother!*"

"Just a little hint, dear, no need to get your chemise all twisted," said Mrs. Ainsworth happily, picking up her embroidery. "You know best, I'm sure. Though speaking of chemise—"

"*Mother!*"

It was all Victoria could do to force her mother to speak of anything else during afternoon tea. It probably did not help that her hair had already been put into rags to give her the curls her mother said were so inviting—"*Mother!*"—as Danvers furiously polished the silver jewelry her mother was lending her for the occasion. "*So much more flattering for your blushing complexion, my dear.*"

That had been two hours ago. Now Victoria was being handed into the carriage while her mother took a hackney cab to Lady Romeril's. "*I insist, my dear, I insist. You cannot arrive at your intended's in a hired coach!*"

Why she felt so nervous, she was not sure. Perhaps it was because she and Danvers had spent longer on her attire this evening than they had in a long while.

Perhaps it was because the last time she had seen Thomas Chance, he'd been sporting between his thighs a... Well. A definite and most obvious regard for her.

Perhaps it was because this would surely be the night—*the* night. The night during which Thomas would propose matrimony for her fortune, though he did not know she knew it, and her seduction would—perhaps—finally be complete.

It was a lot to take in.

"*Let go, Thomas. Take me...*"

Victoria clutched her invitation as she stepped out of the carriage before the tall townhouse that was the Chances' residence in Bath. At least, this set of Chances. There were four brothers in the elder generation, weren't there?

The footman examined her invitation closely.

"It's not a forgery," Victoria tried to jest as he held it up to the candlelight.

He did not smile back. "There are many people in Bath, Miss, who would be grateful for an invitation such as this. Your mother is not here."

"Ah, no, but she—"

"There you are."

Victoria almost melted onto the pavement.

How did he do it? There was something so...so visceral about the way Thomas spoke. Was his voice always like that, or was it something special for her?

He looked more handsome tonight than he ever had. Crisp, white breeches and a dark coat that made his broad shoulders even broader.

Trying desperately not to think about the way he had kissed her, pressed against the velvet sofa in her mother's drawing room, Victoria curtseyed low. "Your Grace."

"Miss Ainsworth is my personal guest, Bradbury, and will be accompanied by—ah, there she is."

"I suppose you know all about this, Miss Ainsworth, and how tiring it all is," said Lady Maude, wearing a dazzling pink gown. Yes, she could see it now, in that small smirk—a slight resemblance, as would befit half-siblings.

Try as she might, Victoria could not prevent her shoulders from drooping, just a tad. "Oh, Lady Maude. I did not intend to be a bother. I—"

"All this 'needing a chaperone' nonsense, I grow quite tired of it," Lady Maude said breezily, taking Victoria's hand without a moment's warning and slipping it in the crook of her own. "I long for the day ladies can gallivant about the place much as the gentlemen do. I'm sure you agree."

"I… Yes, I suppose I—"

"Out of my way, Thomas, you really are most untidy," said Lady Maude to her brother, the Duke of Cothrom, as though he were a mere footman. "Honestly!"

Victoria stifled a giggle as she glanced at Thomas while she and Lady Maude entered the impressive hallway. Then her levity faded.

"We're all at sixes and sevens, I'm afraid. Thomas brought the ball forward by a week, so the place has hardly been spruced up," Lady Maude said airily. "A real shame. I wish you could see the place at its best."

At… At its best?

Lady Maude led Victoria hurriedly through a magnificent hallway lined with ancient portraits, swords on the walls, and a chandelier with more crystals on it than diamonds in Victoria's jewelry box, then along a corridor lined with thick, red carpet and landscapes edged in gold-gilt frames, then across an atrium with a skylight that showed the stars. It was all Victoria could do to keep her breath.

She lost it as they stepped into the ballroom, Lady Maude waving off the butler standing to attention there to announce the guests.

"Oh, my…"

"Yes, a little tawdry, I must say," said Lady Maude with a wrinkled nose. "A tad last century, but Mother likes it."

Victoria was not surprised. The place was astounding. Far larger than she could have imagined based on the front of the house. The ballroom was exquisite: mirrors lined two of the four walls, creating the sensation that the place went on forever, and the genteel muttering and chatter of their guests was tastefully accompanied by a quintet of musicians. There were footmen in the Chance russet livery meandering about the place, ensuring that glasses were topped up with wine and delicacies restored the energy of the dancers in between sets. The ceiling... Oh, the ceiling was a masterpiece. Victoria would not have been surprised to be told that Michelangelo or Leonardo da Vinci had taken a short visit to Bath during the winter months and had decided to paint it...

"You like the classics?"

Victoria blinked. Lady Maude was looking at her curiously.

"My brother is a great fan of the classics," she said, poking the gentleman beside her. "Aren't you, Thomas?"

"I admire the classical form, yes," he said quietly, his gaze not quite meeting hers.

Victoria tried to keep her face reticent and genteel. "Yes, I thought I spotted that."

"Oh, and there's Jessica and Irene—you must excuse me, Miss Ainsworth," said Lady Maude cheerfully, withdrawing her hand and pointing at a pair of ladies who had a resemblance to her. "Our cousins, you know, from the most junior branch. Until later, Miss Ainsworth."

She swept off in a rush of silk.

Victoria stared back up at the ceiling. It was the sort of ceiling one could enjoy over and over again; there was so much to see, so much to attempt to take in. Clouds upon which sat gods and goddesses, fountains, bowls of fruit, stars, cherubs flying in the sky—

"I hope you like what you see," said Thomas's quiet voice.

Her attention snapped to the gentleman who had invited her to the Chance ball. "I-I beg your pardon?"

"It is old-fashioned, I know," he said softly, stepping closer. "I suppose whoever I marry will have to put up with it, however, as the Duchess of Cothrom. My mother wouldn't hear about it being replaced with anything newfangled and modern."

Victoria's nerves betrayed her and her fingers started to fiddle with her fan.

She supposed this was the way of gentlemen, to hint at a thing before one made it, as it were, official.

And she had done her best. Victoria could not think of anything else she could have done to seduce the man before her, short of throwing herself at—no, she had tried that at the Assembly Rooms. It hadn't worked.

Well, fine, it *had* worked—she'd seen the evidence for herself. But Thomas had held back. Held himself back. Yet he needed her money so badly.

So why hadn't he asked her to marry him?

"I suppose it takes a great deal of money," Victoria said quietly. "The upkeep of a place like this, I mean."

When Thomas met her eyes, it was with a knowing look. "More than you could guess. And there's other properties. Stanphrey Lacey. The townhouse in London."

"Very expensive, indeed," she said. "Might I ask, how will you—"

"There you are, Thomas, I—oh. Good evening, Miss…?"

A woman had approached them. She was slender, elegantly attired in the latest of fashions, with diamond earbobs illuminating a charming face with a curious smile. She had to be in her late forties, Victoria would have surmised, but she had retained her youthful beauty. Why, there was barely a line on her face.

"Miss…?" repeated the woman.

"Victoria Ainsworth," said Thomas, his jaw tightening somewhat. "Miss Ainsworth, may I introduce you to the Duchess of Cothrom."

Victoria's jaw fell open. *The Duchess of—*

"My mother," he added with a wry smile.

"Duchess no longer, after my husband gave up the title earlier this month. People have come to call the pair of us the 'dowager duke and duchess,' and it suits us well enough," said the dowager duchess cordially. "A pleasure to make your acquaintance, Miss Ainsworth. I hope my son is not boring you."

"No, no, not at all!" Victoria spluttered, hardly knowing what to do with herself. "No, I—"

"Miss Ainsworth was admiring your ceiling, Mother," said Thomas gently, drawing a hand around his mother's shoulders in a side embrace.

Try as she might, Victoria could not help but stare at the intimacy. She'd never had brothers and never really felt the lack of them. Boys were dirty, unpleasant things when small, and it appeared to be a lottery whether or not they ever grew out of it.

This side of Thomas... It was a softness she had not seen before.

Though really, she should have been paying attention to what the elegant, mature woman was saying.

"—painted near the end of his life, right in his prime," the dowager duchess was saying. She wasn't really a dowager, nor was there supposed to be a "dowager duke," but she supposed the titles fit. "The clouds here, the shadow and light is most impressive, interplaying with the—"

"I hope you do not mind, Mother," interrupted Thomas gently. "But I was hoping to ask Miss Ainsworth to dance."

Heat prickled in Victoria's cheeks and she did not know where to look as his mother said, "Oh, of course, off you go. You young people should share a dance—I know I did, in my day."

"Your day is hardly over, Mother," said Thomas fondly, placing a kiss on her cheek before releasing her and offering out his hand. "Miss Ainsworth."

It was difficult not to feel self-conscious as Thomas's mother watched her take her son's hand, but Victoria managed to not trip up over her own skirts and fall into his arms, no matter how much she had considered it as a ploy to extract a proposal.

This isn't the time.

This was the time for standing in a line opposite the man she loved and she was absolutely not manipulating, probably, with her dowry, and—

"Thomas!" she gasped.

She really shouldn't have gasped. There were probably people who had heard her, heard the shock in her voice, the sudden, desperate need for air...as Thomas took one of her hands in his, placed his other hand on her waist, and pulled her tightly against him.

Very tightly.

"It's called 'a German waltz,'" said Thomas with a grin. "My mother would be horrified—"

"Thomas William Arnold Chance!"

"—yes, there she goes, but I paid the musicians to ensure they played at least one, Mother notwithstanding," he said in a low voice in her ear.

It wasn't a difficult dance to pick up, as the pairs around them managed to imitate Thomas's steps as well. The closeness of the dance, the inches upon inches of herself that was pressed against himself...

"You requested a waltz...for me?" Victoria gasped.

It was difficult, this close, to look up into Thomas's eyes and not kiss him. Thankfully, the myriad pairs of eyes evidently fixed on them were enough of a preventative.

At least, for now. Lord knew what she would do if he said anything ridiculous like—

"I wanted to be close to you," said Thomas quietly.

Victoria swallowed. Hard.

She was not about to lose all self-control. She was not. And yes, it had occurred to her that this would be a very good time to lean up on her tiptoes and kiss Thomas Chance, Lord Cothrom, thereby creating a scandal of such epic proportions that even his mother would be forced to insist on their marrying...

But she did not kiss him.

The realization was painful, in a way, and it was this: yes, she could seduce Thomas Chance.

But she did not want to.

Seducing him, relying on his animal appetites, tempting him to do what he had done with surely countless other ladies... That was no longer enough.

She wanted more.

"You are a very good dancer, you know."

Victoria permitted herself a laugh, letting some of the tension flow from her. "You're the one doing most of the work. I'm...I'm just following you."

There was a twinkle of mischief in Thomas's eyes. "Is that a promise?"

She almost rested her head on his shoulder, unable to bear the intensity of his look. This was a dangerous game she was playing. He wanted to marry her dowry, she wanted him to fall in love with her...but it appeared only one of them was going to get what they wanted.

When she met his gaze again, Victoria's smile faltered. He was a very good actor. He really made her feel...desired. Wanted. More than that, as though her company were something he craved.

It was all part of his ploy. She mustn't forget that.

"Victoria," said Thomas quietly. "Miss Ainsworth, I mean. I...I was thinking, I—"

The music stopped abruptly. He released her just as he was about to say something Victoria was almost certain she very much wanted to hear.

He turned and swore under his breath. "Mother!"

"That's more than enough waltzes for one ball," the Dowager Duchess of Cothrom said with a fiery glare that reminded Victoria very much of her eldest son. "You and I will talk about this tomorrow!"

Victoria could not help but laugh as she saw the look of concern in Thomas's eyes. "Once a mother's boy, always—"

"It's not like that," Thomas said quickly as the other dancers around them began conversing about the familial altercation. "Well, perhaps it is a bit like that," he said with a lopsided grin. "Would you like some wine, Miss Ainsworth, or punch?"

"Yes—anything," Victoria said gratefully. All this pining over a gentleman who was only interested in one's bosoms and banknotes was exhausting.

The place was starting to fill up and so it took Thomas time to find a footman, despite being the host of the ball. As Victoria stood there, wondering just how pink her cheeks were, a pair of ladies walked past her chattering away about something.

"—and I heard that he spent every single penny!"

"What has this ball been funded with, I wonder? Promises? Yes, he'll be needing a wife—that poor, innocent Miss Ainsworth. She has no idea he desires the dowry, not the debutante!"

Their giggles swiftly became swallowed up with the noise as they walked on.

Victoria very carefully prevented her head from dipping.

Well, that was what they were all thinking, wasn't it? She would likely as not have thought the same thing about another woman, if she had seen a brigand like Thomas Chance pursuing them.

But she would have the last laugh, wouldn't she? She would be the one he married. She would be a duchess. If she continued to take her chances, surely, she would be the one with whom he fell in love?

"Here you go."

Victoria jumped. So lost had she become in her thoughts, Thomas had returned to her side without her noticing.

"Here," repeated the duke, offering her a glass of red wine. When she took it, he offered his own up in a toast. "To our future."

Victoria almost swallowed her tongue. "To *our*...?"

"To *the* future, then," he amended, a wicked look in his eyes. "I suppose you do not mind drinking to that?"

To that, to him—Victoria was hardly sure what she was doing. A gulp of the fiery, red wine did nothing to clear her head, but it at least loosened her tongue. "Is that a line as well? A toast you have offered to other young ladies?"

"You think quite ill of me, don't you?" he said languidly, stepping closer to her to avoid a passing footman.

Very close. So close that when Victoria looked up, it was to breathe against his jawline. His immensely kissable jawline. One so sharp, she would not be surprised if the man would cut down ladies in their thousands.

"I don't think ill of you," she whispered.

The moment of startling honesty went unnoticed by Thomas, who was laughing. The musicians had started up a waltz again and Lady Maude appeared to be physically restraining her mother, who was desperately trying to reach the musicians.

"If they're not careful, they'll cause a scene." Thomas chuckled. "Father would not appreciate that!"

In fact, the last time he had seen the man, he had been attempting to hold back the dowager duchess who was muttering something about uncouth dances and inappropriate music.

"Your family have high expectations for you, don't they?" Victoria said without thinking. "You, and your siblings, I mean."

It was a very personal thing to say, but then, she *had* kissed the man. She did plan to marry him.

Thomas nodded, downing the rest of his wine and placing it on the platter of a passing footman. "All we Chance cousins have a lot to live up to, and I... I intend to make my parents happy. One way or the other."

Victoria swallowed. "I—"

"Do you wish to dance again, Miss Ainsworth?" Thomas said with a grin. "Oh, I do apologize, you've not finished your—Victoria!"

She had downed the rest of her red wine in much the same attitude that he had. Unlike him, Victoria had struggled to prevent her eyes from watering at the sudden burn in her throat.

"You know, you are nothing like what I expected," he said, offering his arm.

"Of course not," Victoria said, hoping to goodness the wine would not go to her head—anymore, that was, than the gentleman before her already had. "Lead on!"

Chapter Ten

"**S**ENDING YOUR CARRIAGE home, claiming you'll spend the night under my mother's and sister's eye and then changing your mind, was a foolish idea—"

"It was *my* idea!"

"That doesn't mean it can't be foolish," Thomas said with a laugh at the woman who was confusing him with every passing turn.

Victoria turned up the collar of her pelisse around her neck, as though that would have any impact on the freezing temperatures, and grinned. "Well, what can I say. It's more fun to walk home."

"But I can't let you walk home on your own," he began as he opened the front door of the Chance house, light spilling out onto the icy pavement.

His stomach lurched as Victoria glanced over her shoulder. "Then don't."

She stepped forward without hesitation to the pavement and started walking slowly in the direction of Union Street.

Thomas cursed quietly as he stood there, indecisive. His father was expecting him for drinks in the library. His mother would undoubtedly want to ask about the damned waltz, and if he knew Maude, she would want to know just what his intentions were toward the young woman to whom he was paying such marked attention.

His intentions. An excellent question.

His gaze lingered on the sway of Victoria's hips as she walked. Even through the thick fabric of her pelisse, there was no mistaking those curves.

Thomas's fists tightened, just for a moment. And then the decision was made.

"Victoria—Miss Ainsworth, wait!"

She halted, twisting to smile with a far-too-knowing grin. How had she known? He had barely known himself until a second ago what he was about to do.

Grabbing the nearest greatcoat from one of the family's startled footmen and ramming his hands through the sleeves, Thomas almost slipped as he ran out into the cold, night air.

The freezing, absolutely bone chilling cold air.

Hissing through his teeth, he shook his head as he reached Victoria. "You're being ridiculous, walking home in this!"

"It's only cold," said the shrugging woman playing havoc with his mind.

"It's absolutely freezing! You do not even have a hat!"

"Cold is a state of mind," she said cheerfully, slipping a hand into his—*a hand. Into his.* Her other hand curled seductively around his arm. "Not so cold now, is it?"

Thomas swallowed and looked into the eyes of a woman who appeared to know him better than he knew himself.

Because she was right. The close proximity of the woman he had wanted to kiss so badly ever since he had first tasted those lips was pouring scalding heat through his veins. Hotter than whisky, hotter than rum—he had never tasted anything like it.

"No," he said quietly. "Not so cold now."

They stood there for a moment in silence, the midnight air gently rustling through empty branches.

Then Thomas cleared his throat, looked up, and started forward. "Come on, then. I'll make sure you get home safely."

It wasn't entirely necessary. There were two or three Chance carriages available at any one time, and he did not imagine all of them had been called upon to transport their guests home. Not with Miss Victoria Ainsworth one of the last to leave.

All he would have had to do is ask Bradbury, their butler, to prepare a carriage—or go out into the street and find a hackney cab—to transport Miss Ainsworth home, with a chaperone if needed. A maid, perhaps. With a footman to guard them.

Thomas's fingers tightened around Victoria's own. The idea of sending her off into the night with a mere footman! A blaggard, perhaps, a rogue who would tell the maid to look the other way and take advantage of—

"I had a wonderful time at your ball."

Thomas looked into Victoria's face.

When would he have a handle on this woman? At times bold and brash, at others shy and curious, there appeared to be endless facets to her. Surely, most women were not so complicated?

Surely, most men did not bother to find out.

"I am glad," Thomas said honestly, truth slipping from his tongue far easier than the many lies he had so recently told. "It was... Well. Important to me. I wanted my family to have a good opinion of you."

"And do they?"

He weighed up the truth.

His mother had instructed him to marry Victoria Ainsworth as soon as possible.

His father had inquired as to her suitability as a spouse and had been gratified to discover not the slightest hint of scandal.

His brothers had teased him something awful about the fact that, but for the toss of a coin, he would have been attending the family ball with Lady Marjorie—a comment from Leopold that had inexplicably made Xander's ears redden.

And his sister had informed him, quite calmly, that he was not good enough for Miss Ainsworth, would never be good enough for Miss Ainsworth, and should call the whole thing off.

Thomas cleared his throat. "Yes. Yes, they liked you."

Victoria nudged him in the ribs. "That was far too long a pause to be genuine, you know."

"Honestly, they liked you!" Thomas protested, hating that it had taken him so long to gather his thoughts. He hesitated again. "I think they would not mind I were to... If I... If we..."

Why was it so difficult to get these words out? Why was the challenge of speaking his mind so arduous?

Because, came that irritating little voice at the back of his mind again, *you started all this under false pretenses, didn't you? You lied about the money. You're lying to all of them. You tossed a coin to choose a bride! And she has no idea your only interest is in her money...*

Well. Not the only interest. Not anymore.

"Thomas, what are you thinking?"

Thomas started. "What?"

"Oh, nothing," Victoria said airily with a laugh. "Only that we've been walking now in the wrong direction for about two minutes, and try as I might, I haven't been able to turn you."

He halted in his tracks, looked around wildly, and saw a street sign. Union Street. *Union Street?*

Laughing at how swiftly he could become lost in his thoughts, Thomas changed tack, both with feet and tongue. "Enough about my family—I want to hear about your own."

"Mine?"

He nodded. Yes, that was a safe topic. That couldn't take him closer to danger.

Victoria shrugged, the movement against the borrowed greatcoat shooting sparks down Thomas's spine. "You have met the entirety of my family, I am afraid. My mother and I are all that's left of the Ainsworths."

"And your father—what was he like?"

For a moment, Thomas worried he'd touched a nerve. It could have been the nighttime shadow passing over Victoria's face as they passed a window, light streaming through a chink in the curtains. But then it faded, and her smile returned.

"My father was… He was everything you would want a father to be. Kind, and a tad gruff. He gave so freely to the poor that my mother would jest he would starve us to feed others!"

Thomas stiffened, but only for a moment. *There was no way she could know, was there?*

"His death was quite a shock, and in some ways, I think… I think a part of my mother died with him," Victoria said, more solemnly. "They were so in love—a rarity, I think. An arranged match that ended up in true devotion."

She met Thomas's gaze, and he tried not to show any great depth of feeling. "Indeed."

"*Indeed,*" she mocked with a lilting laugh. "Tell me about the Chance family—at least, tell me that which I do not already know."

"'Already know'?"

Victoria squeezed his hand as they turned a corner. "You must understand that being a Chance… Well, the family has been respected for generations, hasn't it? If you ask me, it's a surprise none of our generation have been knighted yet—"

"Don't tell my brother Alexander that," Thomas said. The very thought of his younger brother prancing about the place with a knighthood—

"—but I have to assume most of the rumors aren't true," Victoria continued, curiosity lacing her voice. "They can't all be true, can they?"

Thomas hesitated. "Well, that depends on what you've been told."

Her eyes widened. "What on earth do you mean?"

"Well, my father is the eldest of four brothers and they were young during the Regency. You know, when Prinny was dancing about the place and excess was the norm," Thomas attempted to explain. *How did one describe the myriad family stories, half of which he didn't even believe?* "My father was always the calm, quiet, devoted one, fearing scandal and attempting to keep my uncles on the straight and narrow—"

"With varying success, I would imagine," Victoria said dryly.

Thomas's pulse skipped a beat as they crossed the deserted street. It was incredible; there was something about talking with Victoria, even about family topics, that made him feel…so comfortable. So safe.

And so in danger at the same time.

"I haven't been told all the stories, and I'm not sure I ever will," he admitted. "I suppose my cousins have different sides of the stories."

"You have a number of cousins, I think."

Thomas nodded. "Uncle John has two daughters and two sons, Uncle George has a son and two daughters, and Uncle Frederick… Well, he's the most prolific of the lot."

"More than four?"

"Five." Thomas displayed a wide grin, thinking of his favorite uncle. "A son and four daughters."

Victoria's eyes widened. "All of you Chances."

"We're all unmarried, so far." The words did not come out nearly so nonchalantly as he had intended. "I would guess that most of my cousins have stories about their fathers and the hijinks they got up to back in the day, but my father and uncles don't like to talk about it much."

"They don't want to encourage their sons to become scandalous."

The words themselves were relatively innocuous, but it was the way she'd said them. Heat shuddered through Thomas and he tried not to think about the way his fingers encircled hers. Victoria. The woman with whom he had wished to be very scandalous, though he had managed, just about, to keep his hands to himself.

Mostly.

"And what about you?"

Thomas blinked. "What about me?"

"Well," said Victoria, biting her bottom lip as she tilted her head on one side. After much consideration, she said quietly, "When are you going to become scandalous?"

Thomas stiffened. "My father would not like me to become involved in anything that could be deemed a scan—"

"Is that why you hold yourself back from me?" Her words were urgent now, low, though there was no one around to hear. "Are you afraid, Thomas? Afraid of a little scandal? Afraid that if you let yourself go, that the scandal would overcome you? You know, if anyone were to see us right now, right here, without a chaperone, as innocent as our behavior might be…"

And that was when it became too much, far too much, for Thomas to bear.

He had been good, hadn't he? Restrained himself, attempted to act the gentleman around her—despite great provocation.

"Damn it, woman, I'm trying to be honorable!"

"Not so honorable that you would propose to me."

And here, in the darkness where no one would bear witness to the outrageous thing he was about to do, Thomas allowed all the pent-up need that he had most studiously dammed to be unleashed.

"Thomas?" Victoria had stopped in her tracks, breath blossoming into mist on the cold, winter breeze. There was a smile on her face—a knowing one, one that told him she was certain he would do nothing about her words.

How wrong she was.

"Thomas!"

Victoria's astonished gasp was full of longing, spurring Thomas on—not that he needed additional encouragement. He grabbed her by the arms and swept her to the left, pinning her against the cold brick wall of the street. The place was empty, not a single pedestrian or carriage disturbing them.

For perhaps the first time ever, they were truly alone.

"Thomas?" The sudden movement had clearly robbed Victoria of momentum and the way she'd gasped his name stirred his loins. "What are you—"

Overcome by need, desiring her more than he had ever desired a woman in his life, exhausted from the ball and unable to fight off his feelings any longer, Thomas lowered his lips to hers and claimed them as his own.

Victoria put up no resistance; if she had, Thomas would have released her immediately, apologized if his mouth had worked, then returned her home.

But she was clearly just as eager for this as he was. Tilting her head and parting her lips to welcome him in, she moaned and Thomas lost his head.

"You asked me once," he growled, wrenching away his lips to look into her wide eyes, "to *take you*. And I didn't."

"You wanted to," she shot back in a whisper, her hands pressed against his shirt.

Thomas grinned wickedly, lowering his mouth to her neck and nuzzling as his hands moved from her arms to her waist, pinning her against the wall. "I did."

Victoria was quivering now, not the shiver cold created but lust. Heat poured through Thomas, egging him on, and he could not help himself. The control he valued so highly, that all Chance gentlemen were taught, was melting away in the heat of their connection.

His fingers needed her—needed more. And he knew just what was to satisfy them.

Returning his lips to hers, tugging out waves of hedonism as his tongue laved her own, eking out a sensual dance that had Victoria melting into his arms, Thomas allowed his fingers to do what they had itched to do for far too long.

The softness of Victoria's breast allowed his thumb to sink into it and he almost wept. *Oh, God, she feels wonderful.* Everything he had wanted, had longed for... *But I mustn't. I must try to control myself—*

"Yes," moaned Victoria quite unexpectedly, arching her back into him, welcoming his touch. "Oh, touch me like that—more, more…"

Thomas groaned in her mouth, the temptation to just take her here and now growing with every passing moment. His fingers scraped past the buttons of her pelisse, freeing it, and heat seared his loins and his rapidly stiffening manhood as his fingers brushed past not fabric, but décolletage.

"Victoria, you feel—you feel—"

He could barely breathe, so how speech was possible, he did not know—but there was just enough power in Thomas's mind for the fingers on his left hand to gently brush along the hem of her bust…then slip into her gown, freeing her breast from its corset.

For a moment, just a moment, Thomas raised his head. It was torture to separate his lips from her own, but he had to check—had to see she was quite as willing as she sounded.

He almost swore. Victoria's hair was mussed; pins had evidently cascaded to the pavement at some point, but he had not noticed when. Her lips were pink, wet, bruised under the passion of his touch. Her eyes were wide, astonished…yet eager.

"I… Oh, yes," Victoria whimpered.

Thomas had barely realized he'd done it. His fingers had gently caressed her breast, glorying in the weight of it, while his thumb moved over to her nipple, twisting it gently and, he knew, sparking an erotic thrum through her body.

Victoria shivered, lifting up her lips to be kissed. "More."

She was insatiable. She was sensual. She was—everything he had ever wanted.

With a growl of answering need, Thomas forced her back against the wall, his right hip pinning her there just as securely as if it had been with his own hand. His left hand continued to lavish attention on her breast and his lips claimed her mouth.

He would, after all, need to keep her quiet for what was about to happen next.

Head spinning at the decadent way her breast felt in his hand, Thomas tried to consider what to do next, but thoughts were no longer possible. This was instinct, and need, and a deep-rooted knowledge that she wanted this.

Victoria ground her hip against his now-throbbing manhood and Thomas gave into temptation.

"God, I've wanted to do this for ages," Thomas murmured against her mouth, grinning at the way she leaned into him. "For so long, Victoria. For so long—"

"Then do it, whatever it is." She gasped, her head lolling against the brick wall, the only thing keeping her upright. "Thomas, I— Thomas!"

He could have wept. *Oh, God, she felt so good.*

While they had been speaking, his right hand had not been idle. It was not exactly easy to lift up the many skirts that young ladies insisted on wearing these days, but Thomas's eagerness to reach his prize enabled his hand to travel through the edge of her pelisse, her skirt, two petticoats, and then—

Her thigh. Warm, and soft, and pliant.

It did not take long for Thomas's wandering fingers to make their way upward, Victoria gasping under his ministrations, her nipple twisted between forefinger and thumb to keep her warmed...

Oh, Christ alive.

Her curls were searing, welcoming, inviting—and wet. She wanted him just as much as he wanted her.

When Thomas's fingers curled and met flesh, hot, quivering flesh that clearly ached to be stroked, he leaned his forehead against hers and moaned.

"I'll give you everything," came her gentle voice. "Everything, Thomas."

That was when he knew he could not take it.

His fingers halted. For a heartbeat, he stood there, uncertain precisely what had happened.

Then realization dawned. With it came regret before Thomas removed his hand and slowly, remorsefully, slipped the heavy breast back into the gown.

"Thomas? Thomas, what is—"

"I... I'm sorry." Thomas had not expected his voice to rasp. Perhaps it was the night air. It certainly could not have been the emotion throbbing through him. "I can't."

Victoria's skirts fell to the pavement, yet Thomas could not let her go. He wanted to stay here, his forehead pressed against hers, the closeness he so desperately wanted literally within arm's reach.

A hand. He blinked. Victoria was cupping his cheek, leaning back so she could stare deeply into his eyes.

"Why not?" she whispered, pain on her face. "Did... Did I do something wrong?"

Pain shot through his lungs as Thomas tried to take a swift breath and speak at the same time. "No!"

"It's just... You were going to—"

"I know," said Thomas heavily.

How could he explain? Were there even words?

This woman, this wonderful woman, this picture of beauty and elegance, this witty woman... She deserved so much more than him. More than this.

If he weren't already choosing her merely for her money—perhaps not merely for that anymore, but that was how the whole blessed thing had started—he certainly wasn't going to ravish her against a wall as if she were a common hussy!

"Thomas?"

"I... You deserve..." Thomas swallowed. He looked into her green eyes and knew he had to tell the truth. A rare thing for him, at the moment. "Your first time, your first pleasure... Damn it, Victoria, that deserves to be in a bed surrounded by candles, with rose petals strewn about the place and—"

"You're babbling."

"No, I'm not!" He hadn't intended to sound so fierce, and she was beaming. She was not angry with him, but she had to understand. "Victoria, you... I couldn't, I can't... It needs to be perfect. Perfect for you, and this... This is not how I would, how I would want to..."

Words failed him as the desire to change his mind, to pin both hands above her head with one of his own and tease her with his fingers until she could take no more, washed over him.

"I'm going to take you home," Thomas said with a wry sigh, stepping back and trying to tell his manhood it would be worth it. *Eventually*. "I'm going to see you inside, and shut the door behind you, and return to my own home—"

"And your own bed." Victoria's eyes glittered.

He took in a long, deep breath, then let it out in a laugh. "Much as I would wish it otherwise...yes. I'm a gentleman, Miss Ainsworth."

"Gentlemen don't kiss like that," she said, stepping toward him. For a moment, he was certain she was going to launch herself into his arms, but instead, she merely slipped hers in the crook of his arm.

"This one does."

Their laughter rang out in the street as they walked toward the Ainsworth house, but Thomas could barely concentrate on their conversation.

He was getting far too emotional. What had happened to the plan, to marry the money? He could not marry this angel, this beauty, this intellect, for her money, but he could not forget how he had intended to do just that.

And yet that did not change the fact that his family needed that money. Because of him.

How could he stop this deep attraction...and this overpowering guilt?

131

Chapter Eleven

January 23, 1840

THE COLD WEATHER was finally thawing and the streets of Bath were subsequently heaving.

"Oi, careful there, miss!" said a man as he marched past Victoria, bumping into her so heavily she almost lost her balance.

Her, be careful? *The cretin!*

Not that she would have said anything—and even if she had intended to, the man had hurried out of sight too fast to catch her words.

Victoria sighed. It was turning out to be that sort of day. The haberdasher had still not gotten the ribbon her mother wanted, which Mrs. Ainsworth was going to be furious about, and the bookshop was still waiting on the order Victoria had made over a week ago. The warmth had brought out the louts of Bath, people jostling on the pavements and carriages hurtling by far too fast.

And worse... She had not seen Thomas Chance, Duke of Cothrom, for two whole days.

"Gentlemen don't kiss like that."

"This one does."

Victoria shivered, hoping any passerby would presume a chilly breeze had precipitated the movement. Only she had to know it was because of the chilly silence from a certain gentleman that had made her tremble.

What more could she do? No more, as far as she could tell. Seducing a duke with a tarnished reputation was turning out to be far more difficult than she had imagined.

As she walked down the street, Danvers loaded up with packages beside her, the two of them pushing past a few people in her path, Victoria tried studiously not to look at the brick wall beside her. It just happened to be the wall where he—

"Your first time, your first pleasure… Damn it, Victoria, that deserves to be in a bed surrounded by candles, with rose petals strewn about the place…"

Victoria swallowed, her mouth dry. Never, in all her wildest dreams, had she imagined something so wonderful, so decadent, so absolutely scandalous.

The man had started undressing her! Had touched her…her *her*!

Yet still Thomas Chance had not been willing to ravish her.

It was most provoking.

The worst of it is, Victoria thought irritably as she waited for a gaggle of schoolchildren to cross the street, shepherded by a haggard woman in a gray coat, *I arrived home that night aching in all sorts of surprising places.* The man had… Well. Riled her up, was that the right term?

She hardly knew. All she knew was that she would give anything, absolutely anything, to see Thomas right now and—

Victoria halted in her steps abruptly.

"Watch out, miss!"

She ignored the startled comments behind her, her feet flying likely faster than Danvers could follow, weighed down as she was with packages. What did it matter if she was now in the way of other pedestrians attempting to get past? She had just seen…

Thomas Chance.

A smile crept across her face that she did not attempt to fight. He was looking remarkably handsome, bundled up in that great coat, a knitted scarf—a badly knitted scarf—around his neck and finishing over one shoulder. He was talking to…to a gaggle of children.

Victoria blinked. That was unexpected. What was Lord Cothrom doing speaking to a group of children? They were all dressed in red, the same sort of red as the Chance livery, and they were...warm. Wrapped up in clothes far more elegant than their general appearance would have suggested.

There were quite a few Chance cousins, weren't there? That must have been it.

After a final word from him, the children grinned then scampered away, leaving just Thomas and...a woman.

She'd been a fool. There she'd been, thinking she would have given anything to see him, and how was she rewarded?

By spotting the tall, handsome, and laughing Duke of Cothrom on the other side of the road...arm in arm with the most beautiful woman Victoria had ever seen.

The world spun. Her mind whirled, her sense of balance leaving her breathless. Victoria put out a hand dazedly, almost blindly, hoping to grasp on to something solid to prevent her falling.

The roughness of the brick beneath her gloved fingertips almost mocked her. The same sensation had covered her back when Thomas had been kissing her. Now there he stood, arm in arm with another woman.

Tears threatened to fall as they prickled in the corners of her eyes. How had she been so stupid?

Of course she was not the only woman Thomas Chance was pursuing. What a fool she had been. She'd heard enough of the rumors about his brothers, the ladies they chased after, the scandal after scandal hushed up.

Why had she thought Thomas, the eldest, would be any different?

The woman had the sort of beauty men sighed over and women desperately craved. Her elegant blue pelisse matched her bonnet, the felt seamlessly crafted with a matching ribbon. Her gloves also matched, as did her reticule. Victoria had never seen a woman look more put together and in control of her own life.

Her stomach lurched. And Thomas was smiling at her. The woman.

It was not a crime. Not officially, at any rate—but the jealousy that rose in her was insupportable.

She had to get away.

The thought flashed through her mind like lightning, but it made enough of an impression to force Victoria's feet into a juddering pace.

She had to get away—get home. Away from the sight of Thomas Chance, away from the reminder that she was not special, not important.

Had he kissed that woman like he had kissed her?

The agony accompanying the thought made Victoria stumble, her world still not yet righted from the shock of seeing such a sight.

"Victoria—Miss Ainsworth?"

And it doesn't make sense, Victoria thought as she fought back tears. *She* had been the one tricking *him*, hadn't she? After all, she'd known his intention had been to merely take her dowry and solve his family's problems with it. She knew that—had known it from the very beginning.

So why did this hurt so much?

The affection she felt was to blame, but then, it had hurt to be apart from him in the year they'd spent apart. Why was this any different?

Because it cheapens what you thought you had, Victoria thought dazedly as she attempted to keep walking. *Because it negates every good moment that you shared together. Just when you...when you thought—*

"Miss Ainsworth!"

Finally, the words shouted across the crowded street registered in Victoria's mind. Looking up, she turned to see who was calling after her.

Her heart skipped a beat.

Thomas Chance.

Absolutely not. Her feet moved without instruction, speeding up in the opposite direction. Where was Danvers? Had she lost her in the crowd? If Thomas Chance thought Victoria was just going to stand there and allow him to talk to her with another woman on his arm—

"Miss Ainsworth, wait!"

Panic flaring in her lungs, Victoria tried to pick up her pace, but her legs weren't obeying. Why was this happening to her? It had to be a million-to-one chance, the streets of Bath so packed today, that she would even see him. Why did it have to be—

A hand on her arm, a sudden jolt, and Victoria was no longer moving forward.

Oh, no...

"Victoria—Miss Ainsworth, I mean," said Thomas with a wide grin. "I thought it was you!"

Victoria wrenched her arm away as the hordes of people meandered past them, like waves encircling a rock in the ocean.

She was going to be calm. That was all—calm. She was going to be calm, and relaxed, and utterly prepossessed. She was not going to reveal just how much seeing him with her—the beautiful woman staring with unabashed curiosity—was hurting her.

She was not.

"Who are you?" Victoria blurted out, glaring at the woman.

The woman raised an eyebrow. "How interesting."

"*Victoria!*" hissed Thomas, as though *she* were the one who had acted indecorously.

Heat was pouring into Victoria's cheeks, but there was nothing she could do about it—it was Thomas who should have felt ashamed!

"I trusted you," Victoria said in a low voice, ignoring the woman for now and concentrating her attention on Thomas. "I-I thought... I mean, it seemed to me as though—"

"Shall I introduce myself, or should I wait for you to get around to it, Tommy?" asked the woman with a frown at Thomas.

Victoria's stomach lurched as she saw the intimacy between them. Oh, this was far worse than she had expected. *"Tommy"?*

"Victoria, I can explain—"

"You know, I don't think you can!" Victoria hated how high her voice was, how she could feel the stares of strangers on the back of her neck, but if it was going to end, here and now, it was going to end on her terms. "You, Thomas Chance, are a complete rake! You are a liar, and a cheat, and a—"

"You know, I quite agree," interrupted the woman in a bored voice. "He always has been."

Victoria gaped at the woman. Well, this was far more ridiculous than she had expected!

"You... You don't care?" she spluttered at the woman.

The stranger raised a sardonic eyebrow. "Why should I? Marrying one's cousin may be deemed acceptable by many, but I would never consider it myself."

Marrying one's...one's cousin.

Victoria realized her mouth was still open. She shut it hurriedly, then looked up at Thomas. He was grinning. She glared, and his face immediately fell.

"Liliana, Miss Victoria Ainsworth. Miss Ainsworth, Lady Lilianna Chance. I was trying to tell you, Victoria. She's only—"

"'Only'? Well, thank you very much, Tommy," snapped the woman. She pulled her arm from his and sniffed. "Don't ask me for a favor again, please. If this is how it's going to end up, I would rather stay at home with Frank, even if they are dull as ditchwater at the moment. Miss Ainsworth."

"Let me walk you—" started Thomas.

"No need. My lady's maid awaits me in the carriage. It was too cold for her out here."

Dropping into a graceful curtsey that Victoria hastily attempted to reciprocate, though hers was in no way as elegant, the woman swept away in a rush of fashion.

Victoria stared. *Cousin. Right.*

And lady's maid. She glanced around and realized she really *had* lost sight of her Danvers.

All the better. She would not have liked her to have witnessed this.

She turned on Thomas. "Well, you could have said!"

"I attempted to!" Thomas said, lifting his hands in mock surrender as he was buffeted by a crowd of young boys. "Lilianna is a menace, but she is my cousin and I had asked her for a favor. Blast it all. She won't help me now."

Victoria deflated just as swiftly as she had been riled.

She looked the complete fool now, she supposed. Getting all hot and bothered because the man she loved—a man who did not love her, and wouldn't even be tempted to ravish her when offered her body on a plate—had been walking about in public with his cousin. A cousin, moreover, who clearly had absolutely no desire to be the next Duchess of Cothrom.

Mortifying did not quite cover it.

"I'm annoyed at you," she muttered to the tall, handsome man whom she loved beyond anything.

"And I have no idea why!" Thomas said, eyes wide as he dropped his hands to his sides. "It is not as though I have done anything wrong!"

He was right. Somehow, that made it worse.

"I have to return home," said Victoria, turning and walking away.

Trying to walk away.

The bounder had caught hold of her arm once again. "Victoria, I—"

"I've just made a complete fool of myself, and I would rather go away and hide than be looked at by you," she said fiercely, tugging her arm ineffectually from his grip. "And people are staring—"

"Let them stare," said Thomas quietly. "I don't care who knows how I feel."

Victoria stopped attempting to escape. When she turned around slowly, arm still in his grasp, she was almost certain she could feel Thomas's pulse through her pelisse.

"You... You don't?"

Victoria could not think what else to say.

How *did* he feel? If the man had been anyone else, she would have presumed he was in love with her. He certainly was in lust with her—no man could falsify the stiffness in those trousers.

But why hadn't he asked her to marry him? What was holding the man back, even though he clearly so desperately needed her money?

"It's not a secret. I may not say it in words, not...not yet. But I am hardly hiding it, am I?"

Somehow—Victoria wasn't sure how—Thomas had closed the gap between them. Despite standing together in broad daylight in the middle of a pavement, where anyone could see them, he was standing... Well, close. Too close. Or not close enough.

Victoria's voice caught in her throat. "N-No."

Her whole body was on fire for him, heating with every passing moment the longer he stood that close. Oh, he was so handsome. And charming. And kind. And idiotic, sometimes, yes. Losing all that money had been a foolish thing indeed.

But there was no harm in him. He wasn't a cruel man.

Victoria swallowed. "What... What favor was your cousin doing for you? May I help?"

It was a foolish thing to suggest, she knew, and her hopes sank as Thomas hesitated glancing about as though suddenly aware he was standing very close to a young lady to whom he was not related, her chaperone nowhere in sight.

He took a step back. "I... Well, I am not entirely..."

"Please, forget I said anything," Victoria said hastily. "I should return home myself. I must find Danvers. She'll be worried, and my mother will be wondering—"

"Yes."

She blinked. "I-I beg your pardon?"

Thomas shifted on his feet, inexplicably uncertain. "It's a small task, but I would really prefer a woman's eye. If you do not mind."

Victoria's shoulders relaxed. *Oh, it's that sort of favor.* The man must have needed to enter a haberdasher, or a tailor, or something of the sort. He must have needed advice on colors, or a fabric, or perhaps the right button choice.

"Lead on, then," she said boldly, though without being bold enough to slip her hand through his arm. "I am more than willing to help."

Poor Danvers would just have to keep worrying.

Still, she had the foresight to tug down the brim of her hat.

Victoria and Thomas walked in companionable silence down two streets. Victoria had never known anything like it; conversation was the adornment of good Society, and she had been brought up to always have something witty, or amusing, or charming to say—preferably all three. The idea of walking with a gentleman, a gentleman to whom she was not engaged, without saying a word was ridiculous.

Yet it felt so right. Being silent with him was better than inane chatter with anyone else.

"It's just down here," said Thomas quietly. "I'd meant to come a few days ago but found myself dazzled by the choice. I thought... Well, I asked Lil if she could help."

"I am sorry to have made her abandon you," Victoria said, attempting levity. Strange, she did not recall any haberdashers along here. Or tailors, for that matter. "Where is the—"

"Here we are," Thomas said, halting suddenly. "Mepham and Sons."

Victoria swallowed.

Oh. Goodness. Saints above.

It wasn't a haberdasher. It wasn't a tailor. In fact, it had nothing to do with men's tailoring at all.

"These are the best jewelers in Bath, according to my mother," said Thomas, calmly peering through the window at the display of fabulous jewels and carefully crafted jewelry. "And you know a duchess has good taste in jewelers. What do you think?"

Think? She thought she was going to have a heart attack.

This was the favor Thomas had asked his cousin to assist him with…to select some jewelry?

If she was not too careful, she was going to expire on the spot. Why, anyone could see them! See them, the new Duke of Cothrom who had come into a title in a most odd way, the penniless Duke of Cothrom who had a reputation as a spendthrift and no ability to hold on to his family's money…and a woman. A lady. Looking at jewelry!

Victoria swallowed, hard. Looking, in fact, at rings. That was the part of the window that Thomas was peering into.

Rings.

"Now, a lady like yourself will have excellent taste, I have no doubt," came Thomas's voice from a long way away. "What do you think—sapphires or emeralds?"

Not for the first time in Thomas Chance's company, Victoria wished to goodness it was the fashion to carry fans about one's person at all times. It would not necessarily have made much of a difference to the heat scalding through her body underneath the pelisse, but she could have at least hidden her face behind it.

As it was, when Thomas glanced up over, he surely saw the way her face was flushed and her lips were parted.

"Victoria?"

"What?" she said hurriedly.

"Sapphires or emeralds." he repeated, turning back to the rings. "I know in a way, it is only a choice between blue and green, but I have to imagine that young ladies think a great deal about this sort of thing."

Victoria leaned forward to place her gloved hand on the glass. It was that or keel over. "'Young ladies'?"

"I have never purchased jewelry for a woman before," Thomas mused, appearing to only be half-listening to her as she was barely able to concentrate on his own words. "My sister much prefers books, or music, or a treat to a concert. She's never been one for finery."

Her pulse was thundering so loudly, Victoria was a little surprised he had not mentioned it.

"And I do want to impress the recipient of this...this present," he continued quietly, not looking at her. "It's important to me. *She's* important to me."

The tightening of her lungs was accompanied by a slight dizziness in her mind, and Victoria focused everything in her being on the most important thing: not falling over.

He was talking about her, wasn't he?

There was no other explanation. Fine, she had presumed he'd been courting more than one woman when she had seen him across the street arm in arm with Lady Lilianna Chance, but that had been a terrible blow, hadn't it? And she'd been wrong.

She, surely, was the only woman Thomas Chance was courting— and that meant this gift was for her.

A ring. To mark their betrothal.

Victoria swallowed. It wasn't the norm, but it was becoming fashionable. A ring, a promise, a deposit, as it were, ahead of the coming together of two people.

It was a physical sign of an ephemeral promise, and here she was, standing beside a man whom she loved and who did not love her in return—for surely, he would have said so—while he attempted to choose a ring for her.

"So?" Thomas came back into view. His head tilted and his eyebrow arched. "Emeralds or sapphires?" he said.

Drawing herself up and deciding she was not going to let the moment overcome her, Victoria looked in the direction he had been perusing. There lay a line of gold rings, each adorned with different stones. One had a single, large, square emerald, another a trio of smaller oval sapphires, and a third had a sapphire surrounded by small diamonds.

All of them were beautiful.

"It's... It's difficult to choose between such beauty, isn't it?"

Thomas shifted beside her, and suddenly, her arm was pressed against his, the man far too close to ignore. Not that she had managed that for the past year or so.

"Beauty deserves beauty," he said softly. "Which do you want?"

"I beg your—"

"I said, which do you like?" Thomas's voice was steady. There was no hint he had changed his wording at all.

Victoria hesitated. Perhaps she had dreamed that first phrase. It was easy to do, as the man's presence was so heady. "I...I like all of them."

"But if you had to choose one." His voice pressed into her, insistent.

It some ways, it was like a dream. The sort of dream in which she had indulged those first few weeks after meeting Lord Thomas Chance, eldest son of the Duke of Cothrom. Dreams about declarations of love, and jewels, and the careful choice of one piece of jewelry in particular.

Victoria straightened up and Thomas mirrored her, and she smiled. This was it.

"—and I heard most of the Chance money is gone!"

Her smile faded.

What was she doing? She knew, better than he understood, just how little money he and his family had. Surely, their creditors would be calling in debts soon, the Chance ball an expense they could ill afford. The whole reason Thomas had started to woo her, after all, had been for her money.

How was he going to afford a pretty bauble like these rings?

"Will you walk me home?" Victoria asked lightly, walking away from the jewelers. "Perhaps Danvers has gone there to look for me."

"Victoria—Victoria? Where are you going?"

She continued to walk along the pavement.

Soon, Thomas was beside her. "I don't—I don't understand. You don't like them? You don't want a ring?"

It was almost exactly what she had hoped for. Only now that the moment was here did Victoria realize that perhaps what she wanted was different. "I want lots of things, Thomas, but they can't be found in that shop. They can't be found in any shop."

Victoria slipped her hand into his without thinking. Thomas squeezed his fingers around hers.

Right. She was so in love with him that she had just refused the offer of a promise ring. Now what?

Chapter Twelve

January 26, 1840

CREEPING WAS A very serious word. A very heavy word. A word filled with negativity and drama and criminality.

He wasn't creeping, not exactly. He was…lurking.

Thomas sighed as he leaned against a tree, eyes trained on the house opposite, wondering what on earth he was doing.

Well, he knew what he was *doing*. He was waiting outside the Ainsworth house, the end of the terrace on this street, hoping to goodness that at some point Mrs. Ainsworth would leave and give him the opportunity to go in there and…

And what?

That was the part of the plan, if it could loosely be called a "plan," that Thomas had not quite worked out yet.

"I want lots of things, Thomas, but they can't be found in that shop. They can't be found in any shop."

The words Victoria had spoken to him just days ago were still rattling around his head. What she had meant, he had been certain of at first. The more time he spent thinking about it, the more he wondered whether he hadn't gotten the complete wrong end of the stick.

It was irksome beyond belief. At first, he had found it fortuitous to have encountered his intended on the streets of London that day, a sign that he'd been right to move past his reservations and ask for her hand. He had really intended, for quite a few minutes, to buy Victoria whichever ring she liked best. It would have been on the ring finger of her left hand before she had returned home, and Thomas in turn could have returned home and announced his betrothal.

Only when Victoria had stridden away from the shop, a strange look on her face, had he remembered.

Damn. No money. No money at all, only debts—and there was the fishmonger to pay, and that looked like it was going to be a large bill. How could so many sardines be consumed by so few people in such little time?

Speaking to Mrs. Ainsworth about the whole thing had been considered and swiftly discounted. He didn't want to give Victoria or her mother time to think about it, to hesitate, like he had. The plan that was now looking like: marry Victoria, take her money, attempt to make her happy.

Dear God, he was in deep. Too deep.

And that meant it was time to confess.

Only that morning he had met with the housemothers of St. Thomas's and promised them that the bills piling up in the small office there, held together by string, would be paid. Soon.

With Victoria's money.

"And where's all this going to come from, if I may ask?" one of the teachers had asked, her brow wrinkled and her mouth pinched.

And Thomas had not been able to bring himself to say the truth: that he was swindling some poor woman into falling in love with him just so that he could get his hands on her dowry.

"From somewhere good," had been all he'd managed to say.

It wasn't a lie. It was most definitely not the truth, but it wasn't a lie.

And now Thomas blew out a long breath as his gaze flickered over the setting sun reflected in the Ainsworth house's windows. The afternoon was wearing on. If Mrs. Ainsworth had intended to leave for an afternoon engagement, surely, she would—

Three things happened almost simultaneously. First, a carriage was brought around to the front of the house. Second, the door to the Ainsworth house opened wide, the figure of a woman illuminated by the candlelight behind her. Third, Thomas slipped in the mud in his haste to hide behind the tree.

"Damn and blast it—"

A bony, older woman in black walking past looked scandalized, picking up her pace so she could swiftly depart from the scoundrel's remarks. At least, that was what it looked like. Thomas supposed it could have been complete coincidence that she almost ran from him, but he doubted it.

Picking himself up and trying to wipe the mud from the back of his greatcoat, Thomas glanced up hurriedly. Was it Miss or Mrs. Ainsworth who was leaving?

A voice rang out across the street. "And when I tell you to ensure Cook uses up the last of that bread pudding, I mean it! I won't have waste, Victoria, you know that, and—"

"Yes, Mother," came the genteel and slightly amused voice of the younger Ainsworth. A footman and the carriage driver were busy carrying a trunk to the carriage, completely ignoring the women and the women completely ignoring the servants.

"Don't you 'Yes, Mother' me! Being away for a night and leaving you on your own. I don't know—"

"You worry too much, Mother." The silhouette of the younger Ainsworth had appeared in the doorway now, and she seemed to be wrapping a scarf around her mother's neck.

"Don't you 'You worry too much, Mother' me! And I forbid you from leaving the house this evening."

"But, Mother—"

"Don't 'But, Mother' me, either!" Mrs. Ainsworth had a set of lungs on her, Thomas would give her that. Her voice echoed so clearly across the street, it were as though he were standing right beside her. "You've been gallivanting after that Chance boy far too much, if you ask me—"

"Mother! I'd hardly call a duke a 'boy.'"

"—and it's time for him to do the chasing. See if he, I don't know, sends you a note. But no leaving the house!"

In the silhouette, Thomas could make out the older Ainsworth woman brandishing a finger at her daughter.

"And have a lovely evening," Mrs. Ainsworth added, pecking her daughter on the cheek before striding down the steps toward her carriage, a servant he guessed to be a lady's maid behind her.

This time, Thomas was much more careful in his retreat around the wide, oak trunk and he did not slip over. He did, however, watch the carriage go off into the increasing gloom of the evening with a thrill.

That solved all his problems. Mrs. Ainsworth was out of the house, as he had hoped—and more than he had ever dreamed, she was staying the night somewhere else. True, Victoria Ainsworth was not permitted to leave the house...but that did not preclude him from visiting, did it?

It did, if he were a gentleman in the truest sense.

But a gentleman in the truest sense wouldn't have done half the things he'd found himself doing with Miss Victoria Ainsworth.

It was with a spring in his step and a thumping pulse that Thomas crept out from behind the oak tree, stepped across the road—narrowly avoiding a yob in a barouche who clearly had no idea how to steer the blasted thing—and almost danced up the steps to the front door.

The bell jangled. Thomas waited.

His excitement made him tap his toes against the step. He would finally have the opportunity to talk to Victoria in the privacy of her own home, without any concern that they were about to be interrupted, assuming her servants kept to themselves. This was his chance to...

Thomas hadn't planned this far. But there were quite a few things left unsaid between himself and Victoria, and though he would never have believed it, his conscience did not permit the situation to go on much longer.

He had to say something. He had to say—

"Victoria," he blurted out as the door opened.

Mrs. Stenton's face grew stern. "My lord."

"'Your Grace,' actually," Thomas said awkwardly. "Though now I say that out loud, I have no idea why I keep correcting people. Is… Is Miss Ainsworth at home?"

"No," the housekeeper said, her wrinkled face impassive.

Thomas's jaw tightened, though he allowed his mirth at the whole ridiculous situation to seep into what he hoped was a charming smile. "Oh?"

He knew damned well she was. Hadn't he just seen her close the door behind her mother? That had only been—what, five minutes ago?

"Miss Ainsworth is not at home," reiterated Mrs. Stenton, adding with a sniff, "and even if she were, which she isn't, she wouldn't be at home for you an' all."

Thomas's eyes widened at this. Well, he knew one of his brothers was no longer welcome in some of the best dining rooms in London because of his nefarious behavior—but he hadn't expected to be tarred with the same brush.

"Not at home for me?" he said blankly. "But—"

His query was broken off by his surprise at a strange noise to the side of the house. Thomas peered around and grinned.

The Ainsworth house, being an end-of-terrace house, had the benefit of something that no other houses in the row had: a side door. Out of that side door at this very moment was a beautiful woman with golden hair and a bonnet skewed to the right.

"Miss Victoria Ainsworth," Thomas said happily.

Victoria jumped. "Thomas!"

"I've just been telling this here gentleman that you are not at home," said Mrs. Stenton peevishly behind him. "And you're not, are you?"

"No, not really," Victoria said with a laugh, stepping toward them both.

"Because you're sneaking out to see him, aren't you?"

Thomas turned and saw a doting expression on the housekeeper's face as she looked at her young charge.

When he turned back to Victoria, she was flushing furiously. "Maybe."

"Well, I think it would be a great deal easier if you were to both come inside and save all this secrecy for another day," said Mrs. Stenton, returning to the front door and opening it. "I've got to go to my sister's, Miss Victoria, and if you give me permission, I will stay with her to help her look after her six boys."

"Six—"

"What a wonderful idea, Mrs. Stenton," Victoria said smoothly, cutting off Thomas's exclamation. "I know that Danvers left to accompany Mother during her outing, but I'll guarantee that Abigail remains, of course. For propriety."

There was something most unpleasant happening to Thomas's ears as he stepped into the Ainsworth house. They appeared, through no fault of his own, to be on fire.

"Well done, dear," said Mrs. Stenton cheerfully, pulling on a pelisse and jamming the most robust bonnet Thomas had ever seen down over her ears. "I'll see you bright and early in the morning, in time to welcome back your mother. Be good, Your Grace."

And with that, she swept out of the house and shut the door behind her.

Thomas stared, agog.

"You can close your mouth," said Victoria cheerfully, taking off her bonnet and hanging her pelisse up on the coatrack by the door.

"She's always like that."

Hastily closing his mouth and hoping he did not look too much like a complete fool, Thomas took off his top hat, shrugged off his greatcoat, and winced at the mud that dropped on the doormat. "Like... Like what?"

"Oh, making sure that I technically keep to my mother's rules, but also making sure that I can enjoy myself at the same time," said Victoria with a grin. "She was my nurse before she was our housekeeper. We've had Stentons in the family for generations. Her son is one of our footmen. He'll go with her, look after her. Tea?"

Thomas smiled weakly as Victoria swept, all calm and confident, into the drawing room.

Right. Good.

The trouble was, the plan was to see whether he could have a private audience with Victoria. His planning had never actually extended to what he would say when he got there.

"Thomas?"

Almost tripping over his own feet in his haste to enter the room, he was just in time to see Victoria ring the bell by the fireplace.

Some of the excitement leached out of him. Of course there were still servants about. It would be far too much to hope that they could be completely—

"Ah, there you are, Abigail," said Victoria cheerfully as she sat elegantly on the edge of the sofa. "I wanted to let you know that I am happy to grant your request."

The young, wiry girl who had just arrived in the door beamed, drawing even more attention to the swath of freckles across her face. "You're sure, miss?"

"Very sure," Victoria said.

Thomas's head jerked from side to side between the two of them as he attempted to decipher this complicated code. *What on earth is going on?*

"It's just, it's only once a year, and—"

"Yes, yes, I said *yes*. And take Cook with you. And Gower—he deserves a night out. You can all stay with your mother, is that right?"

"Oh, she'll be glad to have the company, Miss Victoria, if I'm honest. It's awful lonely for her there."

"Take this, and take a hackney cab—no, I insist," said Victoria sternly, though with a twinkle in her eye. "It's high time you three had a reward in this long and hard winter."

Thomas swallowed as he watched the woman he cared for more than he thought strictly appropriate hand over a five-pound note to the maid.

A five—a five-pound note?

Abigail gasped as she looked at it and quickly bobbed a curtsey. "Oh, thank you, Miss Victoria! I am so grateful. It's just what I—"

"Better make a start now, I think," said Victoria, gently interrupting as she leaned back in the sofa and beamed. "Go on. Have a wonderful time."

Amid a plethora of thanks, which were just as swiftly returned as unnecessary, Abigail closed the door and left them in silence.

Thomas found to his astonishment that he was still standing. *"Have a wonderful time"? A five-pound note? Take Gower? Who's Gower?*

"You look puzzled."

Blinking in an attempt to force his brain in gear, Thomas saw Victoria was smiling. And that was what forced his mind, finally, to act.

Moving across the room without a second thought, he sat—beside Victoria on the sofa. Her smile broadened, just for a moment. Unless he had been looking for it, he would not have noticed.

His own smile returned. She wanted this—wanted him, the two of them, alone. Was that what all that was about? Had she been—surely not. Surely, a young lady with such impeccable breeding as Miss Ainsworth had not sent away all the servants of the house?

As though she could read his mind, Victoria took a deep breath. "Well, we're alone. At least, we will be within ten minutes."

"You sent them away?"

"Abigail has been desperate to go to the circus ever since the posters appeared outside the Pump Room last week," Victoria said. "You must have seen them. And Cook and Gower—he's our other footman—well, they work so hard. They didn't get much of a rest over Christmas, as they went so overboard with the decorations and the food and so... Well. I thought, what a nice opportunity to give them a treat."

Her eyes had been downcast to her lap, but they lifted to meet his with her last words.

Yes, and a nice opportunity for the two of them to be alone. *Completely alone*, thought Thomas with a rush of need. Dear God, this woman was more than he had ever bargained for.

"I am glad you're here," Victoria said softly. "I...I have missed you."

Thomas swallowed. This was the moment, the perfect moment. The introduction could not have been more perfect. Now all he had to do was say that he had missed her.

It was true, wasn't it? So why did the words stick so painfully in his throat?

Just say it. Say it—it's not hard. Say that you missed her. You missed. Just say that—

"What an exquisite doily," Thomas heard himself say, to his own horror. "Did...uh... Did you make it yourself?"

He pointed at the doily on a console table on the other side of the room.

He wasn't surprised that Victoria halted, evidently unsure of what to say next. What did one say to such an inane comment?

"I... No, I did not," she said quietly. "What are you doing here, Thomas?"

Excellent question. "I...am... Well, the thing that I am here for... I am here for the—the thing. You know."

Oh, dear God, my brain must be melting out of my own ears.

Victoria did not look away and Thomas's pulse began to pound painfully as she said softly, "No. No, I don't know."

And he was able to bear it no longer. "I am here for you."

She tilted her head, her lips curling into a delicious pout. "For me?"

"I... Oh, hang it, I was waiting outside your house waiting to see whether your mother would leave and give me the chance to see you," he confessed, hating how swiftly she could wring the truth from him. "Alone, if at all possible."

When he looked up, Victoria's cheeks were pink. "You were?"

Thomas nodded ruefully. "It sounds a bit ridiculous, when I put it like that—"

"We're leaving now then, Miss Victoria," said Abigail, opening the door and letting in the hustle and bustle of people getting ready in the hallway. "You'll have Mrs. Stenton, after all. She'll be able to look after you."

"But..." began Thomas, like the idiot he was.

"Yes, that's right, thank you, Abigail," said Victoria smoothly. "Have a wonderful time at the circus. Real lions, I hear."

Abigail squealed and shut the door. Amidst a great deal of chatter, the front door opened then closed. The chatter disappeared.

"You... They think Mrs. Stenton is here, with you?" Thomas asked quietly.

Victoria did not look up at him but appeared to be inspecting the edge of one of her nails. "It certainly seems that way."

"And Mrs. Stenton left," he continued slowly, "on the understanding that you would spend the evening with Abigail."

She still did not look up, but color was swiftly moving to her cheeks. "So it appears."

Thomas stared for a moment. Then he grinned. "I knew I liked you for a reason."

"You like me?" Victoria looked up swiftly, fixing him with her gaze.

He swallowed.

Far too much. Too much to marry you, worse luck. Perhaps if he had gone about this honestly, had been open with her from the start. Perhaps if he had just told her, revealed to her just how bad things had become, how poorly he had managed everything, she would have…

But no. No woman like Victoria would willingly take on a husband who was such a disaster. Even without her knowing the truth, she surely realized that he was not the sort of gentleman whom a young lady like her sought for matrimony, his title notwithstanding.

Was he about to do the second-best thing in his life, and walk away from a woman he truly cared about…for her sake?

"I like you," Thomas said hoarsely.

They sat for a moment in silence. The inches between them could be easily surmounted, yet Thomas could not bring himself to do it. Once he touched her, which he very much wanted to do, he knew all resolve to be the better man he wished to become would disappear. He would kiss her, and kiss her soundly, and now he knew they were the only two in the house and would be all night…

No, he was not going to be that sort of man.

Even if he wanted to be.

"You see through me, you know," Thomas said softly. "I think… I think sometimes you see right through me. Into who I am. The core of me."

Where the words were coming from, he could not tell, and worst of all, he could not stop them.

"There's so much about me I don't like, and even when I try to be good, I end up getting it wrong," he confessed, longing to reach out and touch her, ground himself with her presence. "And I could offer to stay here and protect you—"

"'Protect' me?" Victoria said, tilting her head on one side again. "Protect me from what?"

Me, Thomas wanted to say. *Me, and all the delicious things I want to do to you.* "Robbers. Bandits, that sort of thing. You're all alone in this house—"

"I'm with you," she pointed out with a mischievous giggle. "Are you saying I need protecting from you?"

Thomas swallowed. *Yes.*

Touching her would be a betrayal of the commitment he'd made when coming here. He had intended at first to spill all—to tell her the truth, about the money, where it had gone, why he had spent it, everything. Perhaps to even tell her that he had first sought her company merely because he needed a dowry. That time was long past, at least. He hadn't even noticed when it had ceased to be true.

Then watching her send all the servants away—Thomas knew he was not good enough for her. That marriage to her now would be a sham, a lie, a trick, a deception he should never have attempted and could not go through with now.

And still, his whole body hummed for her touch, for the slightest hint that she wanted him to take her in his arms and—

"I said," Victoria murmured in a low voice, shifting so she was mere inches from him on the sofa, "are you saying I need protecting from you?"

"Yes," said Thomas hoarsely, fingers inching toward her then balling into fists in his lap. "God damn it, woman, you know how I feel about you."

"I know what you want to *do* to me, to be sure," said the woman he cared about more than anyone, her cheeks flushing and her gaze unwavering. "I know how much you enjoy the kisses we've shared. The first time was on this very sofa."

I am not going to lose control, Thomas told himself firmly. Even if the reminder was like a shot of rum through his bloodstream, slowly tearing down the barriers of control around his will—

"Every time I get close to you, I think… I think we are going to get even closer," said Victoria softly, her voice quavering. "And I want it, and I'm afraid of it, and—"

"You should be." Thomas had not intended to interrupt her, but he could not help it. "Damn it, woman, you're an innocent!"

"And you are not."

Christ, why had he not waited for this marvelous, heady woman? "No," he admitted, hating that he had ever touched another. "You don't know what you're—"

"Why do you find it so hard to admit that you are attracted to me?"

"Because I'm so damn attracted to you, I worry that that's all you'll see." Thomas exploded, standing up. "My need! My arrogant, selfish need for you, and it's so much—there's so much more than…"

His voice trailed away as he stared at the wall before him, not willing to turn to see her expression.

Where on God's green earth did that all come from?

It had been there, deep inside him, for almost so long now, he had barely noticed it. The words he had fought for so long rose, unable to be contained any longer.

"I want you, yes," Thomas said, whirling around. Victoria was standing now by the sofa, her eyes wide. "Christ, I want to plunge myself into you and show you, not just try to tell you, how badly I want you. I want to give you such pleasure that you're not able to walk the next day."

She swallowed. "Thomas—"

"But that would reduce what I feel—what I think I feel—to something, something animalistic, something thoughtless," Thomas said, barreling on. There was no turning back now. "And it's not that—I mean, it is, but what I feel, how I think of you, it's so much more than—more than anything I could… I mean, it doesn't even make sense!"

There was a desperation in his voice that Thomas hated. He hated this vulnerability, hated how she looked without judgment, with pure interest.

How could she do it? Stand there and listen to his nonsense?

"God's teeth—I can't explain it!" he said, throwing his hands up in the air. "If I could, I would have told you already!"

"But you have. You are." Victoria stepped forward as she spoke, hesitantly, like one would approach a frightened dog. "Thomas, you—"

"Don't you go telling me what I'm thinking because I don't know half the time," Thomas said bitterly, pulling his hand through his hair distractedly, light glinting on his signet ring. "If I could explain it to myself, if I had any idea—"

The way she twisted him up on the inside and made it impossible to steady himself—dear God, how did she do it? How had he allowed her to do it to him?

"You've shown me, and told me, countess times." She was standing right before him now, and before Thomas could stop her, she had captured both of his hands in hers. "Every time you've wanted to take from me and stopped yourself, you've told me. When you kissed me, when you—"

"It's not enough," Thomas said in a voice cracked with emotion he could no longer control. "It's not enough. You deserve—"

"I want you," said Victoria fiercely. "Thomas, look at me—*look at me!*"

It felt good, so good, to be told what to do, to be ordered about by this woman whom he craved so desperately. Thomas lifted his eyes and met hers. Within her pupils blazed a fire that she had sparked, and would now never go out.

"I think it's about time you ravished me," Victoria said simply. "And—what did you say? *Pleasure me until I couldn't walk?*"

Thomas groaned. "I could never do that to—"

"I insist," said the woman whom he had only started to court for her money, and who now owned him in a way he had never been possessed before. "I order you to lie with me, Thomas Chance. As man and woman. Right now."

Chapter Thirteen

HER WORDS RANG out in the drawing room and Victoria almost took a step back from Thomas, releasing his hands, at the way he froze stiff, a sudden look of shock on his face.

Ah. Well, she could hardly be blamed for going too far. She was… What was it she had once overheard? Yes—all riled up.

She was all riled up, and it was his fault, Thomas's fault—and she had managed to orchestrate a completely empty house for them. Surely, he would not walk away from—

Thomas released her hands and walked away. He had gotten as far as the door, his hand on the handle, before he spoke. "You don't know what you're asking of me."

And anger flared, roaring through her stomach and settling between her thighs. *What I'm asking of him?*

"I don't think you know what you're asking of *me!*" Victoria said sharply, jutting out her chin defiantly as his eyes fluttered rapidly. "You can't just go around enticing ladies to pleasure and then abandon them before—before you've shown them what it is to be loved!"

Thomas's jaw dropped. "That isn't what—"

"You had your fingers on my—and my breast in your hand, and you were kissing me with—with everything you had," Victoria said, heat scalding her cheeks but determinedly pressing on. "You owe me, Thomas!"

"This is ridiculous. You can't force me to ravish you," he pointed out.

"I...I suppose I can't," said Victoria, her voice lowering along with her shoulders.

And she had never thought she would have to. *Oh, this is so humiliating.* The man had undoubtedly bedded countless ladies and none of them had been forced to beg for it. Yes, she was a debutante, someone no gentleman would ravish lightly, but she was more than willing to marry him after. Clearly, Thomas Chance, Duke of Cothrom, had no real interest in her. If he did, surely, he would...

Something caught Victoria's attention. *It couldn't be... Could it?*

It was. Thomas was eyeing her up, even in the midst of this wild conversation. He wanted her. So what did he need to push him over the edge?

"So... So you don't want me, then."

The words had slipped out of her mouth before she could stop them.

Thomas's eyes widened. "You think that?"

"I don't think I could offer myself more plainly, yet you are rejecting me," Victoria pointed out, doing her best to keep anger from her voice. "I am no fool, Thomas. How much more blatant do you wish me to be? I have rid my entire house of company for you, offered you myself on more than one occasion—"

He took a shattered breath. "But I thought... I mean... Why?"

She swallowed hard. *Ah.* Well, this wasn't precisely the direction of conversation she had expected, and therefore, she had no clever quips or meaningful looks prepared.

"You are so...so beautiful." Thomas's voice was low and he released the door handle, though he did not move away from it. "So beautiful, and young, and innocent—"

Not innocent for much longer, if she could help it. "You think a lady cannot be attracted to a gentleman?"

"Not to me—I mean," he corrected hastily, as though she would not have paid attention to his words. "It's just... Ladies of the *ton* don't—"

"And why not? Because they are afraid of this, of revealing their desires and then being rejected," Victoria said quietly.

The pain in her voice felt evident, and perhaps Thomas heard it. A shadow certainly flickered over his face. "'Rejected'?"

"What else do you call it?" asked Victoria with a shrug. "Thomas, other than stripping off all my clothes and lying here on the floor"—his eyes widened—"I don't think I could make myself more available to you. The actions I've taken, I'd be called a hussy, a—"

"So why?" he whispered.

Did he truly believe himself to be that unlovable?

"Because I want you," she said simply.

"No one has ever wanted me...me, for me, I mean," Thomas said, sweeping a hand through his hair. "You—God, I want you like I have never wanted any other woman, but, Victoria, you can't... I mean, I get things wrong. I'm wrong, I make mistakes. I'm not perfect. I'm not the son or brother my family want... What if I make a mistake with you? What if I'm not the duke you need? What if... What if after tonight, *you* don't want *me*?"

Victoria's mind whirled, countless thoughts streaming through it, until one rose to the surface and threatened to overwhelm them all.

If Thomas was not in love with her already...then he would be, surely, after they had lain together as man and woman.

It was not the certainty she wanted, but it was close.

"Love me," she whispered. "Love me like...like you said I deserved. Do you remember, Thomas?"

Perhaps it was the way she whispered his name, or the fact that she had reminded him of his own words.

"Your first time, your first pleasure... Damn it, Victoria, that deserves to be in a bed surrounded by candles, with rose petals strewn about the place..."

Whatever it was, the fight disappeared from Thomas's eyes, replaced by a heady need she had seen before. Optimism flared in Victoria, a need building she could only hope he would satisfy.

"You really mean it, don't you." His voice was low, factual. He was not asking her—he was stating the truth in wonder.

Victoria stepped toward him and did something she had dreamed of but never permitted herself to do. As a yelp gutted in his throat, Victoria grabbed Thomas's wrists and pushed him against the drawing room door.

"I really mean it," she whispered, leaning forward and permitting her not insubstantial chest to press against Thomas's own. "Take me, Thomas. Wholly and completely."

He captured her lips in a frenzy of need, his tongue worshiping her own before Victoria could catch her breath. Not that she needed it. His touch gave her life in a way nothing else had and she leaned into him, whimpering at the intensity of his ardor.

There was something deeply erotic about the way she was forcing him against the door, and those feelings only heightened as Thomas struggled against her and she kept him pinned.

Well. Victoria was almost certain that if he had truly wanted to get away, he most definitely could. He was a man after all, tall and broad, with all the strength youth and vigor could give.

Which meant he wanted this. *He wanted her.* He truly cared about her.

As sparks of heat roared through Victoria's body, Thomas nibbling expertly on her lower lip to heat the furnace within her, Victoria gloried in the knowledge that he cared for her, perhaps as strongly as she cared for him.

The sham was over. The trick was no longer necessary.

Thomas Chance was in love with her.

How long they stood there, kissing passionately, Victoria was not sure. All she knew was that in a sudden movement she could not have predicted, Thomas somehow had wrenched his arms free of her, captured her wrists with his strong fingers, and twisted her hastily.

Victoria blinked. Now her back was the one against the wall, and her wrists—dear God, her wrists were now clasped together by one of Thomas's hands, held up above her head, and that left her—

Vulnerable.

She swallowed. "T-Thomas—"

"I think you're going to like this," he said softly, lowering his head to nuzzle her neck. "It's something I've wanted to share for a long time. A long, long time..."

Victoria's eyes closed, unbidden, as the sensual thrum of Thomas's voice vibrated down her throat and into her breasts. How did he do that? Find a frequency that made her body respond in such a way? It was surely—what, a million-to-one chance?

"I trust you," she gasped.

Thomas lifted his head and stared into her eyes, his expression hungry yet curious. "You do?"

Victoria was not sure she was up for a philosophical debate at this point. Not based on the way her knees were quivering with longing. "Touch me, Thomas."

The quiet curse only heightened her anticipation, and Victoria was well-rewarded when his free right hand moved to scrape a thumb over her breast—a breast that was swiftly released.

Victoria moaned, leaning against the wall for dear life. Straining against the hold he had of her, there was something charged about the surrender she had to give him.

But then, as she saw the devotion in Thomas's expression, the reverence with which he lowered his head and began to suckle at her nipple, she thought perhaps she was not the only one surrendering.

That was the last coherent thought she had for a while. The absolute devastation of Thomas's tongue laving her nipple, the teasing tugs his teeth wrought around the sensitive skin, was almost too much to bear. Victoria was aware she was moaning, that her gasps were coming fast and few, but there was no way to control herself.

No need to.

And no chance of it. Somehow, Thomas's attention was split, his mouth worshipping her breast while his right hand—

"Oh, Thomas," Victoria whimpered, shifting her feet to widen the gap between her legs.

His hand knew what it wanted and she wished to give it to him. Shivers of anticipation pouring through her, Victoria moaned in sweet ecstasy as Thomas's fingers at first brushed along the secret place between her legs, then more confidently—

Victoria's eyes widened. "Thomas!"

It was unlike anything she had ever felt before. Her whole center was melting, her core molten as Thomas slipped a questing finger into her warm wetness.

Try as she might, Victoria could not arch her back nor push her hips forward sufficiently to take him deeper—Thomas was controlled, controlling her, controlling the pace, controlling himself.

It was so wildly attractive to see him resist the urge to just take her then and there that a jolt of sensual delight roared from her breast to her loins.

"Yes, more, please—"

And he obeyed. Victoria's head fell back as Thomas's thumb slipped inside her, brushing against a sensitive nub within that made her cry out his name even as his finger started to stroke a rhythm—a rhythm that was swiftly echoed by her heartbeat and the way Thomas's tongue twisted around her nipple.

Her hands strained against his hold, but only because she wanted to touch him, feel him, reward him somehow for the intense pleasure that she was receiving. The strength in his hands and his utter dominance of her inexplicably heightened Victoria's gratification of the whole thing.

"Oh, God, I'm… I'm…"

Precisely what she was going to do, Victoria could not tell. There was a pressure building in her, building between her thighs, and if she didn't feel its completion soon, she was going to—

Thomas's fingers stilled as he lifted his head. "I shouldn't do this—not here, not like this. I promised you—"

She snapped her eyes back to him. "Thomas Chance, give me what I need or I swear—"

He groaned, leaning his head against her shoulder as his fingers inside her started up their hypnotizing rhythm again. "God, I love it when you command me."

"Then I'm—I'm ordering you to…to…" Victoria blinked, trying to keep a hold of her words, but it was impossible. Who could possibly be expected to speak when their body was arching, arching upward, up toward the sky, the sensual connection between them building so much, it was going to—

Thomas crushed his lips against hers as his thumb pressed, hard, on that sensitive nub and Victoria came undone.

Every part of her was on fire and the flames did not burn, but satisfy. Her body was exploding, but every part of it was being loved by Thomas, and she would sacrifice herself, again and again, to feel this way, to feel this ecstasy, to know herself well and truly loved by this man. *Oh, this man.*

When Victoria was finally able to open her eyes, the room had grown shadowy and Thomas was breathing deeply.

"I… I did not hurt you, did I?"

Victoria's eyes widened as she looked into the handsome and exceedingly concerned face of a man she could never give up. "Hurt me?"

"I know that sometimes, when a woman—I mean, when it's the first time—"

"You c-could do that to me day in, d-day out, and I would have no complaints," Victoria said in a shaky voice.

Only when Thomas gave her a lopsided grin then released his grip did she realize that he'd still had her pinned to the wall.

Her wrists fell to her side. They felt empty, somehow, without him. Lonely.

But not for long. He'd grasped one of her hands, his fingers interlocking with hers. "Are you ready for more?"

Victoria swallowed, her throat dry. "'More'?"

Thomas's expression was wicked, but there was still an understanding there, something deep, a connection they shared.

To think what she had shared with him—what she had allowed him to do. How could she ever look at another gentleman again? How would she ever look at the world in the same way, now it was changed forever?

"Where's your bedchamber?"

"'Bedchamber'?" Victoria's mind was whirling. She could barely take in what he was saying.

Hot lips crushed against hers, just for a moment. Then—"Lead me."

It was quite a new experience, to be taken by the hand by a handsome gentleman before leading him through her own home, up her own stairs, and toward her own bedchamber. But then, the evening had already given her a few new experiences Victoria had never expected.

Not in the drawing room, anyway.

Her confidence failed her, however, when they reached her bedchamber door. Her feet locked together, halting on the carpet.

Thomas looked around, his brow furrowed.

"This..." She cleared her throat. "This is my bedchamber."

"Yes, I rather gathered that."

This was it. There was no going back. Once a gentleman had been in her bedchamber—this gentleman in particular—she would never be able to go back to being Miss Victoria Ainsworth, an innocent young woman.

She would be... Well, not a ruined woman, whatever Society

might say if it knew. She didn't consider this being "ruined." Not when she was about to experience the heights of pleasure, again, with the man she loved.

But she certainly could not return to being the person she was.

A hand cupped her face. Victoria blinked and looked up into Thomas's understanding eyes.

"This is why I was hesitant," he whispered. "Because you have so much more to lose than I."

How, precisely, he understood her concerns, she did not know—but his disquiet somehow revived her.

Victoria reached out and opened the door. "I have nothing to lose, and everything to gain."

She laughed, her merriment echoing around her bedchamber, as Thomas pulled her inside. A few candles had already been lit, probably by Abigail before she'd departed, and as the door closed, they flickered, casting golden shadows over Thomas's face.

Over Thomas's chest. What the—

"You don't mind?" he asked, halting as he was about to drop his shirt on the floor.

Dear God, how did he manage to do that so quickly? And how had he kept all that muscle, that skin scattered with blond hair, hidden?

Victoria reached forward and placed her palms on his chest, reveling in the softness of his skin and the scratch of his wiry hair. This was, in a way, more intimate than what they had already shared. A piece of him she had never seen before.

"Victoria?"

She lifted her chin to look up at the soft brows, the trembling lips of the man she loved. "Thomas."

When he kissed her this time, it was reverential. The heat was still there, yes, but it had become a white, burning-hot, steady flame, a flame that built between them as Victoria twisted her hands up Thomas's neck and clutched at his hair, pulling him tighter.

"You're so beautiful," she whispered, hardly knowing how a gentleman should be described but knowing she was completely right.

Thomas's chuckle against her neck was accompanied by his questing fingers finding her gown's ties at the back of her bodice. "'Beautiful'?"

"You know what I mean." Victoria gasped as he nuzzled her neck, kissing that delicate part of her just behind her ear that made her knees quiver. "You are. You must know—"

"Not as beautiful as you." Thomas sighed, the tie of her gown falling to the floor as the garment slipped past her shoulders. "Victoria, you—you are everything I could have dreamed of. Everything I hoped for and knew I would never deserve."

The words washed over her like water, like a hot stream, but Victoria could not pay attention to them. Not with her gown now cascading to the carpet, pooling around her feet as she stood here—

Well. Practically naked.

She saw the gleam of desire in Thomas's eyes and stood up a little straighter. It just so happened that this brought the top of her breasts and décolletage right into his eyeline.

Thomas groaned. "I've got to get this corset off you."

"But—"

"I want to see you, all of you," he said, his voice ragged now, his fingers working faster than she could have believed possible. "There we are—and another catch—there."

Victoria gasped as the corset was released in an explosion of boning. The support it gave, the comfort it offered, was gone. Gravity greedily took hold of her breasts, which sagged. The petticoats and undergarments were wrenched from her body, Thomas pulling them over her head in a swift movement that made her breathless.

And there she was. Standing, utterly naked, before a half-dressed duke. *Her* half-dressed duke.

Thomas stared.

And said nothing. For a few heartbeats, Victoria wondered what he had found fault with. She glanced down. It was her body, and she loved it because it was her own. But no gentleman, no person had ever looked at it like this. What flaw had he discovered?

"You... You're exquisite."

Victoria tilted her head as she looked at Thomas, heat searing her cheeks. "You don't have to say—"

"I don't think I have any choice," he said quietly, reaching out to cup her face in his two large hands. "You are one in a million, Victoria, and I'm not going to let you go. As long as you want me to, I won't ever let you go."

She whimpered in delight as he pulled her flush against him, her nipples grazing his chest, the warmth pooling between her legs, desperate now that she knew what she was missing, feeling his—

Oh, that was definitely...definitely *him* pressing up against her hip, wasn't it?

"Victoria!"

"What?" she said defensively, looking up into Thomas's astonished face as her fingers continued to attempt to undo the buttons of his trousers. "Well, I'm naked, aren't I?"

"You are incorrigible." He growled, pushing her toward the bed so rapidly, she fell onto it.

Victoria tried to catch her breath, but it was difficult while watching Thomas slowly undo his trousers, all the while never taking his eyes from hers. "Does... Does that mean I don't need encouragement, or that you won't encourage me any further?"

The growl in Thomas's throat did not really answer the question, but it did not need to. Not when he had practically ripped his trousers and boots from his body, throwing socks to the floor and swiftly covering her body with his as he struggled to put something long he'd pulled from one pocket upon his manhood.

Oh, this was... *That* was...

Nothing could have prepared her for it. Victoria had thought what they'd shared before had been intimate, but having his skin touching hers, touching hers all over, the weighty press of his manhood against her thigh, the way his hands moved, first at her hips then tracing her waist then touching her—

"Oh, you're ready for me." Thomas stroked a finger through her slickness. "Stop me if it hurts."

"If it...?"

The cry Victoria gave out was accompanied by her back arching and Thomas froze immediately, partly inside her as he hovered over her.

"Victoria? Victoria, talk to me. Are you—"

"More," she gasped, looking up through fluttering lashes.

He blinked. He looked stricken, confused, utterly lost.

"I said *more*," Victoria said in a stronger voice this time, shifting her hips so she could take more of him in. "Oh, Thomas, I want, I need—"

He understood. Kissing her deeply, his tongue questing inside her mouth searching for more ways to gratify her, Thomas plunged himself into her, sheathing himself to the hilt.

Victoria hissed through her teeth, but it was not pain she felt, but a mingle of intrusion and intimacy. Having him inside her, literally deep within her—it was a depth of connection she had never expected, never believed possible.

"Ready?"

She stared, hands clutching his shoulders, as though only that would keep her pinned to the earth. "Ready? For what?"

Thomas grinned and her hopes broke into a thousand pieces. *Oh, this man.* He could do anything to her, anything at all, and she would thank him on bended knee.

"This," said Thomas quietly as he slowly pulled himself away, almost until he was no longer inside her, then thrust into her with a precision and depth that quite literally took her breath away.

"Oh, God, that's—"

"I wanted to have you that first time we kissed," Thomas murmured, his voice rough and desperate against her throat as Victoria tried to accept the sensual decadence he was sparking through her body. "Not just because you're beautiful, Victoria, but because I can't... God, I can't stay away from you—"

"Don't." Victoria gasped, her hands leaving Thomas's shoulders, but only so she could cling on to the bedsheets. *Oh, this is heaven, this is—*

"You're everything—everything I want, everything I never thought I deserved." Thomas's lips pressed a kiss onto her neck, then his tongue was flicking around her nipple, then he was back to her neck. "I could spend the rest of my life searching the world, but I would never—Christ, you feel good—never find someone like you. You're... You're..."

Victoria moaned, unable to help the interruption as Thomas quickened his pace. His thrusting was harsh now, deep inside her, yet each movement gave her not pain but an exquisite heat building in her core.

And she knew where that led.

"One in a million you said." She panted, arching her back and tilting her hips to welcome him in deeper. "Oh, Thomas!"

Perhaps it was crying out his name that did it. Thomas fisted the blanket beside her, throwing back his head as his whole body shuddered, his wild thrusting now rapid and purposeful and—

"Yes, yes, yes!"

Victoria knew it was coming this time, but that did not detract from the ecstasy that poured through her body. Again she was falling apart, again her body was exploding, but this time, she was with Thomas and he was exploding inside her.

Together, together, they rode the wave of pleasure. And when it came crashing down and Thomas collapsed into Victoria's arms, she knew she'd done it.

She'd made him ravish her. She'd made him fall in love with her.

Chapter Fourteen

January 27, 1840

I T WAS A rather disorienting experience, waking up in an unfamiliar bed. The last time it had happened, over a year ago, Thomas had vowed he would not do it again.

Somehow, along the way, he had obviously forgotten.

Thomas groaned, half his face pressed into the pillow. Not his pillow. This was covered in a pillowcase edged with lace, something even his butler would have noticed. Fine, so this was someone else's pillow. That had to mean...someone else's bed.

His memories were murky, his mind only just starting to surface from sleep. Thomas was at least aware, however, of three things.

Firstly, he was completely naked. This was not a total surprise, given that he was clearly in someone else's bed, but it was awkward. That meant his clothes were somewhere else. He'd just have to hope they were still there.

Secondly, he felt such an utter calm and peace, he felt as if he were resting on a cloud, not a bed. There was a tension utterly absent from his body. Thomas could not recall the last time he'd felt this...this satisfied.

And thirdly, there was someone else in the bed with him.

Thomas froze as the person sighed, then unstiffened when his reason caught up with him. It had to be the woman he had bedded last night. There was some sort of sensation of joy, or happiness, or something similar settled within him. Almost as though he had fallen in—

Victoria Ainsworth sighed again and turned onto her front.

Blinking, hardly able to believe it, Thomas waited for the dream to end.

Because this had to be a dream, didn't it? After lusting after the woman for so long, it could only be a dream. Surely, he had not managed to persuade her…

Then all the memories of the evening flooded back in, and a wicked smile crept across his face.

Dear God, he'd done it. Or rather, *she*'d done it. Thomas could not pretend the seduction was all one-sided; he'd never met a woman more eager for his touch.

And what a touch it had been.

Memories cascaded through his mind, each one offering something more delicious than the last. Heavens, but he had been treated. The woman was a goddess—she had to know that—and the feeling of pouring himself into her…

Thomas halted that particular line of thinking. It wasn't as though he could expect her to offer herself again this morning, and if he wasn't careful, he would be walking around with tented trousers for the rest of the day.

He cast an eye over at the woman he…cared for. There didn't appear to be a word for what he felt for Victoria Ainsworth. Warmth, yes, and attraction, but that had always been there. This need, this desire, was deeper than mere attraction.

And he liked her.

"You—You're not going to make the decision about the woman you marry based on a coin toss?"

The smile that had creased his face disappeared. It had all started on the toss of a coin. A mere chance.

Thomas swallowed. Well, what did it matter how it had begun? He could not have predicted the way it would continue, and surely, that was far more important?

Apparently not. The guilt ate away at him, nestled around his heart, threatening to poison everything.

I am happy, Thomas reminded himself sternly as he twisted in bed to look at Victoria again. *Happy*. Did he not deserve to be happy? After all he had done—well, actually, now he came to think about it, perhaps he did *not* deserve to be happy. It was the Chance family fortune that was gone, and now he was seeking out a fortune with little concern for the woman attached to it.

And he was late in visiting St. Thomas's again. He wouldn't hear the end of it when he finally showed his face. He was neglecting them. He was neglecting everything he—

"Good morning," said a sleepy voice.

Thomas's pulse skipped a beat. When he blinked, the woman who came into focus was an absolute vision.

Pink tinged Victoria's cheeks. "I... Well, I didn't think you'd still be here."

And that was when Thomas fell hard in love.

Didn't think I'd still be here—where was he supposed to go? How could he even *consider* leaving her while she slept, not speaking to her, not making sure she knew—

Thomas swallowed the declaration of love. Not now. Not here. She would think it only uttered because they had lain together, and while it had been that vulnerability, that moment of shared intimacy that had helped him understand just what he felt for her, it wasn't the sum total of his regard.

There was so much more.

"Come here," Thomas murmured, turning onto his back and extending an arm.

She did not hesitate, and that was perhaps the most comforting thing. Victoria's scent, her closeness, the feeling of her breath against his collarbone and the movement of her chest against his own...that was all wonderful.

But it was the lack of indecision that meant the most. She came to him when he called.

Thomas tightened his grip around her, blinking away tears that came unbidden and did not make sense.

It was all going to plan. And at the same time, this situation was so completely different from his original plan, it was difficult to understand how he had gotten here.

How had he gotten here?

"Thank you," murmured Victoria against his neck.

Thomas shivered, the intimacy making him want to pull away just enough to kiss her soundly. "Thank you? What for?"

A tap on his shoulder, a sense that everything was right with the world and he never wanted to leave this bed. "You know."

"In that case, I rather think I should thank *you*," Thomas said quietly, reveling in the way their voices thrummed through each other as they spoke. "After all, you're the one who let me—"

"'*Let*' you? I almost had to get on my knees and beg," came the sleepy reply.

Clearing his throat, Thomas shifted his hips and tried not to think about Victoria on her knees before him. That was something for another day. Probably.

"I just hope I was... Well. Good enough," she said softly.

He did push her away that time, staring into her eyes with incredulity. "You aren't seriously saying that."

Victoria looked down, golden hair cascading past her shoulders, a nervous tilt of her head the only response.

"Victoria Ainsworth, you were... You are..." Thomas swallowed. *Hell, why is it so difficult to say this?* "Everything."

"You're everything—*everything* I want, everything I never thought I deserved."

His throat was dry, yet she was still staring as though waiting for something. And he knew what, of course. He was no fool. She had bared herself to him, allowed him to take his fill, and he had still said nothing about marriage.

And he wanted to. For her, for the dowry, for everything.

So why were the words sticking in his throat?

"It's early."

Thomas blinked. "It is?"

Victoria turned her head to the left, her hair pooling onto him. Thomas tried not to think about the softness of her locks, the intimacy of the simplest of connection. "Not quite seven o'clock. The sun won't be up yet. My mother, the servants... They're not back yet."

When she turned back to him, there was a strange look in her eye. A look that said... *No, surely not.*

"You cannot be serious."

"Why not?" Victoria wiggled her hips and Thomas groaned as the realization that she was just as nude as he was seared across his thighs. "There's no one here—"

"If I am going to be able to walk out of here, we mustn't," Thomas said, regret blazing but knowing he was making the right decision.

Difficult as it was, he pushed the woman he loved from him and pulled himself out of the comfort of the bed. *Clothes, clothes, where are my clothes?*

She smirked. "I thought *I* was the one who wasn't supposed to be able to walk this morning?"

Thomas gritted his teeth, relieved he was facing away from Victoria so she couldn't see the agony on his face. Dear God, she was enough to tempt the saints themselves. Did she have any idea how difficult it was to hear her say that and not lower his face to hers and—

There was a heavy sigh behind him and the rustle of blankets moving. "Fine. But you must have breakfast before you go."

"What, to gather my strength?" Thomas quipped as he pulled on his trousers.

When he turned to face her, Victoria was smiling shyly. "Strength for what, may I ask?"

Thomas swallowed. She was sitting on the edge of the bed, ankles crossed, hands leaning on either side of her onto the mattress…and she must have known how delicious she looked, her hair falling down over her breasts, her nipples peaked—

Because of the cold, Thomas tried to remind himself, trying and failing to put his own arm through a sleeve of his shirt. *That's all.*

"Dress, woman," he said hoarsely. "Or I'll not be responsible for my actions."

Victoria tilted her head. "That sounds more like an inducement than a punish—"

"*Victoria!*"

It took several minutes for Victoria to attire herself in a way that she deemed respectable. Thomas's fingers fumbled over the ties of her corset, half-hating that he was putting away this delightful body, half-wondering how he was managing to concentrate with so much of Victoria's soft flesh beneath his fingertips.

When she was finally dressed and had slipped a hand in his without a word, Thomas did not notice it until they were halfway down the stairs.

It felt…natural.

As though this were their lives. Their life. As though this were just another morning in which they could enjoy each other's company after a night of passionate touch. As though this were their home, where they could just—

Thomas managed to stop himself—just—before he started to create a perfect domestic image in his mind. He wasn't there yet. He had to propose, and finding the right moment to do that would be tricky.

After all, he had turned up here last night ready to confess to something completely different…

"Now, I'm sure there is some food somewhere," said Victoria vaguely, slipping her hand from his as she opened the door. "It is a kitchen, after all."

It was, but as Thomas had so little experience navigating a kitchen, he wasn't sure where the best place to look was. There were herbs hanging from the ceiling and a trio of small bowls that appeared to contain spices near a large fireplace that was currently cold. There were cupboards and drawers galore, but none of them appeared to be labeled. How on earth the servants knew where anything was, he had no idea.

Victoria appeared to be equally at sea. "I suppose we just keep searching until we find some," she said, opening a drawer and inspecting it closely. "Goodness, who knew there were so many different types of wooden spoons."

Thomas grinned as he sat at the large kitchen table covered in scratches and burn marks. It was the sort of table that graced a kitchen for a hundred years before someone thought to replace it, and even then there was little point. Fine oak was fine oak.

"You won't make a good housewife, you know," he teased, watching Victoria bend over to peer into a deep cupboard with an appreciation of her behind. "Not knowing your way around a kitchen.

It was intended as a jest, that was all.

When Victoria straightened up, however, there was more red in her cheeks than he would have expected. "What would you know about housewives?"

A pulse throbbed in Thomas's jaw as a vision rushed through his mind.

Victoria. Standing by a large bay window, wintery sunlight streaming past her. As she turned, she revealed a child in her arms. A child with her laugh, her eyes, but his sandy hair. They look at him, smiling, the child calling his name. But it's not his name. It's *Papa*—

Thomas blinked. "N-Nothing."

His momentary lapse of concentration, sanity, whatever one wanted to call it, had not gone unnoticed. Victoria stepped to another cupboard, crowing with delight as she brought out a loaf of bread.

"Now all I have to do is find something to go with it," she said, humming.

Eventually, the feast was spread out on the table. If you could call it a feast.

"It's certainly a different breakfast than the type to which I'm accustomed," he said wryly, glancing at Victoria, who was seated to his right.

"You'll never be able to look a normal breakfast in the face," she teased. "Now pass the cake."

It was a motley offering. Some leftover sponge cake, a jar of marmalade, a loaf of bread cut into uneven slices, two jars of pickled herring, and a hunk of cheese that appeared to have seen better days.

"I suppose having servants around the place is more useful than I thought," Victoria quipped as she spread a thick dollop of marmalade on her slice of cake. "Herring?"

"I suppose," Thomas said with a laugh, shaking his head. "A little too early for herring, even for me."

"It's a sad statement of our luxurious lives, I suppose."

He took a bite of the cake and wondered why people didn't have cake for breakfast every morning. "What is?"

Victoria gestured at the nonsensical spread before them. "This. Perhaps if we had lived without servants at any point in our lives, we would have the faintest idea how to navigate a kitchen."

"Or a kettle. I'd kill for a cup of tea," Thomas said jovially, though his levity sank as he spoke.

The servants. Dear God, he hadn't thought about it.

Not that he had servants himself, not really, outside of his valet. They were more family servants, people who kept the Chance family and houses going like clockwork. Sometimes you could forget they were there, which, according to his father, was a sign of efficient servants. According to his mother, it was a sign that one needed to pay more attention.

But they didn't have any money for their wages.

Thomas couldn't understand how this could have passed him so completely by. But with no money in the Chance coffers for weeks now, the day would soon come when the Chance servants would expect to be paid.

What on earth would happen when his father had to tell them, if they did not know already, that the family was quite ruined?

The cake was dry in his mouth. Thomas swallowed painfully, the crumbs scratching his throat as he stared sightlessly at the loaf of bread before him.

He had to marry her—had to get her dowry. What else was he supposed to do, let the servants go hungry? Let them go completely? Reduce the household staff of the Cothrom branch of the Chance family? Here, in Bath?

Perish the thought.

And they were like family. Why, Bradbury had been butlering for as long as Thomas could remember. For as long as, as far as he was concerned, butlering had ever existed.

Bradbury, leave Stanphrey Lacey? Leave the Chance family?

"Thomas."

A touch on his arm. A hand.

Thomas saw the comforting presence of Victoria's hand on his wrist. When he looked up at her face, there was concern there. Concern, for him.

"You look as though all the problems of the world have fallen upon your shoulders," she said quietly.

He couldn't tell her. Not now. This was a perfect morning after a perfect evening, and if Thomas tried to explain…

There were no words for it. *Sorry, Victoria. I only chose to pursue you because I'd quite like to get my hands on your gold? Sorry, it was all a bit of a laugh and a joke, and after a one-in-a-million chance with a coin toss, I threw it again and it decided on you?*

Not the most romantic thing to say to someone after you'd just taken their innocence.

"You mustn't worry," said Victoria softly, squeezing his arm. "Everything will be fine."

"You don't know that," said Thomas as lightly as he could manage, as though they were only jesting. "You can't possibly. I mean, anything can happen. The world is unpredictable."

"But you have everything that you need right here, within arm's reach," came her gentle reply.

Thomas hesitated.

She wasn't wrong. She was right there, her money ready for the taking, her affections there for the plucking. He could make her love him—probably had. Otherwise, what had all that begging him been for?

The need in him as he looked at her, her hand still on his arm, was so sharp, it was almost painful. It was an unknown feeling, an unfamiliar one that settled comfortably within him as though he had been waiting for it his whole life.

And that was when Thomas realized that he wanted this. This, these sorts of moments. Moments between him and Victoria, nothing special, nothing complicated, just a ragtag breakfast of nonsensical items. It was she who made it special, she who made him beam, made this warmth swell in his stomach.

Thomas swallowed.

A proposal. That was what he needed. Right. Well, he couldn't do it now, obviously. Mrs. Ainsworth and the servants would be returning soon and the last place he needed to be found was here, in their kitchen, kissing Victoria Ainsworth silly.

Much as he would like to.

No, he would have to think about this. Plan something, something worthy of her. Worthy of the way he felt, worthy of what he wanted to offer her. What she deserved.

Thomas placed his hand on hers and squeezed it before removing it from his arm. "Come on, eat up. I'll have to be going soon, and we can't have any scandal, can we?"

There was a flicker of something unknowable in Victoria's eyes. Then she nodded and took a bite of her cake and marmalade.

So, a proposal in a few days when he had the opportunity to think of precisely how to do it. He'd propose to Victoria, Victoria would say *yes*, obviously, and within a few weeks, they could be married and he would have access—finally—to the money that would save his family and the orphans at St. Thomas's.

That had been the plan all along, hadn't it?

Chapter Fifteen

January 30, 1840

VICTORIA LOWERED HERSELF slowly onto the chair and made sure not to wince.

She could never have guessed just what an impact such intimacy would have on her body. The mind didn't expect such…such delight. Such stiffness afterward. Such a strange medley of sensations in her body, making it feel as though it were not hers. That it was his.

"You look tired."

Victoria managed a wan smile. "I suppose I do."

It had been difficult, after all, to sleep in her bed after…after he had. It was the most unaccountable thing; Thomas had spent but one night lying beside her, his gentle breathing soothing her to sleep better than any lullaby, and now she was finding it almost impossible to sleep without him. Waking up in the middle of the night, her head jerking around, desperately searching for the man whom, when she awoke properly, she would remember would not be there. Should not be there.

Or rather, should be.

Her mother frowned. "I should never have left you on your own the other night. You must still be frightened! You're still so young, my dear, sleeping here in the house all on your own, I don't know what Cook was—"

"I am tired, but I am not a child, Mother," Victoria pointed out, reaching eagerly for the teapot. *Tea, that's it. Tea will make everything better.* "I can sleep perfectly well, I just… I had a strange dream."

Well, it wasn't exactly a lie. She had had a strange dream. A strange, wonderful dream. A dream that had made no sense, and did not need to, and had washed over her like the painful yet sweet memory of a loving touch.

Mrs. Ainsworth snorted. "You look *exhausted*, my dear. Those bags under your eyes, the red around your pupils—"

Victoria sighed. Well, she had never expected her mother to be charming all the time.

"—I suppose it is a good thing that you will not be seeing that duke of yours today."

Stomach lurching, trying her best to keep her face as impassive as one not deeply in love with "that duke of yours," Victoria lifted a teaspoon nonchalantly and stirred her tea. "Oh?"

"Well, you haven't mentioned any such invitation to me," her mother said, sipping her own tea. "And you would not do anything so indecorous as meet without a prior appointment, would you?"

Victoria tried to smile. "Of course not."

No, that would be far too radical for her mother to comprehend. The fact that she had been soundly bedded by that duke, and in her own bedchamber while the house was entirely empty…that was neither here nor there.

A rustle. Her mother had opened up the newspaper.

"Ah, I see St. Thomas's orphanage has taken on another tutor. Good on them."

Victoria nodded vaguely as she helped herself to three slices of toast, lathering them in the softly melting butter and considering honey or marmalade with a tilt of her head. "Yes, very commendable."

"More people should do such things," her mother was saying behind the pages of the print. "Honestly, the world simply doesn't support the orphans of the world anymore!"

184

"You mean like we don't?"

It was the wrong thing to say. Victoria's mother re-appeared in a flurry of newspaper and frowns. "And just what is that supposed to mean?"

"Nothing, nothing," Victoria said hastily, regretting her words immediately. "I just thought—"

"Ahem."

Both Ainsworth women turned their heads in surprise. Victoria hadn't heard anyone come into the breakfast room—she hadn't even heard the door open.

Mrs. Stenton was standing there with boiling-red cheeks and a hand on her chest. She looked as though something awful had happened.

Victoria's pulse skipped a beat. News had arrived; something terrible had occurred to Thomas. Bad news had been sent. A letter, a footman, perhaps. Couldn't she see the lurking figure of a man in the hallway?

She rose, her napkin falling from her lap unheeded. "What is it? What happened? Is he—"

"The Duke of Cothrom for you madam, Miss Victoria," said the housekeeper, stepping to the left as the looming figure stepped forward.

This time, Victoria gasped, her hand lifting to her chest.

What on earth was he doing here—uninvited, and this early, too? It was unheard of. It was, as her mother would put it, indecorous.

Her mother.

Victoria turned to see the reaction on her mother's face. There was a twinkle in her eye, a softness in her shoulders. She was…delighted?

"Oh, Your Grace, what a delightful surprise. Come on in, help yourself to tea and toast and a chair—"

And my daughter, Victoria thought wryly.

Her mother could not have been more blatant if she had tried. The simpering giggle and the constant curtseying was a bit much, but the way she offered out her newspaper and apologized that she had already turned the pages…

Victoria shuddered, trying to keep the movement in her shoulders to a minimum. It was outrageous. It was embarrassing. It was—

"Come, Victoria, welcome our guest," trilled her mother.

Doing her best not to roll her eyes, Victoria said, "Good morning, Your Grace."

She had expected to have to hide the heat that would flare between them. She expected a shared knowing look and she would be forced to look away to prevent any awkward questions from her mother.

In truth, she almost hoped for it.

Yet she was to receive nothing of the sort. Thomas looked at her coldly, gave a stiff bow, and muttered something that sounded like, "Read the newspaper this morning."

Victoria swallowed, hope sinking as swiftly as it had risen.

This was not like him. She knew Thomas, knew him perhaps better than he knew himself, and this was not right. It was not natural. He was holding himself awkwardly, his gaze never settling, that charm she so loved utterly absent.

What was wrong?

What was he doing here so early in the morning?

And perhaps most importantly, what could be done about her mother?

"—have my own cup. It's perfectly seasoned with lemon and—"

"Mother, Thomas—*His Grace* does not want your cup of tea," Victoria said hastily, hating that she had to correct herself, but not nearly so much as she hated the triumphant look her mother gave her. "Come, sit down. You too, Your Grace."

"I would prefer to stand."

Victoria halted halfway into her seat in astonishment. Preferred to stand? For breakfast?

Perhaps there were still a few things she did not know about him...

"How... How unusual," said Mrs. Ainsworth quietly as she finally sat, still clutching her cup of tea. "Invigorating, I suppose, though. I have never considered taking a meal while standing. I suppose it has many great beneficial—"

"Mrs. Ainsworth, I was wondering whether you would permit a short conversation between myself and your daughter," Thomas said stiffly, his eyes not leaving the Japan cabinet resting against the wall behind them.

Victoria's cheeks burned, and for once in her life—the one time she needed her mother to be quick on the uptake—the older woman seemed utterly oblivious.

"Oh, please do not mind me," her mother said brightly, picking up her newspaper and immediately hiding behind it.

Thomas cleared his throat, and Victoria's attention was inexplicably drawn to the strength of his throat, the curve of his jaw, the way it made her want to—

Well. Perhaps not so inexplicably.

"I actually meant... Well. Alone."

Mrs. Ainsworth could not have leapt up from her chair at a greater speed. "Yes, yes, of course. What was I thinking—alone, far more pleasant. Who wants to stay here listening to you two natter on? I'll just head to the—"

Victoria groaned as her mother's words became incomprehensible.

"—library. So good, much better read library. Newspaper belong library—"

"Yes, thank you, Mother," Victoria said eventually, halting the stream of consciousness. She rose and took her mother's arm, whispering close in her ear, "You're making a mountain out of a molehill, Mother."

"Am I?" Her mother's eyes sparkled in obvious delight as Victoria was shepherded to the door. "Or am I hearing wedding bells?"

Hoping to goodness Thomas hadn't heard her mother's words, Victoria pushed her out into the hallway and came close to slamming the door behind her.

She didn't. But it was a close thing.

Sighing heavily and almost sagging against the door, she turned around and looked straight into the face of Thomas Chance, Duke of Cothrom.

Goodness. When had he stepped across the room? And so quietly too...

"Victoria," he said softly, mere inches from her, preventing her from leaving the door. "Miss Ainsworth."

Victoria swallowed.

Well, this was what she had wanted. What she had hoped for—planned for. After abandoning the delicate, simpering, giggling façade, she had been bold and revealed her true self. She had aimed to seduce him—she had succeeded.

And it had all led to this. And yet...

Something was wrong. There was a strange expression on Thomas's face, his cold eyes not matching the plastered smile across his lips. It was all a little... Well. Forced.

He's nervous, Victoria told herself sternly. *And what gentleman wouldn't be?* It was a very important moment in a man's life, and he couldn't be expected to just immediately know what to say.

What would *she* say, after all?

The thought tickled her, and an impromptu smile lifted the corners of her mouth. "Your Grace."

She had expected him to correct her, to remind her that he preferred "Thomas" when addressed by her.

But he did not. His jaw tightened as he nodded tightly. Then he dropped to his knees.

"Miss Ainsworth, the last few weeks have been the happiest of my life. Make me even happier and consent to be my wife."

Victoria blinked. She had almost missed it.

Was that... Was that all? Surely, there has to be more than that.

Thomas was looking up from his kneeling position, his wan face a picture of...of boredom.

Something twisted painfully in Victoria's stomach. Surely, it was not meant to feel like this? Like... Like rote, following lines from a play. As though all the emotion had somehow been pulled out of his chest. As though Thomas were merely following instructions, allowing himself to be swept away by what ought to happen, rather than what he wanted.

She bit her lip, the silence elongating most painfully. This wasn't what she had thought would happen. This wasn't what she had wanted.

But it was, wasn't it? When she had pictured Thomas Chance, the man she had desired above all others for over a year, proposing to her, she hadn't really thought of the details. It had been Thomas himself whom she had cared about. As long as they were together, what did the proposal itself matter?

This is just one moment, Victoria reminded herself as she reached out and took Thomas's hand. *One moment that will lead to years of wonderful moments.*

That was all. She must not overthink this.

"You love me?" she said softly before she could stop herself.

A flicker of something she did not recognize across his features: not pain, not discomfort, but something altogether most unpleasant.

Then it was gone, Thomas's face calm and smooth once more. "Yes."

Victoria swallowed. It would have been nice if he had said it, but then, perhaps Thomas was not a particularly expressive man when it

EMILY E K MURDOCH

came to matters of the heart. Not everyone was.

She had won, hadn't she? Won him, won his heart. Allowing him into her bed had been a risk that had paid off.

She had seduced Thomas Chance.

"Yes."

A frown puckered in the corners of Thomas's brows. "Yes?"

"Yes, I will be your wife," she said, her voice stronger. "Yes, I will marry you."

His shoulders sagged, the relief sweeping across his face astonishingly clear. And then he was standing up. A box appeared in his hand. "This is for you."

She knew what it would be, but that did not halt the gasp of astonishment as he opened it. "Sapphires and emeralds."

"I had hoped that you would select a favorite," Thomas said wryly, slipping the ring off the velvet bed in the box and taking her left hand. "But you never made things easy for me."

Perhaps not, but it had been worth it, all of it. Victoria gazed in amazement as the sapphire-and-emerald ring, surrounding a large diamond on a gold band, was slipped onto her finger. It sat there, glittering in the early morning night. Her promise ring.

She had barely much time to look at it before he was pulling her into his arms. This was what she had expected: passion and closeness.

"Oh, Victoria, you have made me so happy," Thomas murmured close by her ear.

And she could believe it this time. She could feel the tension leaving his body as he held her, feel the soaring elation that was his racing pulse.

Nerves, that was all, Victoria told herself sternly. And she could hardly blame him. It was a monumental moment in a man's life.

In a woman's life. *Her* life.

Good lord. She was going to marry Thomas Chance.

That wasn't something anyone could just go about thinking every day.

"You make me happy," she said, clutching around his shoulders and breathing him in. There was something so *Thomas* about the way he smelled, that rich sandalwood—and she'd never have to worry about missing it, because she was going to be his wife. They were going to be together, they were going to be happy.

She'd done it.

"I-I can hardly believe it," Victoria said shakily, pulling away to look him in the face, then lifting up her hand to look at the ring. Her ring. The ring he had chosen. This wasn't a dream, was it? "Lady Thomas Chance."

"Your Grace, Victoria Chance, Duchess of Cothrom," he said, the teasing voice she knew so well finally returning.

Her mouth dropped open as he began to laugh.

Oh, Lord. Yes, of course. When she had fallen in love with Thomas— at least, what she had thought had been love at the time, and now that she truly knew him, she wasn't sure if it had been love or lust or infatuation—he had been merely Lord Thomas Chance.

And now he was the Duke of Cothrom. And that would make her—

"Duchess."

Suddenly, the room span. Just for a moment, she was able to gain her equilibrium almost immediately, but there was a sudden sway.

Duchess of Cothrom—a duchess! How could she have forgotten, even for a moment?

"I'm amazed you hadn't put that together," he said jovially, his soft voice stroking along the base of her spine, making her want to sit down. Or lie down. Or lie down with *him.* "When you become my wife, you will become one of the most important people in the *ton.*"

"I-I knew. I just forgot." She really needed to sit.

"What a whirlwind," Thomas was saying, his voice somehow speaking from far away and very close at the same time. "It's strange to think that just a few months ago, we hardly knew each other! Well, there was that series of dinners we both attended a year ago, as my mother reminded me, but we did not speak much then, did we?"

Victoria blinked, her future husband—husband!—coming back into view.

Should she tell him?

She had never considered what she would do after Thomas had proposed and she had accepted. All her thoughts, all her hopes and dreams, everything she had wanted was leading up to this moment. The moment when he requested her hand in marriage, and she offered it wholeheartedly.

But what was she supposed to do now?

She could admit the truth.

Victoria pushed the thought away immediately, not giving it a second look. Admit the truth? Tell Thomas she was perfectly aware he had squandered the family fortune, and more, that he was on the hunt for a rich bride, and even more than that, that her dowry was the only reason he had pursued her?

It was not exactly the opening for a joyful conversation.

Yet they could not progress like this, could they? Victoria was hardly an expert in matrimonial affairs, but her gut told her it was not the best idea to enter into a marriage with secrets and lies.

Well. Not lies. Not exactly.

Victoria swallowed. "Thomas, I..."

Her voice trailed away as her gaze flickered over his impossibly-handsome face. He was so charming. So ridiculously lovely. There was so much good in him, good that the world didn't see because all they cared about was money.

Oh, money. What good had it done her?

Other than attract her a husband, she supposed.

"—tell your mother at some point—"

Victoria's focus sharpened and her lips parted in astonishment. "I suppose we have to tell her now?"

"Soon, certainly," said Thomas airily as he stepped over to the breakfast table and picked up a buttered piece of toast from her plate. He shoved it in his mouth hungrily as though he were starving. Perhaps he had been too anxious to eat that morning. Perhaps that was why he was here so early. "Won't she start to get suspicious if we remain in here alone for too long?"

Suspicious, yes...or hopeful. Aloud, Victoria said, "I suppose so. Then there is your family to tell—"

"Oh, they already know. I told them weeks ago," Thomas said with a grin. Then he saw her face. "I mean...what I was considering. Perhaps. Maybe. I've certainly not been thinking about this for weeks."

Victoria stifled a smile. He really wasn't a very good actor. It was a good thing he had been born into money and nobility. He wouldn't have lasted five minutes on the stage.

"Of course not," she said smoothly. "And the announcements in the newspapers... The church must read the banns. It will take a good few months to plan the wedding, I presume."

"I think we should get married next week," Thomas said conversationally, finishing off her piece of toast.

Victoria reached out for the wall. "Next... Next week?"

He could not have been serious. Heat tingled through her body, tingling at her collarbones and whirling through her fingers. *Next week?*

"As soon as possible, then." He shrugged, as though weddings could be put together in five minutes. "I can procure a special license for us. I don't see the point in waiting."

The look he gave her was one of heat and longing and deep-rooted attraction, and at first Victoria was delighted. He couldn't wait, could he? Well, that was a positive sign and no mistake. One never knew, did one, whether one was adequate in bed. It was nice to receive a positive review.

But that wasn't the only reason he wanted her to become his wife so quickly, was it?

The thought was subtle, but it swam up through the recesses of her mind and presented itself to her as a *fait accompli*.

She had loved him for a year. He had wanted her dowry for a month.

Now they were engaged to be married.

"You love me?"

"Yes."

It wasn't the most resounding confirmation of love she had ever heard. Victoria tried to think back, to when she had been younger and her father had been alive. How had her parents shared their affection?

With kisses. With lingering looks. With laughter, and hands clasped under the table as though no one could guess their fingers were intertwined. With squabbles that ended with her father on bended knee, begging comically for forgiveness, and her mother dropping to her own knees in peals of laughter and begging for forgiveness in turn.

A smile lilted Victoria's mouth. That was love. That was what she wanted.

Was that what she had?

Thomas was chattering on about how easy it would be for them to get the wedding preparations sorted, especially with their two mothers involved, yet she could not quite grasp each word, each phrase. It washed over her like a tide slowly creeping up a shore.

Had he truly fallen in love with her? Or was this still all part of his plan, Thomas's plan, to get his hands on her dowry?

And did she care?

Victoria swallowed. "You're right."

"Of course I'm right. How long does it take to bake a cake—"

"No, I meant about—about getting married as soon as possible," Victoria said, trying to keep her voice level, as though she had not just agonized over whether to entrap the man into marriage before he realized he did not truly love her. "Next week, or the week after. Why wait?"

Thomas beamed, stepping toward her and cupping her face with both hands. "My beautiful Victoria. My beautiful wife-to-be."

Victoria tried to accept his kiss—which was remarkably chaste—with exultation and hope.

She had been certain that allowing Thomas to bed her would make him fall in love with her, and perhaps she was right. Perhaps his nerves had just gotten the better of him. He would not be the first.

Perhaps once they were married, it would be different. Perhaps he would truly fall in love with her when they lived together, or when they explored each other's bodies every morning, or perhaps—

Perhaps, perhaps, perhaps…

Thomas clasped him to her. "You're all I want, Victoria."

All he wants. But was she? Was she all he wanted…or was it the dowry?

The words of Thomas's proposal echoed in her ears, and Victoria could not help but notice that all the words of love, or rather the only singular mention of love, had come from her lips.

"You love me?"

"Yes."

Chapter Sixteen

February 2, 1840

"THERE IS ABSOLUTELY nothing to be nervous about," Thomas said as he ushered her into the cavernous hallway. "Trust me."

Trust me. It was the sort of thing he was finding himself saying often at the moment. *Trust me, Victoria. Trust me that I am marrying you for the right reasons. Trust me that I can be depended on with your immense fortune. Trust me that I love you, even though I haven't said it.*

Why, I don't know myself.

"That's easy for you to say. They're *your* family."

"They're really not that bad," he said quietly, sending away a footman with a wave of his hand before starting to remove Victoria's pelisse.

Thomas swallowed, trying not to let himself get lost in the sensations of Victoria. That delicate, lavender scent that wafted around her almost constantly, making him feel uncomfortably hard whenever he walked down a particular path in the Cothrom garden. The softness, the caress of her skin as he trailed his fingertips around her neck and shoulders to remove the pelisse. The heat of the look she gave him—

It was enough to tip any man over into lust, and Thomas knew precisely what could be gained from that sumptuous form.

Damn it, man, you're about to introduce her to your entire family! Control yourself!

"I suppose they're like any family, really," Victoria was saying, apparently unaffected by his fingers. Which was probably a good thing. "It's just... Well. It's the Cothrom family. The Chance family."

Thomas waited for her to continue as he placed her pelisse carefully on the coatrack by the door, but when he turned back to her with a curious eye, she did not appear to have anything else to say.

"The Chance family," he repeated curiously.

Victoria tilted her head as she finished removing her bonnet. "You really have no idea, do you?"

It was not pleasant, to realize there was something about yourself, about your family, that you did not know. The unpleasantness, however, was mediated by the fact that it gave him the perfect excuse to look at Victoria again. That was not much of a hardship.

She was wearing a delicate cream silk gown, one almost as soft as her skin. It clung to her breasts in all their fullness, making Thomas's mouth dry, then swept down into a marvelous train he was going to have to be careful not to tread on. These modern fashions,—they made it almost impossible for a man to get close to a woman.

His woman.

His stomach stirred, a need to possess her threatening to overwhelm Thomas's senses, but thankfully, at that moment, Victoria continued speaking.

"It's just... Well, the Chance family. You're some of the most popular and impressive people in Society, individually, and as a family—"

"Don't let my sister hear you speaking like that," Thomas warned with a grin as he offered up his arm. "She's big-headed enough as it is."

"It's not Lady Maude, although she's a part of it, I suppose," Victoria said, biting her lip as she accepted his arm, almost as though she did so without thinking.

As though they were meant to be this close.

"Being a Chance, it's like being royalty in my circles. I cannot tell you how pleased my mother is."

She didn't need to. He had seen enough evidence once they had departed the Ainsworth breakfast room three days ago. Mrs. Ainsworth had at first clapped her hands together in delight, then squawked something about being the happiest she had ever been, then yelled for all the servants to hurry, which they had done, despite Victoria's attempts to calm her mother, and then the woman had burst into—presumably happy—tears.

It had been quite the ordeal.

"A shame your mother felt too ill to join us," he said, clearing his throat. The woman's usual energy would have certainly been something for his brothers to comment on later, had she come.

"She is *so* sad to have missed it. But I assured her it was more important she rest, and be healthy for the wedding. Still, I'll not hear the end of her missing tonight."

"It's just dinner with my family," Thomas said confidently, ushering her down a corridor, his pulse thumping too hard for his words to be entirely true. "Just dinner."

Just the first time his future bride would meet his brothers. Just the first time she would be introduced to his sister and mother as his betrothed, the first woman to enter the family in almost two decades. Just the moment when he would discover if he had gained his father's approval in his choice.

Thomas's mouth was unexpectedly dry when he reached the drawing room door and opened it up.

It was just a dinner, as he kept attempting to tell Victoria.

Even he didn't believe that. This was a big moment, one that only grew larger as Thomas took in the scene before him.

Standing by the fireplace were his parents, speaking together rapidly in hushed tones. On the pianoforte was his brother Alexander, a teasing smile already spreading across his face. On the sofa, Leopold and Maude, chattering away happily but falling into silence as they looked at the two newcomers.

Thomas did not even think. He placed a hand over Victoria's on his arm, protecting it. Protecting her.

She squeezed his arm and certainty roared up in Thomas's chest.

Well, this was it.

"Mother, Father," he said confidently as he strode toward the older couple by the fire. "May I introduce Miss Victoria Ainsworth, my betrothed."

Betrothed. Strange. Ever since Thomas had started using the word, he had discovered it fit naturally in his mouth. As though he had been waiting to say it all his life.

His mother was all delight. "Miss Ainsworth, how perfectly splendid to see you again. I was quite desolate that we had little opportunity to speak at our ball, and now you are here for dinner, how wonderful."

Thomas glanced at Victoria and saw to his relief that she was smiling, her charm emanating as he knew it would.

"The pleasure is all mine, Your Grace. My mother sends her regrets. She will be so sad to have missed a chance to dine with the Duchess of Cothrom."

"Oh, I am not the Duchess of Cothrom any longer. That shall be your title! But I am sorry to hear your mother could not come."

And Victoria laughed prettily, and flushed, and said all the right things about not changing precedence and her hopes that they would grow to know each other...

It was everything he wanted. Thomas's chest puffed out, relief and elation mingling in his heart. This was what he had hoped for.

Well. Almost everything.

The Dowager Duke of Cothrom remained silent as his wife and his future daughter-in-law chattered away. His gaze had raked up and down the young woman once. He had said nothing.

Thomas's jaw tightened. It was... Well, not rude. No one would call his father's response rude, though perhaps it wasn't cordial.

Regardless, it was not the warm greeting and welcome he had

hoped for.

I wanted him to be impressed.

The thought could not be taken captive before it had risen up in his mind and Thomas could not deny it. William Chance had impeccable taste—everyone in Society knew that. It would have meant a great deal to Thomas if his father had said a few words of welcome, a compliment, perhaps. Even a smile would have been refreshing.

Yet there he stood, face impassive, eyes cold, tongue silent.

Thomas attempted not to be offended. It was a comment on him, though, surely—wasn't it? Did his father believe he had not made the right choice? Did he think his son should have chosen someone better?

Was there anyone better, in all the world?

Trying to concentrate on the cordiality growing between his mother and Victoria, Thomas extricated his arm and murmured, "Let me get you a drink."

Victoria cast him a momentary look of panic, the absence of him clearly having more of an impact than he thought, but then it was gone. She inclined her head graciously and turned back to his mother.

"You must tell me, Your Grace, just who it was that painted the ceiling of your ballroom. The detailing was most exquisite…"

A smile creased Thomas's face as he walked over to a footman and murmured a request for two glasses of wine. *Well, so far, so—*

"Better make it a whole host of glasses. I think we'll all need it," said a voice.

Thomas groaned as he turned to his brother. "You're not going to make this difficult for me, are you?"

"Wouldn't dare." Leopold nudged his older brother with a wink. "After all, you've won, haven't you?"

His stomach lurched. "I don't know what you mean."

"Oh, yes, you do. You just don't like to admit it," said Alexander, stepping over with their sister and punching Thomas lightly on the arm. "You know, part of me thought you wouldn't be able to go through with it."

Thomas glanced over at Victoria and his parents, hoping beyond hope they could not hear their conversation. The last thing he needed was Victoria suspecting something—at least, before he could explain. And he would explain. At the right moment. When it arrived.

"I like her," said Maude stoutly as the footman returned with a tray of filled wineglasses. She took one. "And I shall be most displeased with you if you hurt her, Tommy."

His jaw tightened. "I don't intend to."

Alexander scoffed. "Well, as long as she's got the dowry—"

"*Xander!*" hissed Thomas.

The man had clearly already been in his cups before he and Victoria had arrived, for he was grinning in that laconic way his brother always did when he'd drunk a little too much.

Their father would be furious.

"It's fine, man. Don't worry, I'm not about to reveal your secret." Alexander winked. "It's bizarre, though, you have to admit. From then to here in what, a month? And all on the toss of a coin."

Thomas tried to grin. His brother was not so foolish as to say something. Even in his cups, the man was clever—far too clever to drop him into a situation he could not talk himself out of.

"I need to take Victoria a glass of wine," he said aloud, hoping to extricate himself from his brother as swiftly as possible and making a mental note to speak quietly to Bradbury to place Alexander as far from Victoria at the dinner table as possible.

"Yes, let's all go and meet her," Maude said, dashing his hopes. "Officially, as it were."

Somehow, all the nerves Victoria had been feeling upon arrival at the Cothrom Bath townhouse had left her and crept under *his* skin. Thomas could feel them churning about in his stomach, making every step a challenge.

The siblings approached their parents and Thomas stood between

Victoria and Alexander. At least that way, he could not directly—

"Pleased to make your acquaintance, Miss Ainsworth," Alexander said cheerfully, lifting his glass. "A toast—to yourself, and this reprobate."

Thomas tried not to snort with exasperation, though thankfully, he was saved the trouble of punching his brother thanks to Maude's vicious elbow.

Alexander cried out. "Ouch. What the devil did I do to—"

"Yes, here's to the happy couple," said Leopold loudly, drowning out their younger brother's nonsense with a roll of his eyes in Thomas's direction. "We look forward to getting to know you better, Miss Ainsworth."

Thomas reveled in the pinkness of Victoria's cheeks as she accepted their toasts and best wishes, his pulse skipping a beat.

This was what he wanted.

This was what he had discovered he had wanted. At first, it had been all about the money—not that he was sure how he would ever explain that to her. Then it had been about burying himself in her arms and eking decadence from every pore of her being. That had been wonderful, and it was most definitely a part of marriage to which he was looking forward.

But now...

Now it was all different. He loved this woman, loved every part of her. Loved the way her eyes crinkled in the corners and the way she sipped her tea, and...and everything.

And he would tell her. Soon.

"—chance of finding one's perfect partner?" Thomas's mother was saying. "I am hardly a mathematician, that's Aunt Dodo for you."

"I am sure she has worked it out," Maude said dryly. "There are few things she hasn't."

"I am serious." His mother nodded pensively. "It must be one in ten thousand, or perhaps more."

"One in a million," said Alexander with a grin.

"A one-in-a-million chance?" Victoria said, her eyes wide. "There must be few other things so rare in life."

There was a tingling panic at the base of his neck and Thomas did not know why. Something was brewing, something his subconscious could clearly see coming, but he could not.

"Oh, I would imagine there are quite a few things," Leopold said, sipping his wine. "The likelihood of finding buried treasure, perhaps—"

"Or discovering Atlantis?" Maude grinned. "Be serious, Leo."

"No, there are most definitely things that happen that only have a one-in-a-million chance," Alexander quipped. "Do you remember that coin toss, Tommy?"

Thomas froze.

Oh, God, no. No, come on, man, this isn't the time to speak of that.

Alexander tapped his chin with one finger. "We were—where were we? I can't remember."

Thomas's mouth was dry and he needed to speak, needed to stop this, needed to head off this disaster and yet the words weren't coming. It was as though he were looking at a portrait of his family and Victoria for all the impact he could have on them, as if they were standing on a tableaux, about to enact a disastrous play.

It was going to happen right here, right in front of him, and he could do nothing to stop it.

"Anyway, Thomas had to toss a coin to decide—"

"You know, I can't really recall," he said hastily, taking Victoria's hand in his and wondering if he could lead her into the dining room right now, before the end of the world occurred. "Mother, do you think we should—"

"—and instead of falling on heads or tails, the coin actually fell onto its edge!" Alexander said triumphantly.

The cries of astonishment and "Surely not!" rang around the drawing room, and Thomas's pulse felt as though it were going to slowly return back to its normal pace.

That was what his brother was talking about. Merely the oddity of the toss, not the reason for the toss in the first place. There was no need to be concerned, no need at all. The story was told, the danger was past, and—

"That *is* remarkable," Victoria said, her eyes wide as she glanced at Thomas. "The sort of thing you could not repeat."

"No," Thomas said tersely, turning back to his mother. "Is dinner ready? I think we should go through—"

"In fact, he did toss the coin again straightaway, as it turns out," Alexander said with a shrug. "To decide between you and Lady Marjorie."

And that was when all chatter ceased.

Thomas could not hear a sound other than the painful throb of his pulse in his ears. Leopold and Maude had both closed their eyes and winced, his parents were frowning, glancing at each other in confusion, and Victoria...

For a series of thumping heartbeats, Thomas did not have the bravery to look. Only when her fingers slipped from his own did he force himself to.

There was...confusion. And pain. And distress, and anger, all flickering across her face like wind across a sail.

Then it settled into...nothingness. "Between..." She cleared her throat. "Between me and Lady Marjorie?"

"You, come on," said Maude sternly, grabbing Alexander by his arm.

His jaw gaped open. "What? Why? Where are we—"

"He always talks nonsense when he gets in his cups, Miss Ainsworth. I would not pay much heed to anything he says," Leopold said hastily, stepping into the gap his two siblings had left as Maude marched Alexander to the door.

"But what did he mean, Leopold?" asked their mother, frowning, and Thomas wished to goodness he had never thought of this dinner. Never lied to Victoria. Never tried to keep the truth from her.

Why on earth hadn't he told her the whole story?

"Between myself, and Lady Marjorie," Victoria repeated, her voice somehow far away. "She is one of the most eligible ladies in Society, true, but...but why would you be..."

That was when she turned her eyes to Thomas and he crumpled, pain shooting across his shoulder blades.

"You were flipping a coin," she whispered, eyes wide. "Flipping a coin to choose between Lady Marjorie...and me? That is all I am. A toss of a coin."

Silence fell in a mortifying heaviness as Thomas tried desperately to articulate a statement that would make her understand. "I... Arghh... Uh... I—"

"Everyone, out," his father said stiffly.

There was no time to speak. The Dowager Duke of Cothrom took his wife's hand as she protested vociferously that she wanted to remain and help. One look at Thomas's brother was enough to send Leopold out with them.

The door closed. They were alone.

"I can explain—" Thomas said in a flash of mortification.

"I don't think you can," Victoria said, taking a step back and placing her glass on the mantelpiece. Her fingers were shaking. How had he not noticed that? "I-I don't think there are words to explain."

"I *must* explain," he said firmly, panic rising.

Because this had to end well—it simply had to. He hadn't come all this way, wooed her, courted her, then gone through the inconvenience of discovering he loved her and could not exist without her, just—just to lose her.

No.

"You think I am just some bauble to pick up and put down, to flip a coin over?" Victoria was speaking quietly, but there was such pain in her voice that it cracked. "How could you? Who are you, Thomas? The man I know, I knew—"

"I am still that man," he said eagerly, stepping forward, needing to be close to her.

His attempt was foiled as she took a step back. "The man I thought I knew, clearly, for you are the same man and you are the man who thought I was so insignificant—"

"Victoria—"

"—so inconsequential to your life that it would not matter which woman you pursued?" Tears sparkled in her eyes.

Thomas's lungs were threatening to tear themselves apart, his whole chest heaving with pain and anguish, and the words he wanted to say mingled with the panic he could not quell.

He was going to lose her. He was going to lose her, and it was all his fault.

"You are not inconsequential," Thomas said fiercely, words finally reaching his tongue. "Victoria, you are—"

"*Miss Ainsworth,*" she said stiffly.

The panic seared into irritation. "You're not even going to let me attempt to explain, are you?"

"There is no explanation!" she shot back. "How can you justify the fact that you saw Lady Marjorie and myself as options on a menu? You tossed a coin to select me as your bride!"

It sounded awful when put like that. Christ alive, he was a fool. "I'm not saying it was the best beginning. The truth is—"

"I can't believe I thought—"

"The truth is worse."

Precisely what had come over him, Thomas did not know. His shoulders were heaving with his rapid breaths, his whole body was tingling with panic and a need to crush the woman into his arms, yet the look Victoria was giving him was so dark, so utterly devoid of passion.

"The truth, please, Your Grace," Victoria said dully. "Then I can go home."

The hell she will.

"Look," said Thomas, hating that the truth had to come out this way but knowing there was nothing for it. "Look, I... Well, I needed money."

And something strange shifted in her expression. Her parted lips grew into a smile. Where fear had been, mirth replaced it.

She was...laughing.

"Oh, Thomas, you really are dense," Victoria said, her tone cutting. "You think I didn't know you were pursuing me for my money?"

Her words echoed around the room, his mind, for what felt like several minutes but could only have been a few seconds.

"I... You..." He swallowed, unable to keep up with the ricochets of revelations. "You knew?"

"I am not a fool, Your Grace. Of course I knew," Victoria said coldly. "The new Lord Cothrom needs money—everyone in the *ton* knows that. Everyone knows you lost your family's fortune."

Pain seared down Thomas's ribcage like a knife. They did? The whole of Society knew how terribly he'd disappointed his family?

Worse, they didn't know the full truth, what he had done, what he had tried to do, whom he had tried to help. And it wasn't about that— but he was no reprobate gambler. He was not that kind of man.

"You're a spendthrift, a wastrel."

"I think you'll find you're wrong there," he said hotly. This wasn't precisely how he had planned to tell her about St. Thomas's, but there was no choice now. "I have actually—"

"I knew you needed my dowry, and I made sure to lure you in." She was speaking so matter-of-factly now, it grated at his nerves, and Victoria kept going. "I thought you would fall in love with me eventually, and—"

"So it's you, really, who is the liar?" Thomas interrupted, a twist in his throat. "You... You were just manipulating me."

"Manipulating a man who chose me thanks to a coin flip!" she retorted hotly.

"I chose you from a coin, but I could have ignored that. I could have pursued anyone—"

Her nostrils flared. "Oh, thank you for devaluing me even further!"

"—but I chose you," Thomas said quietly. All the fight had gone out of him now.

How could it remain? How could he fight for something that had never existed?

She'd never cared for him. Victoria Ainsworth had seen his desperation and used it against him. She'd taken his need for money and twisted it into a sick way to entice him closer. She'd flirted with him all the way into her bed, with her eye on the prize: his title.

She'd known that once he'd been in her bed, he was honor-bound to marry her.

"I think you should leave," Thomas said numbly.

Victoria's eyes widened. "You think *I* should leave? You're the one who—"

"Be that as it may, this is my home, not yours," he said, barely able to see, hardly knowing what to do with his hands, his chest, all these tears that threatened to pour down his face. "Please leave, Miss Ainsworth."

"Gladly!" snapped Victoria, tears now spilling onto her cheeks and his heart ached for her, but what could he say? "You should have this. Sell it if you want, so you can return to your gambling ways!"

Something golden shone in her hand and then it was pressed in his own. Thomas stared at the emerald-and-sapphire encrusted golden ring. Golden promise ring.

She stormed past him in a haze of lavender that made Thomas sink to his knees. The door slammed and there was silence.

Silence except for his quiet, racking sobs.

Chapter Seventeen

February 5, 1840

S HE WAS NOT going to be upset. She was not. She was going to read this book, and not be upset.

Victoria carefully turned a page of the book she was holding up in front of her, whatever it was, and sat in complete silence.

There. That wasn't so hard. Just read this book about...spiders? What on earth had she picked up?

Turning the book in her hand, Victoria was astonished to find the spine read *A Compendium of the Arachnids of South America.*

Ah. Well. How was she to know the book she had been reading for the last twenty minutes had been about spiders? Certainly not her.

A genteel clearing of the throat occurred on the other side of the room and Victoria rolled her eyes as she lowered her book. "You wished to say something, Mother?"

Mrs. Ainsworth was seated with her embroidery in her lap. "I wondered whether you wished to speak about what happened, dear."

"No, thank you," Victoria said smartly, lifting up the book to her eyes once more and delving into the fascinating topic of—oh, bother. Spiders.

Ah well. Beggars couldn't be choosers. That, she well knew.

"Oh, Thomas, you really are dense. You think I didn't know you were pursuing me for my money?"

Pushing aside the memory sternly, as though it had trespassed onto her pleasant and calm afternoon, she also put aside the thoughts of the three letters, now nothing but charred ashes in her bedchamber grate, which had borne the Chance seal. She had not bothered to read them. Why should she? What could Thomas—what could Lord Cothrom say in a letter that he had been unable to say to her face?

No, it was best that the letters were gone, along with any hopes she could be happy.

No one knew for certain he had been in her bed, and fewer people even suspected. She could still marry someday. If she ever *wanted* to marry. She didn't *need* to marry. Her father had left her a fortune, so why did she even care?

Victoria tried to make herself read the lines of blurry text before her.

Blurry text?

Oh. She was crying again.

No matter. Victoria had grown quite accustomed to hiding her tears from her mother the last few days, so it took just a slight twist of her wrist to dislodge her handkerchief. Bringing it up to her eyes was easy, as the book was covering her face and making it impossible for her mother to see precisely what she was doing. All she had to do was dab gently, like so, and—

"I would have thought that handkerchief would be sodden by now. I hope you have not caught my cold on top of everything else."

Victoria allowed her book to fall into her lap. "No, Mother. And I don't want to talk about it."

"I know, and I am sorry," said her mother, and she truly did look sorry, too. "That is why what is about to happen is so unfortunate."

What is about to happen? "What are you—"

"You see, I spotted her from the corner of my eye. I did not mean to," said Mrs. Ainsworth serenely. "I would not have known it was her, of course, except that I had most particularly asked Mrs. Howarth to point out any member of the Chance family to me, just two days ago. How was I supposed to know that you and His Grace would—"

"Mother," Victoria said, trying her best to keep her temper and wondering what on earth her mother was babbling about. "Who have you seen?"

Not the dowager duchess, please. Victoria had done a very good job, she thought, of holding herself together the last few days. Tears, yes, and a slight amount of sobbing, but nothing that would strike someone as out of the ordinary, considering.

"You're not even going to let me attempt to explain, are you?"

"There is no explanation!"

But if Thomas—if Lord Cothrom's mother turned up on her doorstep, begging her to take her son back because the family was in such dire need of funds, Victoria knew precisely what she would say to her.

Probably.

"I don't want to see the Dowager Duchess of Cothrom," Victoria said, a little more fiercely than she had intended. "Mother, you will have to send her away. Tell her—"

The doorbell rang and Victoria's voice halted in her throat.

Oh, this was beyond what she should surely be expected to endure. Was it not bad enough that the man had chosen her on a whim, barely concerned with who or what she was? Did she have to suffer merely because Thomas Chance, the man she had thought she'd loved—and more importantly, he whom she had convinced herself had loved in her return—was desperate to get his hands on her dowry?

Would this pain ever cease?

"The thing is my dear, it wasn't the dowager duchess," her mother said, dropping her voice now to a whisper as the sounds of light conversation in the hallway drifted under the door. "It was—"

"Lady Maude Chance," said Mrs. Stenton triumphantly, as though she were presenting them with a gift.

Victoria lurched to her feet, *A Compendium of the Arachnids of South America* dropping to the carpet with a dull thud.

Lady Maude? Thomas's sister?

But their housekeeper was hardly going to lie about such a thing, and indeed, when she curtseyed and retreated back into the hallway, it was Lady Maude who appeared in the room.

A beautiful pink day dress on, she was laughing breezily, her ringlets bouncing as she stepped into the room. *As well she might laugh.* It was not *her* heart that was broken.

"Miss Ainsworth, how delighted I am that you are home," said Thomas's sister with a broad smile.

"I'm not," Victoria snapped.

It was a foolish thing to say and sadly, there was no way to take it back. Both her mother and Lady Maude raised an eyebrow.

"Indeed," the younger woman said dryly as she brushed some invisible wrinkles out of her skirt. "So I see."

"Well you must excuse me, Lady Maude," said Mrs. Ainsworth cheerfully as she placed her embroidery on her seat, rising in a rush of silk. "I need to see to the kitchens."

"Mother," Victoria said quickly.

She couldn't be thinking of leaving, could she? Abandoning her, right when she needed to defend herself against whatever Lady Maude had come to say.

Not that Victoria had anything to apologize for, naturally.

She pulled herself upright. "Lady Maude, please do not stay too long, I would not wish you to trouble yourself."

"I will stay as long as necessary, Miss Ainsworth," said Thomas's sister, with the same steely glint she'd seen in her brother's eyes. "Good afternoon, Mrs. Ainsworth."

Victoria's mother helpfully waggled her eyebrows over Lady Maude's shoulder before she closed the door behind her, causing Victoria to groan and Lady Maude to jerk her head back.

"I did not realize my presence would be that unwelcome."

"No, it's not that, it's just... Well, my mother was being a tad silly," Victoria said helplessly. "Please...sit."

Well, what else could she say? *"Please go away, I never want to see you again?" "Your brother broke my heart and I didn't even realize that was possible?" "I will never get over him and now I am ruined for other men?"*

Not really the sort of thing one said to a woman one had met fewer than a handful of times.

Lady Maude said nothing for a moment, seating herself in an armchair close to the sofa upon which Victoria sank. Victoria's foot nudged the book, but she did not pick it up. How could she care about such things when she was going to have to face this most embarrassing conversation?

"This is embarrassing, isn't it?" Lady Maude said conversationally, as though she visited spurned lovers of her brothers all the time.

Victoria's pulse skipped a beat. Perhaps she did. Maybe this was all nothing but routine for this family.

"I don't particularly want to see you," she said coldly, trying to keep her shoulders down and her back straight.

Far from being insulted, Lady Maude appeared to be amused, her small mouth quirking on one end. "No, I don't suppose you do, but I am afraid there is no other option. You wouldn't reply to my letters."

Her lips parted in astonishment. "'Letters'? But you haven't sent... I haven't received any—"

"I know you have, Miss Ainsworth, so there is no point in dissembling," said Lady Maude calmly, interlocking her hands atop her lap. "I sent a footman around especially to ensure they didn't get mislaid in the post. You did not reply. Did you even read them?"

Victoria's mind was whirling as she saw again the image of the Chance seal melting as the paper charred.

The Chance seal—yes, but they would all use it, wouldn't they?

"They were from you?"

"I should have thought to use a different seal, I suppose, but there it is. I presumed you would want to read them precisely because they *could* be from Tommy," Lady Maude said with a wry smile. "He did not have the opportunity to properly explain himself, you see."

Victoria's resolve had been softening, but it hardened again at her words.

"He had plenty of time to be honest over the last month, I think you'll find," she said stiffly. "And—"

"You see, my brother had a very good reason to spend all that money," interrupted Lady Maude with a rueful look. "He is still a fool, naturally, as it wasn't his money to spend."

"I don't want to hear about how he almost won his bets, Lady Maude," Victoria said, heart wrenching. "And I wish he hadn't sent you. I believe I made myself perfectly clear to him."

"My brother hasn't sent me, Miss Ainsworth," said her guest softly. "He does not know I am here. In fact, he made me promise faithfully I would not communicate with you at all, so I beg you to listen to me."

Victoria's stomach lurched, a painful twist that sparked up her ribcage and across her shoulder blades.

He didn't know Lady Maude was here? Why, what other secrets could be unfolded? Worse, why would his sister lie to him to come here?

"Tea!" trilled Mrs. Stenton, bursting in with a tray. "I took the liberty of selecting a few biscuits, Miss Victoria. I thought as how you are entertaining your future sister-in—"

"Thank you, Mrs. Stenton," Victoria said hastily. She did not need to have said aloud the very close connection she and Lady Maude would have shared, had it not been for Thomas's rash foolishness.

She swallowed hard as the housekeeper placed down the tray, twittered on for a bit about how delightful it was to be hosting such a refined lady, then bustled out, leaving the two ladies in silence.

It was Lady Maude who broke it. "You haven't told her."

"I have told her more times than I can count, but I am afraid Mrs. Stenton refuses to believe it." Victoria's mouth was dry as she spoke. Mrs. Stenton no doubt assumed what the housekeeper could not *prove* had happened that night. Assumed there was no way Victoria could get out of this marriage now. Why did she have to suffer through this indignity? Such a shame her good manners overruled her. "Tea?"

"Please," said Lady Maude quietly. "You still love him, then?"

It was fortunate indeed that Victoria had only lifted the teapot up a few inches from the tray. Still, a globule of tea dropped onto a saucer.

"He is no spendthrift, truly," his sister persisted. "He had a good reason to spend the money."

"Gambling is not a sufficient good enough reason, not in my book," Victoria said, hardly believing she was having this conversation. She passed over the cup of tea in a saucer—not the one onto which she'd dribbled the tea. "Biscuit?"

"Delightful," said Lady Maude, accepting the offering. "But you have to listen to me, you know."

She didn't have to do any such thing—but it struck Victoria that it was probably the easiest way to get rid of her. Listen to the nonsense the sister would spout out, then vow never to see, speak to, or even think of the brother again.

"Fine."

It was not the warmest of invitations to continue conversing, but her rudeness did not appear to be the reason Lady Maude hesitated.

"I... It's not my place to tell Tommy's secret."

Victoria could not help but snort. "How convenient."

His sister's cheeks colored, some of the passion and confidence seeping away. "He does not even know I know. I only found out by mistake. If you could just ask him about—"

"Absolutely not," said Victoria firmly, reaching firmer ground. Yes, she knew how the conversation would go now. Lady Maude would ask, she would decline, then Thomas's sister could return home with a clear conscience knowing she had tried. "If that is all, Lady Maude...?"

"It is most certainly not all," the woman said fiercely. "And I think you should ask him about it. His reasons are far nobler than you think. Not that I think you'll get a coherent word out of him at present."

Victoria could not help it. She leaned forward, teacup and saucer remaining untouched in her hands. "Why?"

Her curiosity was rewarded.

"Because he is utterly distraught, that's why," Lady Maude said blandly. "Honestly, I have never seen Tommy like this since Harold died."

Goodness, he was that upset? Who was Harold? An uncle? A childhood friend? "You are telling me that he is acting as though he has been bereaved?"

"Harold was his favorite, the most excellent pointer he ever—"

Victoria sagged back against the back of the sofa. "Oh, good. You are comparing me to his dog."

"I didn't—I am just saying, I can't get a sensible word out of the man, and he's driving us all to distraction with his weeping and mooning!" Lady Maude's cheeks were red now. "My brother may think he's clever, but he's not, is he? You were leading him on the chase, pulling the strings, weren't you?"

It was a strange sort of accusation, but not one she could refute. Because she had been, hadn't she? Pulling the strings, making Thomas Chance fall in love—or so she'd thought. She'd known his little plan—perhaps not how it had begun, certainly, but the end result had been the same. Thomas had wanted to marry her dowry, and she had let him court her with just such an ending in mind.

Leading him on the chase, pulling the strings...

It gave Victoria no pleasure to nod. "I-I was."

Lady Maude sighed as she bit into her biscuit and placed the rest on her saucer. "It gives me no pleasure to admit this to you, Miss Ainsworth, but that boy is absolutely head over heels in love with you, and it's destroyed him, this tiff."

"It is not a *tiff*!" Victoria said hotly. "How dare you?"

"How dare I?" Her guest did not even blink an eye. "I know what it is to lose love, Miss Ainsworth."

Victoria had readied herself to refute the nonsense Thomas's sister was next going to throw at her, but it was difficult when the woman looked so…sad.

As though she truly knew, truly understood how Victoria felt.

"I know what it is to lose love, Miss Ainsworth."

How could she? She was known to be past her prime, a spinster by definition, if she had been lower-ranking. Victoria had not heard any gossip about any gentlemen courting the only daughter of the Duke of Cothrom in the years before her own debut. And she was only a sister of a duke now.

She stared curiously as Lady Maude continued to pink.

"Who have you—"

"That is not the point," Lady Maude said hastily.

Victoria's curiosity rose and she leaned forward. "Isn't it? And what *is* the point, then? Why have you barged into my home and demanded I listen to this nonsense?"

"My point is, Miss Ainsworth, my brother was too easily tricked—"

"I did not trick—"

"Not you, himself," said Lady Maude with a sigh. "Don't you see?"

Victoria did not see. The whole conversation had gotten away from her because she could not for the life of her understand what the woman was talking about.

Thomas, trick himself?

After taking a large sip of tea, Lady Maude placed the cup and saucer on the console table beside her. "I will not claim to be an expert in the ways of romance, Miss Ainsworth. Trust me, I am not the sort of person to whom anyone should usually listen when it comes to this sort of thing—but I know my brother. He truly believed, for a short time, that he could just pick a woman out of the air—"

"From a coin toss," Victoria mumbled.

Lady Maude frowned. "Yes, precisely, then marry her. But my brother is not that mercenary. He only managed to keep going with what he thought was his deception because he truly and honestly fell in love with you."

It was just the sort of thing Victoria had wanted to hear. Admittedly from Thomas's own lips, not during a surprise visit from his sister, but still. It would have been so pleasant, so easy to just trick herself into believing Thomas had fallen in love with her.

But he hadn't. He'd never said so, despite multiple opportunities, and when the truth of her "selection" had come out, what had he said?

No words of love, no declarations of affection, not even an apology.

No, he had attempted to justify himself, then accused her of manipulating him.

Victoria swallowed. "I don't want to hear any more. Thomas—"

"You love him," Lady Maude said softly. "Why are you fighting it?"

"Because if this is what love feels like, if this is the consequence of love, then I don't want it!"

Victoria had not intended to shout, had not thought she would so swiftly reveal the thought she had buried deep inside, but it poured out without any control.

Lady Maude was staring. "Oh, Miss Ainsworth."

"You think I want to feel this way? You think I want to feel this alone, this betrayed, this abandoned?" Victoria laughed bitterly, half a sob stifled by her deep intake of breath. "I was so easily selected and so easily cast aside. *You* are here, but where is Thomas? If I meant anything to him, if this between us was real, why is he not here? Why would I not fight this when it gives me naught but pain?!"

Lady Maude spoke softly. "The likelihood of two people finding happily ever after immediately, without any hiccups or confusion. The odds must be—"

"One in a million?" Victoria tried to laugh, but it once again sounded more like a sniffle. "Please, Lady Maude. You may return home, conscience clean. Don't expect anything more than that."

She rose, hoping to indicate by the simple movement that this interview was at an end.

Lady Maude remained seated, defiance in her eyes. "You tricked each other, Miss Ainsworth. My brother managed to trick himself and he's a fool if he doesn't—"

"And yet he doesn't." Victoria waved a hand around the room. "Do you see him? Would not a man in love be here, fighting for the woman he loved, fighting for this 'one in a million' your family appears obsessed with?"

Her guest rose with pressed lips. "I hope you know what you're doing, Miss Ainsworth. Love should never be abandoned, just because it is not easy."

"Is that what you did?" Victoria shot back, pushed now beyond all endurance. What did this woman think she was doing, marching into her home and making demands of her? "Abandon love when it got difficult?"

She had hit the mark. Without another word, Lady Maude's expression hardened, moving in silence as she strode for the door to the hallway. It slammed behind her. There were only the barest of whispers as the footman no doubt appeared to return the guest's outwear. A mere heartbeat after that, the front door in turn slammed.

Victoria sat slowly on the sofa in complete amazement. To be fair, it had not been the most polite of sentences, but it surely had not warranted such a response.

And the pain, the loneliness, the agonizing knowledge that she would now spend the rest of her life alone—for she could not bear to wed another, even if no one ever discovered she had given Thomas her honor—poured over her. Victoria dropped her head into her hands and allowed the tears she had fought all morning to overwhelm her.

Chapter Eighteen

WHEN ONE WAS the oldest son of a duke in a family of four siblings, there were very few places one could go and truly be alone. After all, every room save your own bedchamber belonged to your father, and no one wanted to mope about in the same four walls all day.

It had all become rather complicated since Thomas had become the Duke of Cothrom. He was now the duke...but did that make him head of the family? He had now come into ownership of Stanphrey Lacey, and the London townhouse, and the Bath one, but did that mean both his parents, his siblings, would defer to him?

And just when Thomas would have preferred to be alone, did his mother have to host one of her "little" gatherings?

"It's not 'little' if I can't make it down a corridor without bumping into someone," he growled tetchily.

Thomas's mother raised an eyebrow. "I do apologize, *Your Grace.* I did not realize I had to ensure you approved of all and every action I took."

The flicker of irritation flared, then passed. Thomas pulled a hand through his hair, growling a curse he would not utter in his mother's presence. "I'm going to the study."

"But your father, he will be back at any—"

"*I am going to the study,*" repeated Thomas, walking past his mother and muttering, "He has the whole house to entertain guests. I just want to be alone."

Whether or not his mother had heard him, he was not sure. His father certainly did not enter the study as Thomas whiled away the hours there, bored out of his mind yet finding nothing to do but sit there, staring at the grandfather clock whose hands moved slowly through time.

And when he had nothing to do, Thomas thought. And the thoughts hurt.

"So it's you, really, who is the liar? You... You were just manipulating me."

"Manipulating a man who chose me thanks to a coin flip!"

His jaw tightened, his temple throbbing, and there was pain in his hand—in his hand?

Thomas looked down. He'd clenched his fists, something utterly unconscious. They were clenched so tightly, his nails had dug into his palm. On his right hand were two small semicircle marks in the soft skin.

Forcing himself to relax, though who knew what that meant now, Thomas was astonished to see beading blood along one of the semicircles. He'd gripped his own hand so tightly, he was bleeding.

"I think you should leave."

Growling and uttering words no one could hear, Thomas rose from the armchair and began to prowl about the room like a caged animal.

This was ridiculous. It had all been a pretense, hadn't it—at the beginning? And yet here he was, desperate to understand how the woman could have gained such a grip on him.

A grip from which he could not, would not, release himself.

Thomas sighed heavily as he reached the window, glancing out through the panes at the wintery bustle in the street, and hated himself.

Because that was the truth, wasn't it? He liked this pain. He liked knowing his heart was broken, that he would never be the same again: it meant it had been real. He had really loved her. It was no slight of his imagination, no accidental mistake.

He loved Miss Victoria Ainsworth, and he was going to spend the rest of his life miserable about it.

Thomas leaned an arm up against the frame and stared out. All those people, going about busy with their lives. Did they have any idea what it was to love someone, to lose someone? To realize nothing you had was permanent, that it could slip through your fingers at any—

"Dear God, Mother wasn't exaggerating when she said you were brooding in here," came a cheerful voice. "I feel almost inclined to set up an easel and paint you."

Thomas swore and refused to turn around.

He'd barely seen him. He did not want to see him. The bas—

"You've missed luncheon, you know. You must be starving," said Alexander lightly.

There was the sound of a door closing and Thomas relaxed, sagging against the wall. At least he was gone. He didn't think he could stand much more of him.

"You are going to forgive me at some point, aren't you?"

His brother had not left—and this time, his voice was a little less cheerful.

Thomas still did not look around. Partly because he did not trust himself to be honest. His forgiveness was not something he could just offer, not with the damage Alexander had caused. And partly because the tear falling down his cheek had to be brushed away elegantly so his brother did not notice.

There was a scraping sound, the noise of a chair being moved across a wooden floor. Thomas took advantage of his brother's distraction and used his cuff to dry his eyes. *God damn, I have not let a single tear fall about this whole sorry business. Not until now.*

"So how long are you going to mope in here, then?"

Thomas straightened up, plastered a serious expression on his face, and turned to face his brother.

Alexander was seated in the very armchair he himself had so re-cently vacated, though his brother had moved it to face the window. There were bags around his eyes, which could only mean that he had frequented a gaming hell last night. Perhaps he hadn't slept at all.

He wouldn't be the only one to do the latter.

"I do not know what you mean," Thomas said brusquely.

He was in half a mind to leave the study entirely. That was his purpose as he strode across the room and opened up the door, but the sudden noise of feminine laughter, chatter, the clink of teacups against saucers, and his mother's voice caused him to halt.

"They're here all afternoon," came his brother's helpful voice behind him. "Some sort of charity affair, apparently. St. Thomas's Orphanage. Mother's all for it."

Thomas almost laughed. It was all too ridiculous. Of course he was now trapped in here, unable to escape his pox of a brother, because his mother was hosting an event for the charity he had created. Without them knowing. With their money.

The irony was exquisite.

Taking care not to slam the door shut, though he desperately wanted to, Thomas sighed and turned to face his brother.

Who looked uneasy. "Look, man, I wanted to talk."

"I don't want to talk about it," said Thomas, striding across the room with purpose and throwing himself bodily to lounge on the sofa.

If he had to remain in here, the very least he could do was not talk about Victoria. Not think about her. Not remind himself just how delicate she was, and yet strong, how beautiful and elegant and—

"You must miss her."

All the muscles in Thomas's shoulders tensed. "I don't know what you mean."

Evidently, his attempt at brushing off the topic of conversation was unsuccessful. As Thomas lay there, staring up at the ceiling, his brother's snort was audible even over the noise from the drawing room next door.

"I don't buy it."

"I'm not selling," Thomas said, as lightly as he could manage.

Alexander scoffed. "You can't pretend. You can't lie to me and say you don't care about her."

"As I said, I don't know what you mean." Thomas spoke in a cool, calm voice. At least, it sounded cool and calm in his ears. Perhaps it was fragile around the edges, but then, so was he.

There was a moment of silence just long enough to make him wonder whether his brother had given up the nonsensical line of conversation, until...

"It is ridiculous for you to attempt to pretend you do not love her, you know."

And that was it. That was the catalyst. Had he not earned the right to be left in peace? Had it not been mortifying enough to have such a disaster occur before his whole family? Had he not done enough?

Swinging his legs off the sofa and glaring at his brother opposite him, Thomas hissed, "Fine. Fine! You want me not to pretend? Fine. I will no longer pretend that I don't hate you. I will stop pretending that your idiotic, open-mouthed stupidity lost me someone that I—I cared about, very deeply. I will stop pretending that you are not the reason for my misery, Xander. How do you like that?"

His voice had risen to a pitch and volume he had not expected and Thomas could barely understand how he'd managed to spit out all the words. His lungs were tight, pain aching down his shoulders to his elbows, the stinging in his right palm where he had injured himself now clamoring for attention.

God, what a fiasco.

And Alexander said nothing. He just sat there, face placid, as though he had expected all of this—as if he deserved it.

Well, Thomas thought darkly, *he does deserve it. And the rest.*

"How could you reveal the coin toss to Victoria?" This time,

Thomas was not quite controlled. His voice cracked when he spoke her name. "You're a complete ass—"

"I know," Alexander said softly. "I was."

"—and…" Thomas blinked. "What did you say?"

"I was an ass, a *complete* ass, as you say," his brother said. Only then did Thomas notice his brother had clenched his fists in his lap. There were glowing white marks across his skin where he had presumably recently dug his fingers into skin before. Just as Thomas had.

Thomas found he was breathing heavily, as though preparing himself for a fight. And wasn't he? Hadn't this been coming, ever since his brother had been so foolhardy as to tell Victoria the truth?

"I thought you would fall in love with me eventually, and—"

"So it's you, really, who is the liar? You… You were just manipulating me."

"Manipulating a man who chose me thanks to a coin flip!"

Guilt tugged at his heart, making it skip a beat. He should have been the one to tell Victoria.

"Look, I am not saying what I did was right, because it most certainly wasn't," said his brother, leaning forward and speaking in an urgent tone. "But I can't help but think that at least this way—"

"If you're going to try to convince me of a silver lining, you dolt—"

"—this way, she knows the truth and you don't have to lie to her anymore," Alexander persisted, speaking over Thomas.

There was a moment of silence in the subsequent room. Then the chatter in the drawing room returned, a buzz of noise that was surely echoing through the whole house.

Rather like this conversation, if we aren't careful.

"I wasn't lying to her."

The words had spilled out before he had fully formed them and he could see how ridiculous they were.

Clearly, his brother could too. Alexander raised an eyebrow. "What do you call it, then?"

"I... I omitted a few details."

Even to Thomas's ears, his excuse sounded pathetic. What sort of a man was he?

"Surely, it is better, when one is about to get married, to enter into it with no *omitted details*, to use your phrase," his brother said quietly. "Not that I am much of an expert on marriage, but—"

"You're right, you're not," Thomas barked back. "And you will have to wait longer to see another one close up, because there is not going to be a wedding now. Because of you."

He had intended the last three words to hurt, and for a moment, he did see a spark of pain in his brother's eyes. Only after a few heartbeats did he realize he was seeing a reflection of himself.

"Because of *you*," Alexander repeated pointedly.

Thomas lifted a hand to his face and rubbed at his tired eyes. Was this what it felt like, not sleeping properly for three days? As though the whole world made no sense?

Or was it because he had not seen Victoria in that long?

"Look, you hurt me," Thomas said wearily, dragging his hand across his face then looking up at his brother. "Whether you meant to or not, whatever *noble intentions* you assign to the mistake now, that's essentially immaterial. You did it."

His brother winced. "And I am sorry."

"Sorry doesn't change things, Xander. Sorry doesn't fix it."

"I wasn't the one who—"

Anger flared in Thomas's chest. "If you are going to try to turn this around on me, my boy, I can tell you now—"

"There wouldn't be anything to tell if you had just been honest with her," his brother most inconveniently pointed out. "You were the one who said to me, on that New Year's Day, that you needed to marry a fortune."

Thomas sighed, trying not to think of what he had said. He could not deny it. "Your point is?"

His brother leaned back in his chair, examining him with a surprisingly wise expression. "Well, Victoria—"

"*Miss Ainsworth* to you," Thomas said through gritted teeth.

He rolled his eyes. As if the man had any cause to call her other than by her proper title. She was not his sister-in-law—and never would be. "Lord above. Fine, Miss Ainsworth. She is hardly a foolish woman, is she?"

The cleverest I have ever met. "No."

"And the gossip about our fortune, or lack thereof..."

"Get to the point, man."

A flicker of a smile creased Alexander's face. "Oh, I'm sorry, do you have somewhere to be?"

The glower on his face must have been more amusing than frightening because despite Thomas's best efforts, his brother merely grinned.

"My point is, Miss Ainsworth worked out you were only courting her for the money."

"It wasn't like that, not for long," Thomas protested, as though somehow by saying it, he would make her understand.

She had to understand, didn't she? But he had written and there had been no reply, and when he had gone to the Ainsworth house, he had failed to knock on the door. Cowardly, perhaps, but her silence in regards to his letters had been hint enough at the reception he'd receive.

"Listen, man, for more than five seconds!" Alexander's face was a tad red now, his irritation showing. "You want to marry a fortune— you *need* to, in your own words. You select Miss Ainsworth, it doesn't matter how, and she is wise to your game. Can't you see, can't you understand that she would want to take some control? I mean, how much control to ladies have in today's Society, really?"

Thomas frowned, ready to spur forward with a response that would cut Alexander down to size and demonstrate his affection for

Victoria to boot.

No words came.

God damn it. Did the man have to be right?

"I miss her," he said suddenly.

Readying himself for the expected laughter from his brother, the scorn that would inevitably come, Thomas clenched his teeth.

No such mockery came.

He looked up. There was a look on his face that was altogether too knowing. What on earth did he not know about this youngest brother of his? The man was only four and twenty. He couldn't possibly have fallen in love.

"I can see that," Alexander said quietly.

Placing his elbows on his knees, Thomas dropped his head into his hands.

He missed her. He loved her. This woman who was only supposed to be convenient had most inconveniently wormed her way into his affections, and now he couldn't let go. Let go of the feelings, of the need for her, of the knowledge that he would never be truly complete until he was by her side again.

Christ alive, he would accept just being an acquaintance of hers, someone she saw socially, sharing light conversation with her before she moved on to another.

Just to be in her world. Her orbit. Her life.

"Love is a painful thing, isn't it?"

Thomas's head snapped up, aggression pouring through him, ready to bark back at his brother's teasing—but he halted himself.

There was no ridicule in his brother's face. Instead, there was a... a curiosity, for want of a better word. The man looked interested, the index fingers of both interlocked hands leaning against his mouth.

And he was sitting here, bothering to listen to him. And he had apologized.

Hell, it would be so much easier to just go on hating him.

"'Painful'?" Thomas echoed, leaning back with a sigh. "Yes. No. At the moment, it is. Other moments it was... It was wonderful. It was like sunshine. Sunshine on a wintery day—you almost forget the rest of the world is cold because you're so warm. Everything is warmer, everything is better. Better with her."

He was sounding like a complete sap, but at this point, Thomas hardly cared. What did it matter? The whole world could know how much he needed Miss Victoria Ainsworth.

"She's a woman in a million," he said quietly. "A woman in a million."

He should have known not to use such language, for before he could tell the man to button his lip, Alexander snorted with laughter.

"Yes, just like the coin toss when it landed on its—"

"I swear to God, Xander, I will smack you."

"Yes, yes, sorry," his brother said hastily, putting his hands up in mock—or perhaps real—surrender. "What, so I am never allowed to talk about that moment again? It was fantastic! Something we will never be able to repeat!"

Something we will never be able to repeat.

Thomas's gut twisted painfully, a wave of nausea pouring into his lungs, but he fought it.

Being in love, loving someone like Victoria Ainsworth: that was the one-in-a-million chance. That was the something he would never be able to repeat.

How could he ever feel something like this for another?

"You should go to her."

Thomas sighed heavily and shook his head. The poor lad was so green, so innocent. He didn't understand how the world worked. Yes, he was honor-bound to marry her, but if no one knew what he had done, she might still survive Society gossip to claim another husband. "She'll never take me back."

"Probably not."

"Why don't you keep your mouth shut and your thoughts to yourself?"

"Look, I'm here to help!" protested his younger brother.

Thomas snorted. "Fat lot of good you're doing me, you complete ninny. What have you done? Apologized for a huge mistake that was completely your fault, pointed out I will never have it so good again, reminded me Victoria is far cleverer than I am and totally saw through me, and then suggested I go to her? What sort of help is that?"

His brother's eyes twinkled. "Oh, I'm sorry, what sort of help were you expecting? A fairy godmother to appear, wave a magic wand, and inform you that everything will be well if you can just get to the ball?"

Despite himself, Thomas felt his lip twitch. "I mean, it wouldn't hurt."

Alexander chuckled. "Life isn't like that, I'm afraid."

"When did you get so wise?"

A dark cloud passed over his brother's eyes. "When I... I didn't. It doesn't matter."

"You can tell me," he said curiously, lowering his voice. "I won't tell anyone."

"I'm sure you wouldn't," said Alexander with a bracing smile. "But that's neither here nor there. I'm here to fix *your* life. I'll fix my own another day."

"But—"

"That's another story," Alexander said with a wink. "Besides, you technically wouldn't be in this fix if it weren't for me."

Thomas could not help but snort. "'Technically'?"

"Fine, definitely," said Alexander with a shrug. "The question is, how are we going to get you out of it?"

Thomas sighed. It was a hopeless case, and he knew it. The best he could hope for was a chance meeting somewhere on Milsom Street, or at the Pump Rooms, or—

"I have an idea," said his brother slowly with a grin.

Thomas did not like the look of that. When he spoke, it was warily. "What on earth are you suggesting?"

"Thomas Chance, Duke of Cothrom," his brother declared with a grin, "you shall go to the ball!"

Chapter Nineteen

February 11, 1840

"I DON'T WANT to be here," hissed Victoria, attempting to tug her arm from her mother's iron grip. "Mother, let me leave."

"I will not have you moping about at home any longer. This has gone on quite long enough," her mother hissed back, managing to do it while displaying a broad smile, which even Victoria had to admit was impressive. "Now then, let's introduce you to—"

"I don't want to be introduced to anyone," Victoria muttered, sagging against her mother and allowing her to be sailed through an outer room into a large ballroom. "Not that my opinion matters much here."

They had argued over this quite thoroughly for a day and a half, but Mrs. Ainsworth was determined to have her way and so that was what happened. Victoria had grown so used to it over the years, she found it difficult to deny her mother anything—which was her downfall.

It was also why she was here, dressed to the nines in a gown far too tight for her breasts, forced to talk to the other guests at the Dalton ball.

Instead of at home. In bed. Crying.

"There will be a great number of people here with whom I think you will enjoy speaking," said her mother brightly. "After all, as you are no longer... You know..."

Victoria sighed. Her poor mother had only two days ago accepted her daughter was not going to be marrying the Duke of Cothrom. It had taken a while, particularly because Mrs. Ainsworth had insisted the whole thing was just a misunderstanding.

"A misunderstanding built on lies and deceit," Victoria had said sweetly. "Yes."

There was no arguing with her mother, at least not for long. That was why the two of them were beaming out at the numerous guests of the Daltons as the musicians in the corner prepared to play their first piece.

"Now, I would have you dance," her mother said sternly. "With at least three gentlemen "

"I'm not sure how we'll all fit together, but if you insist, Mother," Victoria said sardonically.

Mrs. Ainsworth tapped her daughter with her fan.

"Ouch!"

"Oh, I barely touched you," she said dismissively. "Now, it's very important you—what on earth is going on over there?"

There was something of a disturbance going on in the doorway they had just walked through. Victoria could not make it out, but heads were turning and it was starting to become impossible for people to walk in or out of the double doors, as so many people were standing there staring, craning their necks to look at something clearly fascinating.

"I suppose it's not possible that... Well, that the queen is here?" Her mother gasped.

Victoria forced down a laugh. "I doubt it, Mother."

"It would be such a coup for the Daltons, and what a thing to be able to say, that one invited the queen to one's ball and she came!" Mrs. Ainsworth's eyes were bright and Victoria did her best not to roll her eyes. "I mean, if you were to become the Duchess of Cothrom, then perhaps—"

"*Please*, Mother," Victoria said tightly.

The pain scratching across her chest was almost visible, heat splattering red across her décolletage. It was most irritating. Most upsetting that just the hint of what could have been was sufficient for her to feel so...so...

So empty.

Victoria swallowed as the hubbub around the door grew. "What do you think is actually happening? Assuming the queen has not..."

Her voice trailed away. She would have kept speaking, if it were physically possible, but all the air had left her lungs and her throat was far too busy knotting itself.

Thomas Chance, Duke of Cothrom, stepped into the Daltons' ballroom. And he was not alone.

He was surrounded by... Well. Not quite children, but not quite adults. Young people. They looked shy, and nervous, and they were all wearing the Chance russet, but they weren't servants. They looked like...family.

"Oh, my," Victoria murmured.

"Is that—"

"It can't be—"

"But I thought he was a spendthrift! A reprobate! What on earth is the man doing?"

"Those are the St. Thomas's orphans, aren't they?"

Victoria could hear every thump of her pulse in her ears, feel every press of its pounding against her ribs. He was here. And he was accompanying...orphans?

Reprobate, spendthrift, she had thought all those things about Thomas Chance and at times, something worse.

And now he was here with a whole host of *children*?

"Miss Ainsworth," Thomas said quietly as he approached her. "Mrs. Ainsworth."

The elder woman practically sputtered. "Oh, Lord Thomas—I

mean, Your Grace, of course. Oh, how wonderful to—"

He did not ask. There was no seeking permission, either from herself or her mother. Before Victoria could open her mouth and say a word, before any thought could rationally express itself through her lips, Thomas had taken her hand and started to pull her away.

"Thomas!"

She should not have shouted. She certainly should not have shouted his name.

Heads turned and whispers started to abound, all with words like "betrothal" and "scandal" and "who?" and Victoria could not stand it.

She tugged her hand from his own—at least, she would have done if he had not such an impressive grip on her hand.

Was this to be her fate tonight? Paraded up and down by her mother and dragged through a crowd by her...whatever Thomas was to her now?

"Thomas, let me go."

"Absolutely not," he muttered, though she might have misheard him in the noise and chatter of the ballroom. "Never again."

Victoria's mind whirled as Thomas pulled her through a card room, along a corridor, toward a door. *Never again?* Surely, she had imagined that. It wasn't possible that he had said that, was it?

Thomas wrenched open the door with his free hand and Victoria gasped as the freezing-cold February air whirled in. "You can't be thinking of going outside! Thomas, neither of us has a coat or pelisse!"

That, apparently, did not matter. There was a grim determination set in his jaw, one she had never seen before, and before she could cry out for help, he had barreled through the door, pulling her along with him.

It was bitter outside. A cold wind blew, rustling the leafless trees and tugging her tresses. Victoria shivered, the cold prickling against her skin. Why, oh, why had she allowed her mother to dress her in such a ridiculous gown?

"That's better," Thomas muttered, shutting the door behind them.

"'Better'?" Victoria repeated, utterly at a loss. "Better than what?"

He did not reply, but he did release her, stomping a few feet away and turning on his heels to look at her.

Look at her with a ferocity that Victoria had never seen before.

Her gasp was captured by the wind and he probably never heard it, but he could surely see the expression on her face. An expression that surely said how confused and pained she was to see him.

Because it hurt. It hurt, standing here before the man with whom she had thought she would spend the rest of her life. It hurt to know she had just been a whim, a casual impulse could have gone so differently.

And it hurt that he loved her, Victoria thought, shivering slightly, and all that love was going to go to waste.

Well, she couldn't stay here all day.

Raising herself up stiffly, she said, "I demand you take me back inside."

"No," said Thomas shortly, still standing feet from her and just...looking.

Victoria's lips parted in astonishment. "'No'?"

He shook his head, his carefully coiffed hairstyle utterly ruined thanks to the wind. Which meant hers was likely just as mussed. It probably looked like...like they had been...

Victoria swallowed hard. "Well, I do not need an escort. I am sure I can find the—"

"I need you to listen to me."

Listen to him? Here? "You had your opportunity."

"I know, but I need another one." Thomas's voice was low, sensuous, just as she remembered.

Victoria was tempted, just for a moment, to close her eyes and ask him to keep talking. *Just say anything*, she wanted to cry out. *I need to hear your voice. I need to know that you're near me.*

One last time.

"I don't have to stand here and listen to this," she said aloud, mouth dry. "Now, if you will excuse me, Your Grace."

She did not curtsey. The man had dragged her out of a ballroom in front of the whole of Bath Society. There were going to be rumors about her all over the place. He did not deserve that courtesy.

Stepping forward, Victoria lifted her skirts slightly off the damp terrace upon which they were standing and made to move around him.

And she would have done, if Thomas had not stepped right into her path.

"You are not excused," he growled. "I need to talk to you."

Her heart skipped a beat. "What makes you think that you have any right to—that I would want to—"

"Because you love me," Thomas said. "And I love you, and this nonsense has to stop."

Fury rose from Victoria's stomach, a dark, sticky fury that coated her lungs and poured out of her. "This is nonsense. It's your nonsense, nothing but your own! You lied, you treated me like a jest, you—"

"You and I care about each other far too much to let this little misunderstanding—"

"'Little misunderstanding'!"

Somehow, Victoria found herself pressing her palms against his broad chest, fingers splayed out. *To force him out of my way*, she told herself. So why wasn't she moving him—why wasn't he moving?

His eyes roved across her features. "I have to tell you about St. Thomas's."

Victoria blinked. "St. Thomas's?"

She knew that place—she had heard about it. Wasn't it that orphanage she was hearing so much about?

The distraction was too much to ignore. *Fine*, she told herself as the wind blew and her spine shivered. She would listen to whatever it was that Thomas—that Lord Cothrom had to say about St. Thomas's, and then she would leave.

"Look," he said quietly, blowing out a long breath. "I've always wanted to do good in the world, real good, good that will matter."

"What are you—"

"So I founded an orphanage last year with most of my money. It... Well, it accelerated from there. More children, more food needed, then I thought, lessons, they can't leave without an education, so I had to find teachers, and they needed salaries."

Victoria stared, amazed, hardly able to think. This—*this* was the great secret of how Thomas Chance had spent his family's fortune? This was what he had chosen to do with his life—to care for those unable to protect themselves?

"They insisted on calling it St. Thomas's, which I loathed, but there it was," he said with a twist of his face. "And before I knew it, the laundry needed updating, and water piped into the kitchens would make such a difference..."

He was babbling now and Victoria stared at the nervous creases in his brow. He was worried about telling her. Worried, about admitting to such philanthropy.

"And that is where all the money went," Thomas said with a heavy sigh almost lost in the wind. "Look, come here."

Victoria allowed herself to be pulled along the terrace and around the corner, her head in a daze. The wind was almost gone here, the shelter of the building making this part of the terrace almost temperate.

He had done it all for children.

She blinked, hardly able to believe it. "Why did you bring them here?"

Thomas pulled a hand through his tousled hair. "I thought, give Society a chance to see them. Perhaps they would be moved to help out."

"Why did you not tell me?"

Thomas laughed bitterly as he dragged a hand through his already windswept hair. "I… It was a secret from everyone. No one knows, in fact."

Victoria raised an eyebrow. "Lady Maude knows."

The duke uttered a very ungentlemanly oath.

"Thomas!"

"I should have known my sister would worm her way into my business," he said ruefully. "I didn't want anyone to know. That was the whole point. Making it public… Well, it would steal away the satisfaction I felt in doing it. It wasn't for other people. It was for me. For them."

So many new thoughts were whirling through her mind, Victoria was finding it rather difficult to catch up.

He wasn't a spendthrift, or a dissolute gambler, or a rake. *Well, perhaps a rake.* He had, after all, lain with her before marriage.

But Thomas Chance was not the fool or the reprobate everyone thought he was. And knowing that, knowing what it was doing to his reputation, he'd allowed everyone to think that.

He was so much more of a man than she had thought.

"I got in too deep, ending up caring far too much about the children," Thomas said with a wry smile. "I gave them everything. Everything I could. That was when I realized I needed to—"

"Marry a fortune," Victoria finished for him quietly.

He nodded.

This man. There was so much more to discover about him. Just when she thought she entirely understood, just when there was absolutely nothing else to learn, he told her something like this.

And so Victoria laughed.

Thomas's frown was swift. "I don't see what is so amusing."

"Oh, Thomas, you utter fool."

"Hang on, that's a bit…"

Victoria giggled, unable to help herself. "Don't you see? This makes you a better man, an even better one than I thought you were, and I will admit I was biased to begin with. Giving up the entire Chance fortune and not to risky stocks and shares, or the gambling den, or the races…but to an orphanage?"

Joy was spilling over into laughter, and there was a lightness across her shoulders she had hardly realized had been absent until now.

His shoulders loosening, his features softening, Thomas's concern was slowly changing into a look of awkward delight. "Well, I wouldn't put it quite like that…"

"I want to give you twenty thousand pounds."

Victoria was not sure what made her say it. She was certain in herself that she wanted to do it, knew it was the right thing—he had already done so much.

Thomas faltered back a step. It was quite a surprise to see a look of devastated horror on his face.

"This is not what this is about," he said quietly, reaching for her. "Victoria, I—"

"Twenty thousand pounds could be invested to create an income, don't you see?" Victoria said urgently, trying not to notice the sparking heat flowing through her body from where Thomas's hand was on her arm. *Oh, touch me…* "It would revolutionize St. Thomas's, allow you to—"

"I made the mistake already of treating you like a bank account," Thomas said fiercely, interrupting her. "You think I want to make that mistake again?"

"I can just send an order to my bank and it will be carried out," said Victoria, exhilaration thundering through her at the look of indignation on the man's face. It was her money, really, to use as she pleased. Not a husband's reward for marrying her. "You can't stop me."

"By God, don't I know that."

And his hands were in her hair, his lips feathering kisses along her jaw, and Victoria gasped at the sudden invasion of his presence but moaned as the ripples of pleasure began awakening in her.

This was wrong, they couldn't—they most certainly shouldn't! And they weren't betrothed, not anymore, and—

"I've missed you," Thomas whispered in her ear in between pressing kisses down her neck, causing undulations of need to bud inside her. "Oh, Victoria, I've missed you."

"You've missed this," she murmured, trying to ignore the frantic pounding of his pulse under her fingertips still splayed against his chest. "You've missed ravishing me."

The kisses suddenly stopped and he was towering over her, staring deep into her eyes as though she were mad.

"You think I would—you think I could do this with anyone else?" he whispered, pain etched across his features. "You think there's anyone else in the world with whom I would want to share this?"

The words felt so good, though not as good as the way he next possessed her mouth, tugging from her a whimper of need that Victoria tried to swallow but could not. She needed him, needed this connection, this closeness. Needed to know she was precious to him. Needed to believe it could work.

"I'll send you the money." Victoria gasped, unsure precisely how she was still standing as one of Thomas's hands snaked to her waist, pulling her even closer into his embrace.

"I'll refuse it."

"That won't matter."

"I'll return it to you."

"I'll send it back." Victoria's eyes fluttered. She was barely able to cope with this onslaught of kisses and debate. "I'll keep sending it to you until you accept."

"I want you, Victoria, you!"

She opened her eyes. Thomas was gazing down, lips wet and parted as though he were about to kiss her again, and she would have welcomed it except they had somehow verged into territory far more dangerous than the discussion of money.

Thomas was panting, his grip on her waist tightening. "I want you, not the money—hang the money!"

This is not happening, she told herself firmly. *And at any moment, you can disentangle yourself from this gorgeous rake and return yourself to the ballroom.*

Any moment. Any moment now.

Her feet remained resolutely where they were.

"I need you—your joy, your laughter, your wit. Do you think I can put a price on that?" Thomas slipped the hand that had tangled in her hair to her cheek, cupping it and lifting up her head.

Slowly, slowly, he lowered his head and pressed his forehead against hers. He was so close, so achingly close. Victoria nudged his nose with hers and she felt him shudder with repressed need.

"I'll sell the house in Bath."

Victoria jolted, accidentally pressing a kiss onto his lips before saying, "You wouldn't!"

"I'll sell everything the Chance family owns, down to the last silver spoon, if it means you will marry me for *me*, Victoria," Thomas murmured, the aching so potent in his voice, she could almost taste it. "I don't want your dowry. You have to believe me."

And she did.

She kissed him, hard on the mouth, and Thomas responded in kind, both arms wrapped around her as if he hoped by the intense pressure she could feel the passion within him.

And she could. Not just in his frantic kisses, or the way his laughter and relief mingled with hers, or even in the way that there was a certain stiff…organ, in his trousers, pushed up against her hip.

No, Victoria couldn't understand it exactly, couldn't explain it: but she knew. This man loved her, and for herself. For what and who she was, not what she owned.

Eventually, they had to lift their heads for air, their panting filling the cold night with blossoming breath.

"You thought you were swindling me," Victoria said with a wry laugh, elation flooding through her.

Thomas snorted. "And you were most definitely swindling *me*— ouch!"

She had tapped him sharply on the chest. The broad, muscular chest that she very much wanted to see again.

"I think we were tricking each other."

Thomas nodded with a mischievous look. "I can believe that."

"You're a chance in a million, Thomas."

Victoria wasn't quite sure what had prompted her to say such a thing, but the words made his face grow serious for a moment as his hands stroked her lower back, sparking a need below it she knew only he could fulfill.

"You're a woman in a million, Victoria Ainsworth," he said seriously. "I… I have something for you."

She could hardly think so could not guess what it could have been—but if her mind had been able, it certainly would not have guessed…

Thomas held out a ring. It was gold, like the last one, but this had a single emerald, smaller than any of the stones that had appeared on the first ring.

"It's different," she said foolishly.

His face became crestfallen. "You don't like it? I… Well, I bought the other one on credit, with the assumption of your dowry. I bought this one with my own money. I wanted it to be mine."

Mine. Victoria swallowed, and only then did she realize that something was missing.

The signet ring on his left hand. It was gone.

Her throat tightened. "Thomas, you didn't—"

"And I… Damn, I should kneel for this bit."

"Don't you dare," she said warningly, clutching on to him. "You're the only thing keeping me warm out here."

He snorted, but seriousness returned to his eyes as he beheld her. "I've proposed to you before, Victoria, and I was so anxious, so nervous, I don't think I gave you much justice."

Victoria's lips parted in astonishment. *That cold demeanor, that stiff speech—he was nervous?*

"More than nervous, I was ashamed. I didn't want to marry you without telling you everything, but I was afraid once you knew, you would leave." He swallowed. "I want to tell you all sorts of things about love, and need, and want. About how I always feel safer, more alive, when I'm with you," he whispered, never taking his eyes from hers. "About how life without you isn't worth living and a life with you is the best and only one to live—"

"Thomas."

"But I can't do that. I can't do you justice with words," he said ruefully, a wicked glint in his eyes. "So I think I'll try the next best thing, and show you."

Victoria blinked. "'Show me'?"

"For the rest of our lives," Thomas said simply. "That's all I want. Your life."

She smirked. "You don't ask for much—"

Her words were stopped with a kiss: passionate, yet reverent. The sort of kiss a man would give his wife, say, on their wedding day. It was deep, his tongue twisting torturous pleasure from her mouth. Victoria clung to him, her hands gripping his lapels, as though he were the only man left in the world.

When the kiss ended, she said, their breath misting in the air between them, "Yes."

"Yes?"

"You think I could say anything else after you dragged me out of that ballroom and caused a scandal?" Victoria quipped with a laugh, and Thomas joined her. "Come on, then. We'd better go back inside and make my mother a very happy woman."

Chapter Twenty

February 28, 1840

THOMAS HAD NEVER been so nervous in his life. Hopefully, he never would be again.

"You look like death warmed up," said Alexander cheerfully, clapping a hand on his shoulder.

Shoving his brother's hand off him but managing to laugh through the tension, Thomas snorted. "You always do, but you don't hear me complaining."

"Oh, good. How wonderful to see that some things never change," quipped their sister. "Now are you going to behave today, Xander?"

"*Me?*" The youngest Chance placed a hand on his heart and arranged his features into an astonished expression. "I can't believe you would even have to ask."

"Really?"

Thomas chuckled at their sister's sardonic word. Anything to distract him from the anxiety prickling around his temples.

This was it. It really was. It had finally come—though arguably after making an agreement with the Archbishop for a special license, and unleashing his mother onto London to get it all organized within days, Thomas supposed he really shouldn't be describing the time since Daltons' ball and today as "finally."

Still. As he stood there in the drawing room, his family happily chattering around him, Thomas could hardly believe it was happening.

His wedding day.

"—look very handsome," his mother said fondly.

Thomas blinked. He hadn't noticed his mother step forward. She was fiddling with his cravat, moving the pin to the left then the right as though attempting to decide which she preferred.

"Thank you," he said stiffly.

Alice Chance flashed him a smile. "You look just like your father did on our wedding day."

"I was less nervous," came a serious voice behind him.

Thomas turned and tried to beam at his father as the Dowager Duchess of Cothrom said fiercely, "You were terrified!"

"Never been terrified in my life," said William Chance, slowly stepping toward them. "Except once. May I have a word with my son, dear?"

Fear—no, not fear, but something very like—bristled up Thomas's spine and neck. Oh, hell, what had he done now? There was always something. No matter what he did, no matter how hard he tried, there was always something he'd done wrong.

His father had not been pleased with the fact that all of their money was gone—though he had softened when Thomas had finally admitted to the reasons behind that. The dowager duke had not been entirely unaware, it turned out, as the solicitors and banks had revealed the checks written to pay off expenses related to the orphanage. He had just been waiting for Thomas to admit what he'd done.

And his father was ready to work with him moving forward, to invest Victoria's money—her own money—in such a way to afford both the estate's expenses and everything the orphanage could need. The latter with help from others of the *ton*.

Still, Thomas had left the conversation feeling a bit scolded, like a helpless child. Of course he never should have taken on all those expenses on his own. Not just for his own family's sake, but for the children's. His coffers would only empty at some point without careful planning, and then where would that have left the orphanage?

Thomas's mother gave William a knowing expression then meandered over to Leopold and started fiddling with her second son's cravat.

"Perhaps just a little to the left," she murmured.

"I know how to dress myself, Mother!"

Thomas grinned, then arranged his features into an expression far more grim. He would hate for his father to think he wasn't taking today seriously.

"Never terrified except once," said his father quietly. "Do you know when that was, Thomas?"

It's going to be some sort of moral lesson, Thomas thought with a sinking heart. That was just what he needed the hour before his wedding: a teachable moment. An opportunity for his father to demonstrate there was still so much for him to learn, so many ways to make more mistakes.

"When?" he said aloud.

There was something twinkling in his father's eyes. "When you were born."

Thomas's eyes widened. "When I was born?"

"It was a difficult birth, as your mother still delights in telling me," his father continued, as though he had not spoken. "For a few hours, it looked as though I was going to lose everything precious, everything I wanted. My wife. My second child. I had Maudy, obviously, but the thought of being her only family…"

Never before had Thomas's father spoken of this—but then, there were few times in Thomas's memory that he and his father had had a conversation of this magnitude.

"Well, it all ended happily," he said, more hoarsely than he'd hoped.

William Chance, the Dowager Duke of Cothrom, nodded sagely. "Yes, but I did not know that, in the moment. All I could think of was

EMILY E K MURDOCH

the idea of losing the woman I loved, and the child who was an emblem, a proof, of our affection. And here you are. On your wedding day."

Thomas shuffled on his feet awkwardly. This was most definitely not what he had expected. "Father, I—"

"I will admit, this is not the day of yours that I am most proud of," his father said quietly in that slow, steady voice Thomas depended on far more than he would like to admit.

"Not today?"

William shook his head. "No, the other day. When you finally told me just how you've been putting the family money to good use. Of course, your sister came to me with her suspicions long before that."

Thomas snapped his head around to glare at Maude, who was studiously not looking at him but instead gazing at Leopold. Just for an instant, she met his gaze and grinned. Then she returned hastily to her conversation.

"I should have known," Thomas muttered. "First Victoria, then—"

"I wish you had come to me earlier. When you had the idea. When those expenses started piling up. I should have paid closer attention and stopped you as soon as the solicitors and banks contacted me about your withdrawals instead of just waiting for you to confess. I was in charge of the household at the time, and I should have taken responsibility." His father cleared his throat. "I don't think I made that clear when we discussed how best to handle the finances going forward."

Thomas's neck ached from whipping it back to his father, but Thomas could pay that no heed. Had he just said... Had his father, of all people, just said...

"I'm proud of you, son," William said, grasping Thomas's shoulder. "I may not be the most approachable father in the world—"

"Father—"

"—but I have created some remarkable sons," his father continued quietly. "And I am proud of you."

Thomas blinked back burning tears. It wasn't supposed to be like this; he wasn't supposed to be so affected by such a small amount of approbation from his father.

But any man would be a liar if he said he did not long for such a thing. Long for a connection, long for the knowledge that one's life had not only purpose, but approval.

"Thank you," he said gruffly. "I-I wouldn't be the man I am today without you."

For a moment, just a heartbeat, William nodded and squeezed his shoulder. "I know."

The moment passed. His father released him, both he and Thomas cleared their throats loudly. and Thomas tried to grin.

"You don't have to worry about Victoria's funds, by the way. After what I discussed with you, our solicitors are putting together a plan, an investment plan, with additional funds from others throughout the *ton*. The future Duchess of Cothrom herself gave her approval. We'll make St. Thomas's self-sufficient." His father nodded with a knowing look. "And if I weren't impressed enough with you, I would have to be with that wife of yours. Which reminds me. Weren't we supposed to be going to a church?"

Thomas started, turning to look at the clock. "Oh, hell!"

They weren't quite late. Late would suggest that the wedding had attempted to start without them, and it hadn't. Still, Thomas did not relish the idea of parading his entire family down the aisle full of wedding guests because they hadn't paid enough attention to the time.

"Really, Your Grace," hissed the vicar as he snuck them through a side chapel and across the vestry. "I was about to send a note!"

"I know, I know," said Thomas, his pulse hammering. "Is she here?"

The vicar raised a sardonic eyebrow. "Not officially."

Thomas discovered. later that day, that what the reverend meant was that Victoria had arrived—at her mother's insistence—over an hour before the wedding ceremony was supposed to take place. The vicar had taken pity on her and hidden her in one of the side chapels and then taken even more pity on her and encouraged Mrs. Ainsworth to sit in the church to welcome their guests.

And so it was that when the organ began to play and Thomas rose, it was Mrs. Ainsworth who tapped him on the shoulder.

"Your Grace," she said in a whisper and with a wide grin. "Congratulations."

Thomas's mind was whirling with so many thoughts and emotions that he blurted out, "Congratulations for what?"

Leopold, standing beside him as his best man, groaned.

"Congratulations," Mrs. Ainsworth said with a knowing look, "on a one-in-a-million bride."

Thomas would have replied. He had intended to, but his attention had meandered from Mrs. Ainsworth to the figure walking up the aisle. Both of them.

His mouth fell open.

Oh, she is a vision. Dressed all in white, as was the newest fashion due to Queen Victoria's famous dress during her recent nuptials to Prince Albert, there was an elegant simplicity to her attire that made her all Victoria Ainsworth, even with the bridal veil partially obscuring her face. Her breasts—and Thomas's manhood lurched just to think of them—were delicately covered by reams of lace, but there was no disguising that delicious figure.

Beside her, walking her sedately and serenely down the aisle, was Alexander.

"I still don't know why you asked *him* to give her away," muttered Leopold in his ear. "The boy is an absolute menace."

Thomas chuckled, pushing aside the memory of what their younger brother had said.

"I'm here to fix your life. I'll fix my own another day."

Menace, yes, but *boy?* Not any longer. He would have to remember to ask the scallywag more about what he'd meant later.

"I didn't ask him," Thomas muttered, unable to take his eyes from his upcoming bride.

"Then why—"

"Victoria asked him. Said it was all his fault the wedding was delayed," said Thomas with a grin, "so she would make it his fault if she was late to the altar."

All speaking had to cease at that moment. Victoria and Alexander had reached Thomas and Leopold, her lavender scent making Thomas weak at the knees, and the vicar began his welcome as Thomas's heart thrummed.

"Dearly beloved, we are gathered here today in the sight of God..."

The wedding definitely happened. Thomas was sure. When he looked at his left hand hours later, the wedding celebrations at the Ainsworth house in full flow, there was the proof. A golden ring.

"You don't have to wear one, you know," Victoria had said to him only two days ago. *"It's quite unheard of for a man to wear a promise ring. Most gentlemen would balk at the idea."*

And he had smiled, and said, *"Most gentlemen don't have the chance to marry Miss Victoria Ainsworth."*

So, the wedding had happened. He'd been there. But the moments had mingled and rushed through his mind, every moment a shock to the system. Repeating his vows, hearing Victoria return them in a clear voice, the lifting of her veil, the desperate need to kiss her and scandalize the whole wedding party...

Thomas blinked, shaking his head. It was all like a dream. A dream he had longed for. Just like that, they were married.

Victoria squeezed his hand and the strangeness of the ring on his finger tightened. "Thomas?"

He looked up from their intertwined hands. This was where he belonged. This was whom he belonged to.

"You know," murmured Thomas, reveling in the way her hair fluttered at every movement of her head, "everyone seems to be entertained."

Victoria arched a brow. "Yes, they do."

"So much so that they don't really need us."

Both of her brows were now raised. "Thomas..."

"Well, no one would notice," he said, giving up all pretense. "And after all, your bedchamber is right—"

"We are *not* sneaking out of our wedding reception to—to go and ravish one another!" Victoria hissed, her cheeks pink.

Thomas grinned. He could see the desire in her eyes, hear it in her voice. His eyes trailed the pink rising up her décolletage as her lips parted, her tongue darting out to wet them.

Dear God, but if she didn't say *yes*, he wasn't at all certain how he was going to hide the stiffening in his trousers.

"*Please*," he begged in a low whisper.

Victoria's eyes widened. Then she was pulling him by the hand through the crowd of well-wishers, smiling at their guests, nodding her thanks but not halting. Not even for a moment.

Aching need poured through Thomas's body as anticipation started to rise. Christ, they were going to do it. They were going to march out of here and upstairs and then they would—

They did not march upstairs. To Thomas's utter bewilderment, Victoria pulled him into a room in the Ainsworth house he had never been in before. It appeared to be a—

"A storage room?" he said, blinking around him. "What on earth?"

There were mops and brushes and a few console tables in need of repair. A pot of paint had crusted over and there were several chairs and a stepladder pushed up against one wall.

Thomas's shoulders sagged. *Ah. So this isn't a clandestine encounter, then.* "Victoria—"

"They'll suspect if we go upstairs," she said, and she was pressing up against him now, her fingers scrabbling at the buttons of his trousers as though craving what was inside. *Perhaps she is.* "But here—"

"No one will think to look for us," Thomas breathed, surrendering immediately to his wife's intoxicating desire.

Christ, was there anything more attractive than a woman attempting to undress a man?

"Hurry up," she said impatiently, her fingers struggling to release him. "How on earth do you—ah!"

Her sigh was exquisite. The sound was the nectar of the gods, and Thomas's body responded in the only way it knew how. The trouble was, his trousers were slipping down and pooling around his boots now, so the very physical response to her was... Well. Front and center.

"I've wanted you all day," Victoria said fervently. "How are we going to—"

"Here," Thomas said hastily, trying his best to walk a few steps forward with his trousers around his ankles and his manhood leading the way. "Come here."

His wife halted for a moment. "You—You're sitting down. Where am I going to sit?"

It was difficult not to grin at such an innocent question. *Oh, this wife of mine. I still have so much to teach her, just as I have so much to learn.*

"Right here," he said pointedly.

For a few heartbeats, Victoria just stood there, staring. Thomas had selected what he considered to be the most sturdy of chairs—after all, it would need to be—and he lay against its back languidly, holding out a hand.

"I-I don't know what you mean," Victoria said hesitantly, stepping forward and halting just before him. "You want me to sit on your lap, you mean?"

Thomas bit down the groan her naïve question heralded. "Here, like this..."

It was easier to show her than to explain. Victoria's eyes widened as he pulled her toward him, nudging her legs apart with his free hand so she straddled him and the chair. When he tugged her down, his manhood pressed against her hip, she squealed, a noise quickly halted by his passionate kiss.

"Oh, Victoria," he murmured.

He couldn't help himself. The feeling of her astride him, the closeness of her, the fact that they could do this now without any fear of discovery or scandal—

Well, perhaps a *little* scandal. Brides and grooms were not supposed to consummate their wedding in a storage room.

But there was no time to think about that. Not with Victoria's hands in his hair and her thighs pressed against him and his manhood desperate to reach her core and his hands cupping her buttocks under her skirts...

"That feels so good." Victoria panted, squirming in his lap and making stars appear in the corners of his vision. "But I don't understand. How will we—"

He claimed her mouth again, thirsty for the sweet nectar of her tongue, and as his lips played with hers, eking little squeaks from his wife, Thomas's hands were not idle. Her skirts, her petticoats, all of them were moved aside until his fingertips brushed up against—

Victoria ground her hips forward and welcomed him in, Thomas moaning at the unexpected closeness.

Christ, he could pump into her just a few times and find his release at this point...but he mustn't.

The thought sharpened his resolve. He was not going to begin this marriage by leaving his wife unsatisfied.

Trying desperately to control himself, willing himself to stay resolute, Thomas lowered his mouth to the swell of Victoria's breasts and laved along the top of her décolletage as his left hand clasped her buttock and his right thumb slipped inside her wet folds.

All the saints in heaven, but she was ready for him. How long had she been wanting this?

Probably as long as he had.

It wasn't enough—he had to taste her. Ignoring her shocked gasp and reveling in the way her head immediately fell back in uncontrolled passion, Thomas tore the front of Victoria's gown with his teeth and pulled at her corset.

There wasn't a great deal of movement, but there was sufficient for one nipple to peek out and Thomas claimed it with his teeth and growled.

The thrumming vibration through her body made Victoria shudder, or perhaps it was the way a finger had joined his thumb in stroking her. Gritting his teeth and praying he could prevent himself completing against her hip, Thomas concentrated on nipping her breast, feathering it with soft kisses then aggressively demanding her nipple.

"Thomas, more! More..."

And he gave her more. He gave her everything, everything that was in him. Thomas's thumb brushed against her nub and Victoria jolted in his arms, and he knew she was close. Ready to be pushed over the edge.

Without mercy, his thumb, finger, and tongue worked in harmony until Victoria cried out his name.

He could weep, she was so beautiful coming apart in his hands. Thomas captured her mouth, allowing her to scream into his lips as she quivered, until all the aftershocks had subsided.

Victoria looked up with bleary eyes. "But, Thomas, you haven't—"

"Not yet," Thomas rasped through gritted teeth. "But give me a moment."

She allowed him, through a lust-sodden gaze, to gently lift her up. When he lowered her onto his manhood, Victoria hissed at the sudden intrusion.

It was all Thomas could do not to come right away. Oh, she was wet, and dripping, and ready for him, but there was so much more than that. She was sweet, and hot, and designed somehow to perfectly fit him. The squeeze of her inner muscles as she sighed was almost too much and Thomas burrowed his face against her neck, breathing her in. He wished to goodness this was the rest of his life.

It is the rest of my life.

"And now I-I ride you, I suppose?"

Thomas barely had the strength to give a reply, but it appeared Victoria did not need one. Her expression curious as she explored this new sensual territory, she pushed herself up on her toes, slowly threatening to release his manhood, then spurted down, sheathing him.

Thomas juddered. "Yes, yes, yes…"

Whether anything else he said made sense, he did not know. How long it took for Victoria to ride him to the very edge of ecstasy then push him off into bliss, Thomas could not have said.

All he knew was that if someone had happened to walk past the Ainsworth storage room for the next hour and a half, they would have heard some very interesting noises indeed.

Epilogue

March 1, 1840

WELL, SHE'D DONE it. She could hardly believe it, but she'd done it.

"Now, you mustn't attempt to memorize all the cousins in one go," Thomas said blithely, patting her hand as he led her through corridor after corridor. "There are quite a few of us."

"I'm still astonished you know your way around this place without a map," said Victoria in awe, gazing around herself and trying to take in every tiny detail.

Her new husband's laughter rang out as they stepped into the next room.

"Look, this is all a bit much," gasped Victoria, staring around herself in astonishment. "Didn't you ever consider a smaller home? I mean, only one smaller home?"

It was magnificent. Oh, she had heard Stanphrey Lacey was one of the most impressive mansions in England, but that was easy to say. Only now she had been here a few days, still getting lost every morning in an attempt to find the breakfast room, could Victoria admit she had never seen a place so wonderful in her life.

The architecture was exquisite, the selection of furnishings phenomenal, and every time you thought you had seen the best room in the place…

"What? It's just an orangery," said Thomas with a shrug. "Ah, there they are. Uncle John and Aunt Flo only arrived an hour ago, apparently."

Victoria allowed herself to be pulled over to the gaggle of elegantly attired people standing several yards away, though she spent most of the time staring around her.

Just an orangery? Did her husband have any idea it was not normal for a house to have an orangery this size, the glass towering above her, the stars blinking in their heavenly settings, the scent of oranges and green earth filling the space?

When she blinked, she was being introduced to what felt like half the Chance family—which, now she came to think of it, she probably was.

"And Uncle John and Aunt Flo," said Thomas, "my unruly uncle and his charming wife."

"You little toe rag," Uncle John said with a charming grin. He was remarkably similar to his older brother, the former Duke of Cothrom, but there was a little more gray in his hair and a little more mischief in his eyes. "How dare—"

"Oh, I d-don't know, he's got a p-point," said the beautiful woman on his arm with a laugh. Her dark eyes contrasted with her pale skin, and her lips pressed together in a teasing smile. "How lovely to s-see you again, my d-dear. The wedding itself was s-such a rush and we couldn't seem to f-find you at the wedding breakfast."

Try as she might, Victoria could not prevent her cheeks from pinking. *Well, there was a reason for that...*

"It was such a crush there, Mother, I wouldn't worry," came a refined and snooty voice. "How pleasant to meet you again, Miss Ainsworth—I do apologize, *Your Grace.*"

Victoria tried to smile. "Oh, please, Lady Lilianna, we are family. Call me 'Victoria.'"

The woman raised an eyebrow and Victoria immediately wondered what sort of etiquette she had breached this time. She had been raised well, gently and genteelly, yet the Chance family was quite literally a cut above the rest.

"Ah, and here are some of our local friends," said William Chance, striding forward to clap his son on the back. "I'll go and greet them. Lil, there are a few gentlemen I think you may wish to meet again. Lord Zouch in particular was very desirous of having the pleasure of your—"

"I am sure he was," said Lady Lilianna, causing her mother to elbow her in the ribs. "But you will have to make my excuses, Uncle William. I am indisposed."

The dowager duke cocked his head, his concern for his niece evident. "'Indisposed'?"

Victoria felt a pang of affection for the man who could never replace her father but who had done a sterling job in welcoming her to the family.

"Yes, Lord Zouch makes my stomach churn," Lady Lilianna said with a haughty laugh. "I'm going to the music room. Your Graces."

For a moment, Victoria was not sure to whom the lady was talking, but her cheeks burned as she realized that the woman was taking her leave of them—of herself and Thomas.

She was not the only person in the gaggle whose cheeks were red.

"You must excuse m-my d-daughter, Your—I mean, M-Victoria, if you insist," said the woman Victoria had been instructed to address as "Aunt Flo." "She is… Well. Sh-She's a Chance."

"And if that doesn't tell you enough about us by now, I don't know what will." Thomas winked. "Come over here. I want to show you something. Excuse us."

Without giving her the option to say goodbye to those to whom she was talking or welcome those new guests entering the orangery shepherded in by William, Thomas pulled Victoria through the orangery and through a door she had not noticed. It led them into a corridor she had not yet walked down—though thanks to the size of

Stanphrey Lacey, that was not saying a great deal.

"Your cousin Lilianna, she is... Well..."

"Arrogant, I think is the preferred family term," Thomas said with a laugh. "Yes, I suppose she is arrogant. Very certain of what she is worth is Cousin Lilianna."

"You're not that different, though, all of you," Victoria pointed out wryly as Thomas pulled her into a room that looked nondescript. "You all have the sense that you are slightly above everyone around you."

Thomas adopted a ridiculous hauteur as he shut the door. "But aren't we?"

She could not help but laugh. The man was infuriating, yes. He sometimes had bad judgment, and if she didn't keep a close eye on him, he was liable to give away all their money again.

Too big a heart, that was Thomas Chance's problem.

"You Chances are too arrogant by half," Victoria said, stepping forward into waiting arms. "There you were, thinking you could marry my dowry—"

Her husband groaned. "I thought we were past that!"

"You think I am ever going to let you forget your utter nonsense over my money?" Victoria kissed him hard and swiftly on the lips. "Never. It's the perfect thing to hold over you for the rest of our lives."

His laughter echoed through her chest and Victoria could not believe how happy she was. How had she managed it?

Oh, there had been the little something of a seduction. Thomas had to claim at least some of the credit too, she supposed. Not much. But some. And that accursed coin deserved a little credit, too.

But in many ways, it was a complete coincidence that everything had worked out so well. They certainly could not have predicted such a wash of happiness surrounding them each and every day.

"I should have known I was marrying a merciless woman," Thomas murmured, trailing a kiss down her cheek and toward her ear.

Victoria shivered. "We mustn't…"

"Why not?" he shot back with a chuckle. "We're married. This is our home, our family's home, at least. If not here, where?"

It was tempting indeed to permit her husband to remove just enough of her skirts to give her a good loving, but Victoria managed to maintain some decorum.

After a few more minutes of kissing, that was.

"Look, I mean it. You can't just drag me away from your family to kiss me," she said a little breathlessly.

Thomas raised his head and straightened yup. "Dear Lord, you're right. This isn't why I brought you here at all."

He released her in a rush and Victoria wavered, unsure precisely where her husband had gone. "You didn't?"

"No, I wanted to show you…this!"

With a sudden sweep of silk, Thomas had removed a sheet of fabric that had been covering up a table in the corner. Though now Victoria came to look at it properly in the candlelight, it wasn't just a table. It was…

A model. A model of a building. A large building. On the front was a little carved sign.

Sts. Thomas and Victoria's Orphanage.

Victoria sighed.

"You don't like it," said Thomas immediately. "I should have known it was foolish. I don't know why I—"

"You are far too kind for your own good," Victoria said softly, reaching out to touch the model with a delicate finger. "You will bankrupt us, you know."

When she looked around, some of his excitement and confidence had gone. She ached for him. How would she love this man? To the best of her ability, yes, but where was the balance between enthusiasm and practicality?

Wherever we find it, she realized, joy bubbling up inside her. They

EMILY E K MURDOCH

would make mistakes, yes. But they would make them together.

"It's going to be an exciting project," she said quietly.

Thomas perked up. "You think so?"

"It's ambitious," Victoria said, placing her hands on her hips. "You are certainly thinking big, my love, and I applaud that. How long do you think it will take?"

"Oh, years—years to do it properly," said Thomas eagerly, pointing here, and here, and here, his mind clearly excited as his smile broadened. "I was thinking we could do it cheaply, yes, but then wouldn't we just end up doing it again, and again, and again, replacing the shoddy workmanship? So I thought…"

Victoria could not help but beam as she watched her ridiculous husband babble on about his project.

There was so much about him she had not known when she had fallen head over heels in love with him the first time. Things about him that no one, she was almost certain, could guess. The eldest Chance son of the eldest Chance brother, one would have expected him to be mostly rake and partly rascal.

Yet here he was, dedicating his time and energy on something that would benefit not himself, nor his family, but those who could never repay him.

"—and something here for when they are of age but not ready to leave," said Thomas with a flourish of his wrist. "So tell me what do you think? Do you love it? Do you hate it? Do you think I'm being foolish—I am, aren't I?"

Victoria responded the only way she could: with a kiss. "It's marvelous. *You're* marvelous."

His cheeks colored and he looked at his hands, as he always did whenever Victoria wrongfooted him. "You don't have to say that, just because we're married."

"You're right, I don't," said Victoria cheerfully. "And yet here I am, saying it anyway. Though if I may make one suggestion…?"

Her voice trailed off as her stomach lurched. Thomas was watching her, waiting for her to continue, his patience clearly warring with his desire to say something of his own.

"'One suggestion'?"

Victoria nodded. It wasn't exactly the way she had planned to reveal the news, but was there only way to do it? She did not think so.

"If I were you, I would see if I could make the project—at least the first, major part of it—organized so it was complete in seven months," she said softly.

Her husband's eyes widened. "S-Seven months? From now?"

He looked back at the model. The candlelight was flickering around the room and Victoria could not help but feel a sense of foreboding.

This wasn't part of the plan. At least, not part of her plan. Who could plan such a thing? But they had not yet discussed... After all, they had only been married for a few days.

"Why seven months?" Thomas said with a frown.

Victoria took a deep breath and plunged ahead. There was, after all, no going back. "Because in seven months I will be finishing a project of my own."

Surely, that would make him understand...

"You haven't mentioned a project before." Her husband's frown deepened.

She had to laugh at that, and finally, the words spilled out from the very depths of her heart. "Thomas, I'm... I'm with child."

The words echoed around the room and Victoria stood there, lungs constricting with anticipation, as she saw her revelation sink into her husband's mind.

"You... You are?" he said hoarsely. "Oh, Victoria!"

"I know it's soon, perhaps sooner than we would have expected," she said quickly, desperate to get the words out. "I know we haven't talked about—"

"We haven't because—well, I thought that would come in time, but not immediately!" Thomas's expression was one of unadulterated delight. "And for it to happen so soon... Oh, Victoria, you clever thing!"

"I'm not sure I'd go that far," Victoria said wryly. "If I'd been more careful—"

"If *we*'d been more careful, I think you mean," said her besotted husband, reaching out and taking her hands. "Oh, a baby. A baby!"

A baby. Victoria had hardly been able to believe it when her courses had not appeared, but there was no other explanation for it, or the horrendous nausea that had arrived just a few days ago. She was ready to say goodbye to that.

"God, I am so fortunate to have you." Thomas sighed, ignoring the model and pulling her toward him.

Victoria allowed him to do so, knowing she could never have expected her plan—such as it was—to have gone so well. A husband she loved and who adored her, a child of theirs to come, and a lifetime of looking after those who could not look after themselves.

And the Chance family, heaven help her.

"I love you, Victoria Ainsworth."

She tilted her head with a laugh. "You know, this may have passed you by, but I actually changed my name recently. You may not have seen it in the paper."

"Oh?" Thomas raised a quizzical eyebrow and Victoria wondered, with a jolt to her thighs, how she managed to ever stop kissing him. "It sounds like a happy marriage."

"Oh, very happy," she said, grinning. "Husband's a bit ridiculous, but—ouch!"

"And even after that dreadful slander, I am still fortunate to have you," Thomas said genially, his warm gaze resting on hers. "A one-in-a-million chance, and here you are."

Victoria raised a hand and stroked his cheek with the back of her fingers. "A one-in-a-million chance, and here we are. Together."

"For the rest of our lives," breathed Thomas as he leaned forward.

And from that point on, for a very long time, talking was neither possible nor necessary.

A Short Letter From the Author

Hello! Thank you so much for reading *A Chance in a Million*, the fifth novel in my The Chances series. I truly hoped you enjoyed it and fell in love with Thomas and Victoria just as much as I did.

If you've read the first four books of this series (which I strongly recommend!), then you'll have seen the four uncles fall in love. I had always wanted to write a series of brothers, but I could never 'meet' the characters who were quite right. After waiting years to meet them myself, I have had a lot of fun writing the four Chance brothers—and now we're diving into their children. Make sure you go back and read them!

If you're desperate to read the happily ever afters of Thomas's siblings, then you'll want to look out for Book 8, *A Sporting Chance* (Leopold's story); Book 12, *Don't Fancy Your Chance* (Alexander's story); and Book 17, *Let the Chance Slip By* (Maude's story). Our next Chance adventure is going to jump to a different branch of the Chance family…

Being an author can be a lonely business, but knowing that there are readers from all over the world who are going to adore my stories makes it all worthwhile. Thank you for your support, and I hope you love reading more of my books!

Happy reading,
Emily

About Emily E K Murdoch

If you love falling in love, then you've come to the right place.

I am a historian and writer and have a varied career to date: from examining medieval manuscripts to designing museum exhibitions, to working as a researcher for the BBC to working for the National Trust.

My books range from England 1050 to Texas 1848, and I can't wait for you to fall in love with my heroes and heroines!

Follow me on twitter and instagram @emilyekmurdoch, find me on facebook at facebook.com/theemilyekmurdoch, and read my blog at www.emilyekmurdoch.com.

Made in the USA
Monee, IL
10 March 2025

13577515R10154